A
sweeping
novel of
Old California
by a superb
new writer
of frontier
fiction

LARRY
JAY MARTIN

A MAN TO BE RECKONED WITH

Clint turned away from the window to face the two vaqueros. "Inocente Ruiz and I have an appointment—face-to-face this time. I intend to teach him some tolerance, if I have to do it with my knuckles, the heel of my boot, or, if he prefers, with the blade of my knife. If he wishes the blade, then God will judge him. And that's no brag, just fact. It's a foolish man who writes a draft with his mouth that his abilities can't cash."

"Inocente's skill with the blade is renowned," Alfonso warned.

A loaf of bread rested on a table across the room; behind it a thick hardwood cutting board leaned against the wall—eight paces away. Almost before Alfonso had finished his statement, Clint's blade appeared in his hand and flashed across the room, pinning the loaf to the cutting board with a quivering thump.

Alfonso's and Ramón's eyes widened.

"And mine," Clint offered quietly, "has come from a thousand ports in a hundred countries full of hard, skilled men who fancy themselves and their abilities."

"He will not back down," Alfonso said.

"Nor will I."

EL LAZO

Larry Jay Martin

BANTAM BOOKS
NEW YORK • TORONTO • LONDON • SYDNEY • AUCKLAND

EL LAZO

A Bantam Book / March 1991

Bantam Books are published by Bantam Books, a division of Bantam Doubleday Dell Publishing Group, Inc. Its trademark, consisting of the words "Bantam Books" and the portrayal of a rooster, is Registered in U.S. Patent and Trademark Office and in other countries. Marca Registrada. Bantam Books, 666 Fifth Avenue, New York, New York 10103.

PRINTED IN THE UNITED STATES OF AMERICA

OPM   0 9 8 7 6 5 4 3 2 1

ALTA CALIFORNIA

✝ Mission

Scale of Miles

0   25   50   75   100

Eldorado

California has always been a land of contrasts.

Her geological diversity astounds. The burning Hades of Death Valley, 200 feet below sea level, and the 14,700-foot icy peaks of Mt. Whitney lie just 100 miles apart—the lowest and highest spots in the contiguous forty-eight states. The fastest-falling river on the North American continent, named La Pornicula, the Exuberant One, by the padres, then renamed the Kern in honor of Fremont's topographer, tumbles westward from Mt. Whitney toward the sea.

California's thousand miles of seacoast range from the redwood-forested cliffs of Mendocino to the sand dunes of Pismo and Guadalupe. Her coastal mountains shield the world's most productive agricultural valley—at mid–nineteenth century a marshy maze of tules, quicksand, water birds, wild mustangs, elk, and grizzly—from the world's largest ocean. Inside her borders, the Great Basin and the Mojave Desert kiss, dry-lipped and covered with the bones of the brave and the foolish, yet teeming with life.

From gigantic redwood to withered bristlecone pine, great grizzly to tiny white-footed mouse, condor to Allen's hummingbird, minute and tenacious desert pupfish to massive gray whale, her diversity astonishes.

California's earliest-known human inhabitants, twenty-six primary tribes, were capable, enterprising, and fascinating—until conquered by malaria, lues, cholera, and a hundred other maladies against which they had no immunity. Customs that included the killing of their firstborn and the free sexual exchange of their women, and rites that included use of deadly jimson weed were common. Great whales journeying offshore were taken by Chumash hunters in thirty-foot whaleboats. Whale bones fill thousand-year-old middens on California's coast. Some of America's finest basketwork adorned native villages. Trails historically claimed by Gaspar de Portola, Jedediah Smith, Ewing Young, and John Fremont were tracked by moccasined traders for forty thousand years before boots or iron-shod hooves touched the earth. Open-armed, smiling, and hospitable in the beginning, the California Mojave, Paiute, Yokuts, Shoshoni-Commanche, and Modoc finally rose up against their guest-turned-invader and fought for their way of life.

The Russians, French, and English recognized California's bounty and claimed a good share of it. The Spanish saw a country their padres could tame, expending little shot and powder, but did not claim her secret treasure—gold.

The Anglos from the United States, believing in manifest destiny and concerned with the intent of the British, moved against Mexican California under secret presidential orders that have never been verified, while Mexico was busily defending her territory of *Tejas*, or Texas. California, with the help of many *Alta Californios* who felt themselves stepchildren of faraway Mexico City, fell happily into the open arms of the Union.

The great harbor of San Francisco welcomed first the Spaniards, then the Americans, then the hordes of a hundred different lands. And the wide Sacramento River that feeds the bay opened inland to goldfields and beckoning riches.

In 1847 California recorded a population of 14,000 Mexicans and an estimated 30,000 natives. By 1852, she was home to 350,000 people from all over the world. In those same five years, her homicide rate increased 10,000 percent. California would never again be host to the simple and gracious lifestyle of the rancho and the mission. She would forever teem with enterprise, both legal and illegal.

Just as the Spanish had displaced the natives, the new immigrants displaced the Spanish. Americans, Europeans, Chinese, Peruvians, Australians—men and women from all parts of the world rushed to claim her riches or prey on those who had. Black, brown, yellow, red, and white—hundreds of thousands of adventurers—those were the Californios.

They may not all have found her gold or tangible riches, but all found ELDORADO.

EL LAZO

One

John Clinton Ryan crashed to the holystoned deck of the fo'c'sle.

Instantly awake after being thrown from his bunk, he strained in the darkness for sounds of what was happening, but heard nothing over the wailing wind and the sea pounding against the hull of the brig.

The *Savannah* listed sharply to port, then stayed fast. Clint cleared his head and tried to collect himself. The ship was not rolling, not pitching and diving in the huge swells as she had been all day and night. He gained his feet, but the ship lurched again with a wrenching sound that echoed against the bulkhead.

Shattering timbers—the splintering cry of a ship dying in the darkness.

"*Madre de dios*, we are sinking!" a shipmate cried out.

"It's every man for himself!" yelled another of the dozen sailors in the fo'c'sle.

"Don't panic, lads," Clint managed, then grunted as a man stumbled over him with a muttered oath. The sailor drove a knee into Clint's chest, knocking him back to the deck. Clint lurched to his feet before another stumbled into him. Men cursed and cried out, fighting for the ladder and the relative safety of the open deck. Another man crashed·into him, and Clint shoved him roughly away.

Sinking back into the recess of his bunk, he calmly checked his waistband. His knife was still there. He had been too exhausted to remove it when he collapsed into his narrow recess at midnight after twenty-four tortuous hours on deck. Taking a deep breath, he waited for the panicked men to clear out. It appeared that after twelve years at sea, having been a cabin boy at fifteen, he was experiencing his first grounding—and possibly a sinking.

When the clamoring died, Clint made his way to the hatch, groping in the dark until his foot struck something solid. Kneeling in the four-inch-deep water, he realized one of his shipmates was down. Hoisting the man over his shoulder, he started up the ladder to the main deck.

As Clint reached the wind-whipped darkness of the deck, stinging spray lashed at his face with a banshee wail. He strained his eyes but could not see beyond the deckhouse. His burden moaned, and Clint gently lowered the man to the pine. When the man's swarthy face was lit by a flash of distant lightning, Clint realized it was the Turk, a man who had signed on at Pernambuco. The man rolled to his back and sat up, shaking his head, throwing water from his curly black hair and mustache. Again the brig listed badly. Clint grasped a line to keep from sliding to the rail and knelt beside the sailor.

"Are you all right?" he shouted over the wind.

"Aye," Turk said groggily. "Struck my head. What happened?"

"We're hard aground, fast on a reef. But she's givin' way. I fear she'll broach soon."

As Clint regained his feet, Mackie, the second mate, grasped his shoulder and leaned close, shouting to be heard. Mackie's eyes were wide and wild with fright, and even in the wind and rain, Clint could smell the rancid breath of a man who had been at the grog.

"The captain . . . the cap'n called all hands," Mackie slurred, "all hands to scuttling cargo from the forward hold—"

Before he could finish, the foremast snapped with a cannonlike report, and sixty feet of Sitka spruce crashed to the deck, carrying with it yardarms, rigging, and two thousand square feet of furled canvas. Tangles of stiff, tarred stays and fiddle-string-taut running rigging crossed and crisscrossed the deck, snapping like musket shots as mast and yardarms tumbled overboard. Instinctively, Clint leapt back into the safety of the fo'c'sle hatchway, clinging for his life to the handholds. Hearing anguished screams over the moan of the wind, he spun to see the two men before him grasping at the deck with taloned fingers as they were carried away in a snarl of line and timber. They were overboard and underwater before he could reach them.

Wind and gravity tore at him, and the ship listed even more. *She's doomed,* he thought, and clawed his way back on to the deck and into the mess of line and cloth left aboard. He swiped water from his eyes and strained into the darkness.

The rail. He had to make the rail. If she broached, being trapped in the spiderweb of line was sure death.

A tar-covered stay looped his ankle like a constricting black snake, and he went down—but had his knife in hand before he hit the deck. He slashed at the hemp that tried to drag him into a mishmash of splintered wood and canvas, and stubbornly it parted. He careened to the rail. There would be no need to dive. The ten feet of freeboard had disappeared, and her scuppers lay under surging water. For a moment, he stared at frothing dark death, wondering if he should try and ride it out with the ship. Then she listed more, and without hesitation Clint stepped over.

A crashing wave slammed him back against the taffrail, knocking the wind from him, then the backsurge sucked him into the darkness, and the cold black waters of the Pacific dragged him under.

With powerful strokes, he fought for the surface. A yardarm slammed into his chest and knocked the wind from him again. As he gasped for air, he took water, burning lungs and throat, but he clung onto the floating savior.

He slashed at the lines that bound the timber to the ship. Finally he and the flotsam were heaving and dipping but moving away from the vessel that would suck them down in a whirling maelstrom when she slipped from the reef.

A breaker rolled over him, and his end of the yardarm dove deep. When he surfaced, gasping from the water he had taken, he made his way to the middle of the twelve-foot-long timber, and it stabilized.

Backhanding the water from his eyes, he could just make out the outline of the ship. The *Savannah* slithered from the reef with a shuddering moan and disappeared into the deep. The ship where he had lived and worked for six months and the men he had lived and worked with were gone. He thought he saw the outline of a boat and men, then water covered him again. He kicked and fought toward where he hoped he had seen the boat, but the wind and smashing waves tossed him back.

Lightning split the sky, followed by the staccato cannon-fire thunder of the unhappy gods. The fleeting flash revealed nothing but heaving water and lashing rain.

Taking a racking breath, he coughed scorching salt water from lungs and throat. He shivered as an icy chill sliced his spine like a frigid blade.

It seemed a bizarre time to feel fortunate, he thought, looking into the howling blackness where the ship had been, but he knew most of the twenty-four-man crew of the hundred-foot hide, horn, and tallow brig could not swim. He was one of only a few. In the intermittent bursts of light, as the yardarm dipped and dived and tried to lose him, he madly searched the surface of the water for his shipmates. The boat, if it had been there at all, was gone. With a quiet dread knotting his stomach, he spotted no other survivors.

Finally, after hours, the wind abated, and the twelve-foot battering waves became a steady six. Crashing tons of water became lapping whitecaps. Fingers of lightning no longer flicked death crackles at him, nor did his ears ring from the bombardment of the gods' cannons. After the bellow of the storm, the silence hung ominously. Yet, with the reprieve, the first rays of light grayed the sky over Alta California's mountains, and with a burst of glory, burnished the mountains gold. For the first time in hours, Clint lifted his eyes, taking a fleeting moment to revel in the distant beauty and his own survival. Then reality swamped him like another crashing wave, and he wondered which way he was drifting.

Just surviving had been the challenge of the night. Now living became a high range of mountains on the horizon. He had clung on through the night, a triumph over shipwreck and storm and fatigue, and the dawn cheered him with its promised warmth. Maybe he would make it.

He had no idea how far offshore they had been when they took the reef, but they could not have been far. Soon it would be light enough to judge, and it could mean whether he lived or died—whether the night's torture was merely prelude to a deep cold death.

With daybreak, he began to make out the features of the distant shore, but just as the first of the sun's warming rays touched him, a cold numbing fog crept across the water like a wet white muslin sheet, enveloping him in dank confinement. *Damn the bloody mess*, he thought, then reasoned, *Better fog than blistering sun*.

As he drifted, to keep his mind busy and away from what might be lurking beneath him, he calculated how long they had been at sea. They had departed Boston in late October and rounded Tierra del Fuego at Christmastime. Then the long northerly trip up the west coast of the Americas. Five months and twenty-four days, Clint calculated. They had made only three stops in Alta California—one at Santa Catalina Island to offload and bury cargo, so the trade goods would not be taxed by the Mexicans, and a stop at the capital, Monterey, to gain passport and pay the tax on what few goods were left on board, then another anchorage at Santa Barbara to begin trading shoes, boots, iron, and cloth for hides, horn, tallow, and otter and beaver skins.

Clint snapped alert. Out of the corner of his eye he spotted a fin slicing the water and wondered if he could scale the narrow yardarm.

Two

Captain Quade Sharpentier snarled a rebuke to his oarsman. "Row, you sogger! It'll be a month to Santa Barbara at this rate."

His eight-foot-long captain's boat held his first mate, Cecil Skinner, a barrel-chested pig-eyed Englishman, and the cook, Wishon, a wiry half-Carib–half-African from Martinique. Sharpentier reclined against the bow of the boat while Wishon, the smallest of the three, stroked the oars with a smooth steady rhythm and Skinner squinted into the morning sun, manning the tiller.

They had salvaged the boat, launching her from the tilting deck of the doomed *Savannah* into the dark promised death of the angry sea. The boat had survived, and with the light, they had managed to raise her cat sail, but the fickle wind was not being kind at the moment—dead still except for the sea heaving and dropping in great sheets of flat gray. Both Quade's boat and the larger shore boat that followed lay adrift in indolent doldrums. The sail whispered a quiet complaint, luffing uselessly.

Six others had managed to gain the safety of the shore boat. Eight of twenty-four men, nine if Ryan still lived.

He had lost many a man at sea, but this was the only time Quade Sharpentier had marked a ship with the bottom, much less lost one. And he knew he was at fault. *Damn the grog*. He glowered at the horizon. He had made an oath to himself to curtail his drinking but again had broken it. He, and every man in the crew, knew that he should have been topside during the storm, but he had not been. Anger gnawed at his gut and competed with the wretched throbbing head he had earned from too much rum. He set his jaw, and his rawboned knuckles whitened as he grasped the gunwales.

The worst of it was not the loss of ship and men but the potential loss of his captain's papers—or worse. If the owners brought charges against him—and he knew they would—he could face the gallows. No, the blame must be laid elsewhere.

"Hell will find the bugger," Sharpentier mumbled for the hundredth time since they had managed to escape the wrecked brig, "if the cold deep hasn't already claimed him." He scratched his salt-and-pepper beard, and his eyes, cold and blue as chipped ice, bulged. "As God is my witness, I wish Mackie would have lived. I'd relish the opportunity to stretch his Irish neck."

"You may still get a chance at an Irishman," Skinner, the Englishman, placated his New England–raised but English-blooded captain. "John Clinton Ryan is Mystic reared, but he's also an Irish blackguard, just as Mackie was. And it was Ryan that Mackie called to the bow watch. How a man could miss that reef . . . ?"

Sharpentier had already begun to plant the seeds of blame on Mackie and Ryan, and the first mate believed it.

"He's no man!" Sharpentier snapped. "He'll be bait for the gulls when I finish with the bloody bloke, if he's not fishbait already. And Mackie, he got his comeuppance in the fires of perdition, as God willed."

They had found Mackie's body in tangled rigging during their desperate struggle to escape the broaching brig. Mackie would not testify at any owner's hearing. But the owners would want to wreak havoc on someone. As second mate, Mackie, cold in Davy's locker, could bear the lion's share, but the owner's would want a live body to vent their wrath upon, or know that their captain had done so. Skinner should heartily go along with it. During a shore leave, Skinner had had his head knotted soundly by Ryan, so there was no love lost between the two. Skinner had been at fault for the confrontation, but Sharpentier had been unwilling to punish the common sailor—he would have had a mutiny if he had done so. Sharpentier knew that the still angry first mate would back any play he made against the Irishman Ryan.

Sharpentier shaded his eyes with a reddened hand. "A little breeze would be a blessing. . . ." Then his voice lowered. "John Clinton Ryan, a sogger and a shirker."

The captain rearranged his reclining position in the bow and mopped beads of sweat from his mottled brow. "The man who allowed my brig to go aground. An Irish bastard. When we reach Santa Barbara, I'll buy the best piece of hemp in Alta California and take the thirteen turns. I pray on the grave of my sainted mother that the bastard lives, so I can stretch his cowardly neck and watch him do the hangman's jig. He's a man deserved of a piece of new hemp."

"Few lived," Wishon said between oar strokes. "Few. And Cap'n, pardon me for sayin', but I never see de man, Clint Ryan—never see him to shirk."

Sharpentier leaned forward and glared at Wishon with cold blue eyes. To the Carib they seemed like two gun-barrel muzzles.

"You watch your tongue, you African devil." Sharpentier's voice was as cold as his eyes. "You'll find yourself swimmin' back to join your sorrowful mates."

Den who'll row de boat? Wishon thought, but said nothing and kept up the steady pace.

Sharpentier eyed the Carib harshly but hearing no more from him, reclined again. He picked up his log and thumbed through the pages, grateful that the weather had been so bad that no entries had been made. He would fill in his own version of the night's events long before he presented it to the owners. "If the Lord smiles upon me, John Clinton Ryan lives." He shaded his eyes. "I believe the breeze is rising. She's rippling the surface and coming our way. Bring her ten degrees larboard."

Clint Ryan will have to wait, Sharpentier thought, *but he'll keep. I'm a patient man. A patient man.* He shooed pesky kelp flies, a sure sign of the beach, from his sweat-glistening brow. "There will be a breeze, and before long, a reckoning," he growled. *And someone to offer up to the owners' wrath*, he thought. *A sacrificial lamb—and a log to report his malfeasance and his hanging.*

Clint exhaled a long audible sigh of relief as he realized the circling fin was only that of a porpoise. It was a good sign—the sailor's friend. It dove under him as if investigating an interloper, then disappeared as quickly as it had appeared.

He shaded his eyes and searched the far-off shore for recognizable landmarks. As an oarsman, he had gone ashore at

Santa Barbara for a few hours. Only to help with the loading of supplies, but he had enjoyed terra firma for a few precious minutes. Across the beach, he had seen two of Alta California's renownedly beautiful señoritas in the distance watching the *gringo marineros*. What a sight to behold: all lace and crimson and turquoise and turtle combs, one with long black hair and one with chestnut brown, and both with flashing dark eyes. He had been months at sea and had forgotten how soft a woman could look, how musical her laughter could be.

Then they were bound north again, through the Canal de Santa Barbara where the channel passes between offshore islands and the mainland, toward San Luis Obispo, where the captain had heard there were hides aplenty. But the spring storm had struck off Punta Concepción.

California's coast was usually calm, almost lethargic as her people often appeared to be, but this storm had come with a vengeance. Taking water over the bow—the worst they had suffered since the horrific pounding of fifty-foot waves off Tierra del Fuego. And this storm, though less harsh than that, had driven them onto the merciless rocks.

Again Clint opened his eyes and tried to find the horizon. The morning fog was lifting, and the gray sea was calm. *Deathly calm*, Clint thought, then wished he had not. With surprising haste, the sun began to penetrate the dank fog, glinting on the surface of the water, and gray brightened to glimmering blue. At first Clint welcomed it; then, though it was only May, the heat of the burning rays began to beat unmercifully. He had been worried about the cold and prayed for the sun's warmth. Now he was intermittently dunking himself to escape it.

Clint squinted and shaded his eyes, scanning the distant shore. Not a ripple blemished the surface—he would get no encouragement from the breeze. He worked his way to the end of the crossarm, pointed it toward what he figured was the nearest landmass, and began to kick rhythmically with his long, muscular legs.

Drifting and dying of thirst were not a part of his plan. A ship of his own was what he wanted and worked for, not a slow, throat-closing death on a flat gray sea.

After three hours with the sun high above him, thirst began to tickle his throat, and he fought the urge to take in salt water. Drinking it would do no good. He had seen men with lips and tongues swollen from drinking sea water.

No. Better no water at all.

Put your head down and kick. Each stroke takes you closer to shore. Ignore the scorching sun. Fresh water awaits you. Life awaits you.

Stroke.

Kick.

Raising his head, Clint wiped his eyes and realized it was getting dark. He had been stroking and kicking for hours, and his tongue had swollen. His mouth was packed with tongue, not a good sign, and his vision blurred. He wondered if it was lack of water or merely exhaustion.

He stroked on, driving himself half the night, until cramped legs did not answer and exhausted arms knotted and ached with pain. Binding himself to the yardarm with what line was left, he slept.

The sun came and went a second time, and he again pushed himself, ignoring his shrieking muscles. More and more he clung to the yardarm, hoping his arms and legs would still function. Then a breeze tickled his back. He lifted his head. A good sign. He tried to focus his eyes, but the shore seemed no nearer.

Hoping for the strength to resume, a sea chantey came to him, and he hummed quietly and sang the words in his mind.

> *I knew my love was drowned and dead,*
> *He stood so still, no word he said.*
> *All dank his hair, all dim his eye,*
> *I knew that he had said good-bye.*
> *All green and wet with weeds so cold,*
> *Around his form green weeds had hold.*
> *"I'm drowned in California seas," he said,*
> *"Oh, you an' I will ne'er be wed."*

The devil with that, he thought. *To hell with that.*

There was no one to mourn him, so what was the use of drowning? He began to paddle slowly.

But by night he wondered if he would ever again see the dawn.

Three

"**A**ye, *Alcalde*, he is a tall man, blue-eyed, sandy-haired. Thick of shoulder and chest. Nothing more than a common sailor. Goes by the name John Clinton Ryan."

Captain Sharpentier sat across the wide carved table from the justice of the peace, the *alcalde*, of Pueblo Santa Barbara and eyed the rotund bureaucrat, resplendent in a high-collared scarlet coat sporting large buttoned revers and gold-braided epaulets over a purple velvet waistcoat. Don Francisco Acaya's coat and waistcoat contrasted with his light blue trousers with gold stripes down the outer seams. A leather shako hat lined with gilded braid and topped with a red-feather pom-pom rested on a narrow library table behind his desk along with a Bilboa sword with silver-trimmed handguard, sheath, and belt. He was the quintessence of pomp—and plump.

But Sharpentier was not impressed. He had seen his share of peacocks before—though never such a fat one—and he was here on a mission. The captain wrinkled his nose as the unpleasant spicy odor from a small brass incense burner wafted across to him. He took a deep draw of the surprisingly good brandy the man had served him.

"I want him," Sharpentier continued. "If he appears, hold him in irons."

Don Francisco cleared his throat, and his jowls vibrated. He blinked wide-set, docile eyes. "I assure you, señor, we have a stock that will hold any man, and my *juzgado* is among the finest in Alta California, but—"

"But?" Sharpentier raised bushy eyebrows.

"But, it is a matter for you Anglos."

"He will be in your country without passport, a trespasser."

"This is true, but not of his own doing."

"That is where you are wrong, Don Acaya. It was 'his doing' that the *Savannah* was wrecked. 'His doing' that more than half my crew is drowned. 'His doing' that thousands of dollars of cargo—goods that would have been traded to your countrymen for hides and horn—lie at the bottom of the sea off Point Conception. I want this man, *Alcalde*."

"I will write the governor, *Capitán*. He will instruct—"

"That will take weeks!" Sharpentier snapped. Rising, he downed the last of the brandy. "I want this man, and I want to hang him, as the laws of the United States dictate." Steel-gray eyes honed into the Mexican. "I will go to the *majordomo* at the presidio if necessary, and he will—"

"No, you will not, *Capitán*." Don Francisco Acaya puffed up like a strutting cock, and his docile eyes narrowed. "This is a matter for my office, or the governor, not the military." The judge snapped to his feet, surprisingly light-footed in his brilliantly polished black half boots, his trousers fastened under the insteps. He marched around his desk to the office door.

"You, señor, are not in the Unites States. You are in Alta California as a guest of the Mexican government." Don Francisco opened the door and stepped aside so Sharpentier could exit. The captain worked his jaw so hard the muscles ached. He marched through the open door, then spun back to continue his tirade.

Don Francisco, slightly calmer, nodded politely and clicked his heels. "As I said, señor, I will write the governor. If he concurs—"

Sharpentier angrily turned on his heel and left the anteroom, stomping past a clerk who looked up in surprise over his quill pen and journal, and slammed the outside door behind him.

Out in the square, Skinner unlimbered his apelike bulk from a bench under an equally massive live oak. The bench overlooked the pueblo's main road, Calle Principal, and most of the little town. He squinted his small eyes in the bright sunlight and cautiously surveyed his boss. "Didn't go well, Captain?"

"It matters little," Sharpentier said. "When the time

comes, if the Turk is right and Ryan lives, we will stretch his neck—if we have to do it from this oak, right in front of the public house."

"Do we have to stay around here and wait to see if the shirker shows his face?" Skinner asked as he eyed the strong limbs of the oak. "Not that I would mind tightening the noose around his Irish neck. I never favored the man." *And you, Captain,* he thought, *need someone to blame for the loss of the brig. A man who's done the hangman's dance talks to no one.*

"Yes, sir," Skinner said, "it's the hangman's rope for the Irishman."

Sharpentier smiled tightly. "The *Charleston* should make Santa Barbara soon, then I'll be a bloody guest on a company ship until I can make passage home. I pray it's not before Ryan shows up. A signed confession, before we hang him, would bode well with the owners. God knows they'll be an angry lot, and hell could freeze before I get another share as captain."

"I'll speak up for you, sir. Odds are, Ryan's drowned."

"The Turk seems to think not. He was the last to see the sogger and swears he was afloat and clinging to some flotsam, well clear of the ship. If we're to decorate this oak with Ryan's rotting carcass and smell up the *alcalde*'s square, I hope he's right."

"The *alcalde* would not like that much." Skinner furrowed thick eyebrows and displayed a mouth full of rotting teeth.

"I don't give a damn what the fat bastard likes. The only good thing about the *alcalde* is his brandy." Sharpentier lowered his voice and checked to make sure he was not overheard. "Unless I miss my guess, if President Polk has his way, California will be a part of the Union before long. From the Atlantic to the Pacific—that has always been our destiny."

He leaned close to his first mate. "When we were in Monterey, I called on Thomas Larkin, the American consul, and from those gathered at his home I heard more talk of rebellion."

Again Sharpentier glanced around but saw only two *paisanos* busily negotiating the road with a *carreta* overflowing with hides, well out of earshot. "The nine of us can handle a hundred of these Mexes. At least we could if we had our Aston muskets or, better yet, a few of those new Walker Colts I hear the Texas Dragoons are using." He motioned toward an adobe. "Come on, we'll bide our time in the cantina."

As they made their way across the courtyard, Skinner assessed the presidio, the military headquarters of Santa Barbara. "Maybe we should be figuring a way to relieve the *alcalde*'s armory of a few of those Spanish flintlocks I see the *cholos* carrying. They're not much, but in the hands of a few fine sailing men . . ."

Sharpentier laid a sun-reddened hand on his first mate's shoulder. "By the gods, Skinner, you'll make captain yet if you keep up that kind of thinking. Let's gnaw on it over a mug of that godawful *aguardiente*, brandy, these papists drink. It would be a pleasure to throw the fat judge—and the mayor with him—in their own *juzgado*."

"*Juzgado?*" Skinner repeated clumsily.

"Gaol to you, my English friend, jail to the Americans." He laughed. "Sounds good, the judge and the mayor in gaol. Captain Quade Sharpentier the new alcalde of Santa Barbara . . . and a town full of señoritas left to us." He scratched his beard thoughtfully. "There be no need to keep our tail between our legs now . . . we don't have to kiss the fat backsides of these heathen Mexes now that we've no ship to haul hides on and no goods to trade for them, thanks to Clint Ryan."

They reached the cantina, and Skinner pulled the hide door cover aside so the captain could enter. The rousing sound of seven other surviving members of the *Savannah*'s crew singing a lively sea chantey rang out into the square. Sharpentier paused in the doorway before he got within earshot of those inside.

"Ryan and his confession, and a sweet señorita's virtue, may be the last and only pleasure we take from Alta California."

With that, Sharpentier laughed deeply and stepped from the noonday sun into the dark cantina. Smoothing the two patches of stringy blond hair that edged his bald pate, Skinner lumbered in behind.

At first he thought someone was calling him. No, not someone. Many! The caterwauling of the dead? His companions? It was too soon to be dead . . . or was it? He thought the raucous sounds must be Gabriel's trumpets announcing his arrival in heaven or, more likely, the keening of the devil's helpmates in hell. He forced open his eyes, looking directly up to the blazing sun.

Burning hell!

At the touch of cool fresh water trickling into his lips, he choked and coughed, then opened his mouth like a young robin receiving a fat worm. Clean, life-sustaining water caressed his parched tongue and throat. Not part of what he envisioned as hell.

He heard the sounds again—seabirds. And he smelled wet sand and the pungent odor of rotting kelp. Flies tickled his face. He brushed at them with a weary arm. Rolling to his side, he rose to an elbow and waited for his salt-burned eyes to adjust.

The men who surrounded him stepped back as Clint propped himself up on one hand, shading his eyes with the other.

He felt quietly ecstatic. He was alive!

But they were not smiling.

He tried to smile, but his dry, cracking lips refused. He blinked and moved his gaze from man to man. Dressed only in rabbit- or fox-skin loincloths, each man held a weapon. Several held bows with arrows notched; many clutched war clubs with stone heads. All had knives of chipped stone or metal. Each man wore a carrying net of woven milkweed about his shoulders. Some held shellfish, and Clint recognized a few seabirds among the bounty in the nets.

They must be on a hunting or gathering trip, Clint reasoned, but then noticed they were painted. Body paint of red and black covered the exposed body parts. War paint? Clint tried to gain his feet, making it to one knee before a broad-chested warrior with a feather cloak about his shoulders stepped forward and shoved his stone ax against Clint's chest, pushing him back to the sand.

A creeping dread filled his gut, and he prayed for strength. Clint rolled to his side and covered his head as the man raised the ax. He heard an urgent shout, and another warrior, his chest painted pure white, stepped forward and grasped the man's wrist in an iron grip. The two men stood eye to eye, trading guttural remarks, then the white-chested man shoved the other back. Feathercloak stumbled a few steps, then regained his threatening stance. A few of the men gathered behind him, and a few gathered behind Whitechest.

Clint found himself in between. He glanced at the scrub oak forest at the edge of the beach and wondered if he could run. Again he managed to get to one knee. Feathercloak stepped forward, his ax raised, and Whitechest lifted his stubby three-foot bow and drew the arrow a few inches. Both groups were silent, the tension so thick it hung in the air like a bank of fog.

Two tall sinewy men flanked the white-chested warrior, each with a six-foot stone-headed lance. Feathercloak curled a lip, made a guttural remark, turned on his heel, and led his band of supporters away. As Whitechest moved forward and knelt beside Clint, the others in his band returned to their search of the beach. Clint heard the sound of hoofbeats in the distance and presumed that the opposition had left. He breathed in relief.

Whitechest sat, folding his legs and setting his bow aside, then handed Clint a gourd of water. The Indian was as tall as Clint and broad-chested, with a full head of braided and coiled hair. A stone knife was worn in the braids. A necklace of haliotis shells hung down to his muscle-defined belly, and olivella-shell bracelets encircled knotted biceps and calves. His eyes were inquisitive, and wrinkles at their edge hinted of times both joyous and sad. Clint nodded gratefully, managed to sit and raise the water to his lips. As he carefully sipped, letting the water rest in his mouth and relishing the simple wetness of it, the warrior gave him the slightest hint of a smile and patted his white chest.

"*Soohoop*," he said.

Clint wondered if the man was trying to tell him his name and tried Spanish. "*Su nombre?*"

The man shook his head adamantly. A young boy approached, and for the first time, Clint noticed that a group of women and children rested and watched from a nearby sand dune. The boy stood at a discreet distance. "*No español.*"

"He doesn't speak Spanish?" Clint asked in that language.

"He *won't* speak Spanish," the boy replied. "His name is Soohoop, Hawk."

"I am Clint . . . Clint Ryan. Hawk," Clint repeated, and the warrior smiled.

The warrior rose and spoke to the boy in his guttural tongue, then walked away.

"He wants you to rest until the gathering of shellfish is over. Then he will take you to our camp."

"Suits me," Clint managed. The boy wandered away and began digging for clams with a sharpened fire-hardened stick. Clint worked his way to a rock and leaned against it, sipping water, watching, and feeling his strength return as the water worked its wonders in his system.

He took a second to admire his surroundings. The sea broke in long rolling waves against the wide beach, which gave way to low dunes that in turn gave way to a brush and scrub oak forest. Beyond, sharp hills of laurel intermixed with tall arroyo willow, with ravines of short, brilliant green-leaved sandbar willow, rose to high live-oak-covered mountains. Great sandstone shoulders protruding out of green meadow and stately live oak rimmed the skyline in the distance. Seabirds—plovers, and stilts, and sanderlings—worked each wave's edge, scampering back and forth across the hard-packed sand just ahead of the surf. California and Heerman's gulls winged overhead, flashing white and black and gray. A flight of brown pelicans winged low over the water.

He studied the men, women, and children who moved about the beach and the edge of the nearby woods. Each of them wore shell beads. For the first time he noticed two men stationed behind him, watching him closely. It seemed their only duty. Was he a prisoner? Did the man called Hawk save him only to kill later? He had read of the strange rites of primitive tribes. But the man seemed sincere in his friendliness. Clint hoped he was, for he was too weak to do much about it, at least for a while.

All the men wore shell armbands about their biceps and calves, and the women long necklaces that hung between exposed breasts. Even the children wore chokers of colored shells. The women too had skin loincloths and unlike the men, wore vests of skin or woven reeds, but they provided little modesty. A few of the men wore leather moccasins and leggings, but most, and all the women and children, were barefoot. The women wore carrying nets like the men, but also carried intricate conical baskets strapped to their backs. While they worked, they dropped shellfish and an occasional decorative shell over their shoulders. Some of the women bore a double load—basket in back and baby bound to chest in a woven reed carrier.

Clint caught the eye of a young woman, slightly taller than the others and finer featured. She rose from her digging and crossed the sand to where he rested. He smiled, but her gaze remained serious and concerned. She knelt beside him, reaching into her carrying net to fish out the shell of a snail. Clint tried to keep his eyes on hers, as dark as the wing of a raven that cawed overhead, but could not help but lower his eyes to admire her proud breasts as she worked. She hardly noticed his gaze—or at least pretended not to.

Dipping a finger into the snail shell, slowly so as not to startle him, she extended her hand and began to apply a greasy substance to his lips, then to his burned forehead. He closed his eyes and leaned back against the rock to let her work.

He heard the gruff voice of one of the warriors and opened his eyes to see that one of the men stationed to watch him had risen and come over to chastise the girl. She stopped and moved away, and Clint admired her calves, exposed upper legs, and swinging buttocks as she walked. "Thank you," he called after her. She glanced over her shoulder coquettishly and smiled, but said nothing.

The warrior gave him a hard look, then silently returned to his post.

Clint's sunburned skin felt smoothed by the gel she had so gently applied. She had been kind, as had the warrior who had kept old Feathercloak's ax away. But the two men between Clint and the shelter of the forest did not look in the least benevolent.

And they watched him closely.

Four

Clint moved unsteadily along behind the women and children. Every step a chore, he stumbled at first, but soon got into the rhythm and was able to keep up. His stomach roiled with nausea, his arms and legs knotted with pain, his skin burned, his lips cracked, and his vision blurred at times—but he was alive. He hoped that at the end of the walk he would find more water and a soft place to rest and heal. And he hoped he would not find the hostile men who had ridden out ahead of them.

The young boy, who like Clint walked instead of rode, kept glancing back at him. Finally, Clint mustered a smile, and the boy dropped back beside him. His hair had been recently trimmed, much as it would had he been in a New England town. Only shoulder high to Clint, with the fresh face of youth, he flashed Clint a shy grin before he questioned him.

"*Cómo está usted?*" The boy asked him how he was.

"*Bien*, all right," Clint answered.

"My mission name is José," the boy said.

"You speak Spanish well."

"All of us used to speak Spanish."

"Used to?" Clint asked.

"I have only joined the band this moon and have not taken the vow yet. But I caution you, do not speak Spanish to them. It is now considered an insult."

"The vow?"

"The vow of Sup. Our god."

"And what is the vow?"

"It is the oath of the old ways. All of these men were at the mission; some of them born there. But the mission ways

19

changed. No longer was there enough food. The cholera took many of us . . . and lues, the rotting disease that makes you loco. We are returning to the laws of Sup, the old ways that made the Chumash great, before the Spanish came and brought their god."

On the trek, Clint learned that the boy had been at La Purisima mission, a few miles inland from Punta Concepción. His father had fallen out of favor with the padres and, with the *cholos* at his heels, left the boy and his mother and fled back into the mountains to join Hawk's band. Soon many of the others joined them. The boy too fled into the mountains. He had heard of the band of converts and sought and found his father there.

The boy's Spanish was much better than Clint's, but soon, the boy said, he would never be allowed to speak the *Mexicanos*' language again. They talked until one of the men reined his horse around and started back to the end of the procession; then the boy hurried forward to join the women and children. The white-chested warrior called Hawk scolded him, and the boy did not come back again.

Clint looked over his shoulder and noted that the same two men who had been stationed between him and the forest were now riding drag and keeping a constant eye on him.

To hell with them, he thought. Picking up a dead laurel branch, he used it as a walking stick and concentrated all of his effort on keeping up.

Señorita Juana Maria de Alverez y Padilla sat ramrod straight in the rear seat of the family caleche. Her black Portuguese lace mantilla lay properly arranged along her beautiful blemish-free cheeks, her lips slightly reddened, her bright crimson gown full and covering all but her long sculptured neck. Her *dueña*, or chaperon, *Tía*, Aunt, Angelina Alverez, faced her. Riding in the rear-facing front seat, also ramrod straight, her *dueña* was dressed in black from head to toe and noticeably less slender.

With a gold family crest painted on the door panels, the caleche glinted in the sun. Juana's father, Don Estoban Padilla, had imported the carriage all the way from Baltimore in the United States. For almost half a year the carriage had sat, wrapped tightly in oilskin, on the pitching deck of a hide brig. Now, with the tireless hand-rubbing of a dozen Chumash who worked at the rancho, it gleamed. Black lacquer side panels reflected the passersby, and bronze side lanterns with cut-crystal panes refracted the sunlight, throwing a rainbow of color. The matched gray Andalusian stallions proudly sported plumes of white ostrich on brass-trimmed headstalls. The rest of their tack was trimmed in polished silver in Californio style.

Every *paisano* in Santa Barbara was proud of the coach, a far finer vehicle than the rough two-wheeled *carretas* of the pueblo, as they had always been proud of Don Estoban Padilla, his family, and his fine Andalusian horses.

The caleche was driven by a Chumash, booted and dressed in black, and followed by five vaqueros from Rancho del Robles Viejos, the ranch of the old oaks. A well-dressed young Californio in velvet jacket and trousers paused at the approach of the carriage. "Señorita Juana! *Buenos días.*" He doffed his flat-crowned hat, bowing deeply as the carriage passed.

Juana cut her eyes to him but covered the lower half of her face with her fan. Her dark eyes flashed in recognition, eliciting a wide smile from him, but she did not speak.

"There is no need to gawk," her *dueña* instructed. "There will be plenty of time for the young men when you are a little older."

"That may be so, Tía Angelina. But I am certainly old enough. Both you and Mama were married younger than I am now. And there is no harm in looking."

Her aunt moaned. "You will not think 'no harm' if your father, or that wild young mestizo he sends to watch over us, takes offense." She glanced back at the escort. "Look behind you, little one."

Juana turned in her seat to face the rear, and her dark eyes widened. All five vaqueros had reined up, and Inocente Ruiz, the tall, slender vaquero her aunt had referred to, leaned far out of the saddle, his quirt shaking in the face of the frightened young man who had called out to her.

"Inocente," Juana called loudly, "*vamos!*"

The vaquero looked up, turned back to the young man and shook the quirt once more, saying something Juana could only imagine. He wheeled his horse, galloping to close the distance between the escort and the carriage. Juana turned her attention back to her aunt, who continued to chastise her.

"It is rude and impolite to raise your voice in public, Juana," her aunt scolded.

"And it is worse than rude to accost a man for offering pleasantries," Juana said. "Inocente is many things, I think, but 'innocent' is not one of them. Sometimes I—"

"It is not your place, Juana, to judge your father, your *dueña*, or your father's appointed protectors. You just be thankful for those who love and look after you. Inocente is faithful and would lay down his life for you."

"For that I am grateful," Juana said. *Protect is one thing,* she thought, *smother is another. And Inocente Ruiz is half Chumash, a mestizo. His temper will come to no good.* For a mestizo, he was far too arrogant, though he was rather handsome. He had the straight fine features of the Castilians, but he could be cruel, and as deadly as a rattlesnake.

She stared at the adobes they passed, lost in her thoughts. She had known Inocente Ruiz most of her life and never had more than a few words with him, and those only when she asked him to do for her. His responses had been limited to "*Sí,* señorita." He was no talker, more of a brooder, a man who seemed to simmer, like a pot ready to boil over. Why would Father have such a man shadow her? It was enough that Tía Angelina heard and saw everything she did.

She sighed and sat back as the two beautiful matched gray Andalusians picked up their gait across the town's central square, their hooves ringing on the cobblestones. All heads in the square turned to admire the beautiful carriage and one of Alta California's most beautiful señoritas. They cut their eyes away when they fell under the cold hawklike stare of Inocente Ruiz.

Captain Quade Sharpentier stepped out of the cantina to watch the carriage approach. "Come here, Skinner," he called over his shoulder.

The sun shone brightly on the square, with just enough of a sea breeze to keep from shedding jackets. A boy moved a herd of spotted goats down the road and was yelled at by a presidio guard, a *soldado*, who kicked at one errant goat that had the audacity to pull a few daisies from one of the planted areas surrounding the paved public area. The guard returned to his position in front of the presidio at the base of the flagpole that proudly displayed the red, white, and green, serpent-and-nopal banner of Mexico.

The boy hurried the goats along, threading them around a *carreta* pulled by a single coffee-and-cream brindle-colored ox and loaded high above the driver's head with stiff dried cowhides—so stiff that some sat on end, becoming sideboards. The cart's solid sycamore-slab wheels began to clatter as it reached the cobblestones that lined the road surrounding the plaza.

The cart driver's bean-brown face broke into a broad grin as one of the goats reared on his hind legs and, with full-curled horns, ambitiously butted the ox in the side with a thump that carried over the goats' bleating and the clamor of sharp hooves on stone. The massive beast looked back with bovine indifference, reassuring himself that the pest was going on his way, then continued to clomp ahead.

The caleche reined up to give the boy and the *carreta* time to clear the way.

The first mate hulked into the doorway, his mug still in hand. "Aye, sir?" A number of other men from the crew followed Skinner and stood squinting into the afternoon sun.

"Am I mistaken," the captain asked, "or is that a fine caleche coach?"

The huge man squinted his pig eyes. "It 'pears to me to be, sir. And, by the gods, will you look at the fancy señorita riding in her."

All the men stared in silence while the coach passed. Sharpentier locked eyes with Inocente Ruiz, and both men attempted to stare each other down until Ruiz had passed so far he was forced to turn or rein the horse back.

"Now that," Quade said, watching the caleche and the beautiful girl disappear around a bend in the road, "might be worth starting a bloody revolution over."

Clint and the Indians followed a small freshwater stream, its banks lined with cattails, then sandbar willows, fresh with new green, as they rose higher. Dragonflies competed with mayflies for space, creating little concentric waves as they teased the water where it slowed enough to pond. A snake, a black yellow-striped racer, slithered with the speed for which it was named, staying ahead of two of the Indian boys, then cut a wake through the creek and disappeared into the thick willow stand. It flushed a pair of western meadowlarks, their bellies as yellow as the snake's stripes, who broke their repertoire of song with sharp clucking insults as they winged away.

Clint managed a few more swallows of water as they moved up the creek and though he was still nauseous, felt his strength ebbing back.

Soon the canyon deepened, and willows gave way to sandpaper oaks and laurel, then a few huge canyon oaks and twisting sycamores with hand-size leaves. Clint's legs ached with exhaustion, and his face and shoulders burned from the sun, but the earth was solid under him, he had all the water he needed, and even the pain felt good.

They paused among a grove of red-barked, wax-leaved trees—*madrones*, Clint remembered hearing them called in Santa Barbara—and the Indians paused to gather clusters of bright red fruit, filling their carrying nets and baskets.

Clint needed to relieve himself and walked into the nearby brush. Almost immediately, he was flanked by the two horseback braves. They watched him closely until he finished. He was becoming a little irritated at their constant vigil, but still he said nothing. It wouldn't do to have his tongue wager what a tired body couldn't back up. He kept quiet and bided his time.

The canyon widened, and tangled scrub oaks opened onto a broad flat. Two dozen huts of bent willow, woven grass, and mud lined the creek. Some of the huts were small, no more than three paces across, but most looked to be as much as six paces. Other Indians, men, women and children, stood along the path, watching Clint. Some of the younger women, bare-breasted under rabbit-skin or woven reed vests, observed him with obvious interest.

He realized his boots were salt-stained and cracked, his duck pants torn and ragged, his long sandy hair filthy and matted, and his shirt in tatters. His leather belt, cracked boots, sheathed knife, and ragged clothes were all he had in the world.

Ahead of him, grinding stones lay near piles of acorns, and mussel and abalone shells formed deep piles beyond. Women stood near hooped willow stretchers, scraping hides with shells and the sharpened scapula of the very deer whose skins they dressed. Others worked over stone mortars, grinding wild buckwheat or other seeds and acorns. *These heathens eat well*, Clint thought. He dropped to the creek and took one more long drink, then followed on into the center of the village. A few children, naked and playing with tubular bird-bone whistles, followed along behind him.

One larger round hut in the middle was sturdily framed with timber and a dozen paces from side to side. A baked-clay deity hung from a tree-trunk doorjamb, gracing the entrance with a scowl. On the other side of the opening, his arms folded and feet widely placed, stood the feather-cloaked Indian, his stone ax swinging casually at his side. Though shorter than the man called Hawk, he was powerfully thick-chested. His flint-hard expression outdid the deity's. A feeling of dread gnawed at Clint's already nauseous gut, but his gaze never left Feathercloak's hard eyes. Clint passed by without hesitation, entering the large hut, followed closely by Hawk. As his eyes adjusted, Clint could see that the hut was dug into the ground. After descending a two-foot ladder, the leader motioned Clint to a dark corner of the hut. There, on the far side of a fire pit that fed a trail of smoke to a single opening in the reed roof above, a pile of deerskins lay scattered haphazardly.

Hawk pointed around him at the structure. *"Temescal,"* he said, and Clint nodded. Smoke hung in the hut and burned Clint's tired eyes. Hawk pointed to the pile of hides, indicating that Clint should rest there. Collapsing on the hides, he let his lids lower but opened them quickly when the resentful Indian entered behind Hawk and again they argued. Eventually they sat around the fire and were joined by a half-dozen others, Clint's presence apparently forgotten or at least ignored.

It's rest I need, Clint told himself. *With old Feathercloak and his followers, I need all the strength I can muster. Until then, whatever these people want to do with me, they will.*

It was a feeling he did not relish. He closed his eyes, but tried only to rest, not sleep.

Five

Startled, Clint awoke to the deep-throated chanting of a dozen naked, sweaty men who surrounded the small blazing fire in the center of the room. The room lay dark and hot, and the men swayed and sweated as they sang, their shadows on the wall dancing in hypnotic unison. Hawk glanced at Clint, motioned him over, then shifted aside to make room for him in the circle, patting the earth beside him. Clint moved to the spot and sat, crossing his legs like the others.

He could not understand the chant, but was soon caught up in the rhythm and the swaying, and, to his surprise, found himself joining in. He removed his shirt to resemble the nakedness of most of the men. Accepting a shell, he scraped the sweat away as the others did. Hawk seemed pleased. Clint, still weak and at their mercy, was damned glad he was.

The chant increased in tempo, and the hostile Indian rose. He donned an ankle-length cloak of black raven feathers, trimmed at the neck in brilliant red-woodpecker head patches. This was topped by a five-strand necklace of limpet shells that hung to his waist. He began a stomping dance around the outside of the circle. With small turtle shells filled with pebbles tied to each ankle, he made his own rhythm.

"*Truhud*," Hawk said, motioning to the dancer, and Clint presumed that was the man's name.

Dancing and chanting, Truhud seemed to be acting out a one-man play of strife and turmoil. He must be a holy man or the chief, Clint thought, but as he thought back on the day, realized that the group seemed to obey Hawk's commands. He decided Truhud must be the holy man, the shaman, and Hawk the chief. The holy man was a bad enemy to have in any society, and probably the worst to have in a heathen one. He hoped Hawk was a powerful chief.

Clint's stomach grumbled. He had not eaten in more than two days. Eventually the chanting ended, and Truhud hung his brilliant cloak aside and returned to his place in the circle. After a few more scrapes with the shells, they all rose and filed out of the stifling sweat-house. Outside the *temescal*, Clint breathed deeply, and the cool night air refreshed him. While Truhud, followed by three warriors, stalked away into the darkness, the others made their way to the deep creek and plunged in. The only ones who remained out of the creek were the two who had been dogging his steps all day. They remained behind, flanking him at a distance. Clint followed the bathers in and emerged feeling better than he had in days. His fatigue had lifted, at least for the moment.

He eyed the distance to the shadowed forest and wondered if now that his strength was beginning to return, he could outdistance the guards. He had always been fleet of foot and had legs like a ship's pump pistons from years in the rigging, but he knew he was far from his best. He would bide his time, he decided. He was uncomfortable in the strange surroundings, worried about his shipmates, and his gut was flapping inside him with emptiness. Leaving for Santa Barbara was topmost in his mind. If only he weren't so damned weak. He knew he should take advantage of the Indians' hospitality, however tenuous, until he was ready. Then he could take matters into his own hands.

Clint followed the men back to the center of the village where they sat around a large rock covered with grinding holes, and to Clint's relief, the women served them cakes of baked unleavened acorn bread, mussels, madrone fruit, berries, and roasted insects. The food arrived in finely fashioned soapstone bowls and intricate baskets. Fresh water, in baskets lined with asphaltum, accompanied the meal.

Hawk studied him with quiet amusement as Clint turned the grasshopper over and over, eyeing it uncertainly. The first many-legged morsel was a chore to put in his mouth, but to Clint's surprise, he found the fire-browned grasshopper, which he disguised among a handful of berries, pleasantly nutty. He ate his fill of the varied fare and, that necessity satisfied, admired the full-breasted girls who served him, particularly the one who had applied the salve to his lips and forehead. She continued to pamper him, keeping his bowl full. When they had finished, the tall Indian led him to a willow hut, and the girl followed. She spread a bed of deerhides for Clint.

With a nod of approval, Hawk excused himself, but the girl remained.

Hospitality at its finest, Clint decided. Shedding his shirt and boots, he watched the girl, who, to his delight, shed all—dropping her rabbit-skin vest and reed skirt in a pile. She turned and adjusted a hanging skin over the opening. Then she joined him on the mat.

He knew the guards were close by. *To hell with them,* he thought, encircling her in his arms. Then the thought struck him that maybe she was meant to be the sexual equivalent of his last meal.

If so, he decided, he was going to make the most of it.

In Pueblo Santa Barbara, just as the sun topped the mountains to the east, a huge man lounged in the shade of a low shrub, coal-black hair swept low across his brown eyes, covering his wide brow as he watched the scene unfolding in the road. His nut-brown skin made him almost invisible in the shadows, even as huge as he was.

If he had even a few *reales* or pesos in his pocket, he would have been in the cantina, but it had been a long while since he could afford a mug. He had been part of a shore crew, a hide gang, but had been on a meandering walk in the hills behind Santa Barbara when his ship returned for the hides, so he had been left behind. But he cared little. He had always been able to fend for himself. Pele, the goddess of the volcano, would watch over him. He would mind his own business and wait until another ship came along.

Still, he watched with interest as the captain and first mate of the ship that he had heard was lost to the rocks quietly crossed Calle Principal.

Captain Quade Sharpentier and his first mate, Skinner, carried the jug of *aguardiente* across the dirt road to the presidio, the military headquarters of the pueblo. They walked casually to the edge of the building and rounded the corner. Near the rear, a thick timber door sat deep in the adobe wall. Thick iron hinges and a brass padlock, green with age, the size of a man's palm, gave notice that whatever was inside was valued, as did the armed *cholo* guard who had been outside the door all night.

"That must be the armory," Quade said quietly as they approached the man. "We'll know soon enough. I never knew one of these cholos who would turn down a little dollop of this cactus killer."

The guard watched warily as they approached but did not bother to pick up his musket that leaned against the door.

"You have had a long night, amigo?" Quade asked, smiling.

"*Sí*, amigo, a long night."

"I guess you are about to be relieved."

"As soon as Pablo has taken his tea."

Skinner slapped the man on the back. "Then a little of this nectar will do you no harm." He offered the jug of *aguardiente* to the man, who looked hesitant.

The guard checked over his shoulder, walked to the corner, and peered around it, making sure his *commandante* was not in the area, then returned and took the jug. "Just a taste, to wash the cold night away."

"*Sí*, amigo, wash the cold away. Then when your shift is over, join us at the cantina. There is more where this came from."

The guard drank deeply, smiled, and belched. "*Sí*, the cantina. But, amigo, I prefer *pulque*."

Sharpentier waved, trying to keep his smile from becoming a smirk as he retreated.

"That was too easy," Skinner said, heading back across the road.

"Those *cholos* are dumb as jellyfish," Quade said, "and as cowardly as a sardine facing a shark. We'll know just what the *alcalde*'s armory holds long before we have to buy the *cholo* more than what this jug holds . . . long before."

He chuckled to himself. This was going to be easy. He had seen only two cannon in the presidio, and one of them had been spiked, an iron nail driven into its touchhole so it could not be used. The other was hardly more than a signal piece. The whole of California was undermanned and practically unarmed. Though the officers and politicians wore uniforms that would put Napoleon's generals to shame, none of the soldiers Sharpentier had seen had been more than a ragtag, disorganized bunch.

It would be nothing to take Alta California away from Mexico. If a rebellion would only come . . .

Clint awoke from his second day in the Chumash camp feeling strong. He stretched and yawned, and stepped out of the mud hut. Chahett, as the girl had carefully indicated her name to be, had left the hut before he woke.

At less than a half-dozen paces on each side of the hut, the guards lay curled in deerskins. One of the men reclined on a willow backrest. He stretched when Clint stepped from the hut, then walked over and kicked his fellow guard. They followed Clint as he walked into the brush to relieve himself. The men made no move to restrain his freedom but shadowed him a few feet away.

When Clint returned, the camp was busily at work. Unlike the activities he had witnessed the other day, this time most of the women were mending long lines of woven, then braided, fibrous reed, and the men were busily sharpening flint spears and checking the binding of twelve-inch flint heads to long wooden shafts. Truhud and his followers were nowhere to be seen.

Something's up, Clint thought, but had no idea what the excitement could be. He helped himself to a handful of berries, then sat down to watch. He wandered about the village and watched for hours as the preparations went on; then the whole tribe gathered near the fires. He realized that there were more families in the village than he had originally guessed, for each of the larger houses held as many as four families.

As the shadows grew long, the men began to dance, but this time Hawk motioned for Clint to follow him away from the fires and into the darkening forest. At first Clint was apprehensive as he trailed Hawk, but he watched carefully and saw that the two guards did not follow. His curiosity was aroused. They walked up and over a nearby hill, then Hawk reclined against a rock covered with lichen. He fished a stone-bowled pipe from his carrying net, packed it with tobacco, and lit up.

"*Pestibaba*," he said, motioning to a small antelope-horn tobacco container. He handed the pipe to Clint and smiled as Clint winced after taking a small draw.

"It is very strong," Hawk said in Spanish.

Clint snapped his eyes up at the man, who stared off at the

distant mountains, now shimmering golden in the setting sun.

"You've decided to talk to me?"

"We have taken a vow to go back to the old ways," Hawk said, taking another draw on the pipe. "The better ways, we have decided. But I must admit, the Spanish tobacco is better than ours." He gave Clint the slightest hint of a smile, then his face hardened again. "Do not let my people know that I have spoken to you in the Spanish tongue."

"Why have you decided to 'go back'?" Clint asked.

"It is enough for you to know that we have. I will not speak the Spanish tongue again, so listen carefully. Truhud is a powerful man among the Chumash. He is our *paxa*, a shaman to you. He thinks we should kill you and any who discover where we are. By not killing you, I am taking a great risk. Should you tell the missions of our whereabouts—"

"I owe the missions nothing, and I didn't exactly *try* to come among you," Clint said, taken aback at what Hawk was saying, even though the *paxa* had already made it plain enough. "It was the will of the sea and the wind."

"And the will of Sup," Hawk added, "but the *paxa* says it is Sup's way of testing our resolve and we will offend him if we do not kill you."

Clint did not respond. Silently, his fists balled at his sides, he watched as Hawk took another draw on his pipe.

"There is a hunt planned. Afterward, if all is well, I will take you to Santa Barbara where there are others of your kind who trade there. Stay out of Truhud's way. He is well named, what you call the rattlesnake. He strikes with little warning."

Clint nodded as Hawk continued. "Stay with me. Do as I say, and you will be among your kind again."

"Why do you help me?"

"There are good and bad among all people . . . even ours. And if I learned one thing at the missions, it is that there is wrong thinking in all peoples . . . and you were brought to us by Sup, our god."

"What is your trouble with the missions?"

"It is not of your concern. Let it be enough that I will help you return to your people."

"Thank you," Clint managed.

"It is nothing," Hawk said, and started back to the camp. "Remember, I have not spoken with you. And take caution with Truhud. Even *my* power is limited. He is a powerful man."

As they entered the village, Truhud, the rattlesnake, stood with three ominous, frowning warriors who watched Clint and Hawk return to the fireside.

Clint and Hawk sat for a while, and the women served them. When it grew fully dark and the moon appeared, Hawk rose from his cross-legged position in front of the fire and began a slow rhythmic dance. As it progressed, other men joined in while still others shook turtle-shell rattles, beat hollowed-out logs, or played low-toned bone flutes. The women did not join in, but clapped in rhythm.

Soon two men, their bodies completely blackened, joined the dance. Hawk circled them, feigning with the spear. The blackened men danced with their arms tightly held to their sides, their bodies swaying like snakes. Finally, Hawk feigned driving the spear home, narrowly missing the men, who fell to the ground, and the women fell upon them, pretending to hack at them with stone knives, and the dance was over.

Clint went to his hut with the ever-present guards flanking him at ten paces, and wondered what the dance signified. He waited for a while, anticipating Chahett's arrival, but she did not come.

That night he slept lightly, an ear tuned to the silent step of the *paxa* and a quiet dread of what the morning might bring.

Six

Turk, among the lucky survivors thanks to Clint Ryan, sat in a dark corner of the cantina. A wide-hipped señorita served as *camanera*, barmaid, and kept the *marineros'* mugs full.

Wishon sat across the plank table from him, away from the rest of the crew of the *Savannah*. Six men sat around two larger tables near the light of the open doorway. One group was rolling dice carved from pieces of wood; the other was playing whist.

Captain Sharpentier and Cecil Skinner, the surviving officers of the *Savannah*, sat in a far corner with a *cholo* guard, talking in low tones. The *marineros* sipped the murky brown grape brandy, *aguardiente*, and the guard clear, white-hot *pulque* made from mescal, and cooled its bite by nibbling equally scalding chiles from a wooden bowl in the center of the table.

The *Savannah*'s officers and crew drank and ate by the grace of the owner, who kept a chit and counted on the good graces of Bryant and Sturgis to pay the bill the first time another ship of their firm called at Santa Barbara.

A short, powerful man, Turk sat low in his chair, his head hanging, his whiskered lips almost touching the mug on the table. "It not be right," he mumbled drunkenly.

"What?" Wishon, the dark Carib cook, asked, squinting his eyes to focus on his Turkish friend.

"It not be right, by all that's holy."

"You been mumbling dat for de last hour. What de hell 'not be right'?"

"John Clinton Ryan was not the man at fault for sinking that rat-infested tub," Turk muttered. "He was below."

33

"So?" Wishon scratched his tightly curled salt-and-pepper hair.

"So . . . he was never called to watch."

"Hell's fire, man. He must have been called; he jus' did not show. Wit de weather like dat, who de hell could stay on deck a minute longer dan he had to?"

"A bloody sot, that's who."

"What you mean, man?"

"That sogger bastard Mackie," Turk said. "He always shirked, and he was always in the grog. Clever bastard, though. I never knew him to get catched. The cap'n would have cagged him right and good, but he never got catched."

"He was supposed to call Ryan to de watch. I bet he was in de stores, suckin' at de grog barrel, when he shoulda been fetchin' Ryan to de watch." The Carib took a deep draw on his mug, draining it. "I never knew Clint Ryan to shirk, dat's a sure ting."

As a member of the starboard watch, same as Ryan, Turk was expected to stand up for his watch mate. Even the second mate was expected to stand up for the crew since he ate with them and slept in the fo'c'sle. But Wishon was one of three independent members of the crew—the captain, the first mate, and the cook.

Turk eyed the Carib, wondering if he might have some influence with the captain. He shook his head to clear the fuzziness away. "We should speak to the cap'n."

"No, man. I wants to work on anudder Bryant and Sturgis ship. They has some fine full-rigged ships. Not all be rat-infested brigs like the *Savannah*. Why make de trouble?"

"But Clint'll be hanged, for a wrong he didn't do."

"He be a dead man. He drowned. Why worry de cap'n wid a dead man?"

"Maybe he's not dead. He's strong as a young ox. If any survived, it would be Clint Ryan."

"Den if he not be dead an' he show up, we go talk to de cap'n."

"He may have saved my life."

"De cap'n?"

"No, fool, Clint Ryan."

"I carve you ears off and feed the gulls wid'm, you calls me fool again," Wishon growled. "Why you tink Clint Ryan not on de watch?"

"He carried me on board after I took a dive into the foremast. I guess I knocked myself out when we reefed." He furrowed his brow and looked puzzled. "I been thinkin' on it ever since we got ashore. Ryan was below. He carried me topside, and he couldn't have been on watch, 'cause he was below."

"Den here be to Clint Ryan." Wishon offered his mug in toast. "An' to both ends of the busk."

They drained their mugs, and Wishon rose and stumbled toward the bar. "I be gettin' us anudder mug of this slop, an' we talk on it some more."

Soohoop, the Hawk, awoke well before Father Sun began chasing Daughter Moon across the sky. It was the day of the great hunt, one the tribe had planned for during the whole of the awakening moon. They had fared the sleeping moon well, the women and children were fat with the plentiful food from all four moons of last year, and again the land was greening. It was good.

Hawk rose, stretched, and stepped from his hut. Tuhnow, the badger, was awake and had the communal cooking fire stoked. The rest of the tribe still slept.

Hawk eyed the small hut where the Anglo slept and wondered about the man. The *marinero* Ryan had seemed nearly dead when the tribe had found him on the beach, but he had recovered quickly. The *paxa* Truhud wanted the man dead. He was of no use to the tribe, Truhud argued. Ryan had nothing but hunger, and that the tribe did not need. And he was an Anglo, almost as much of an enemy as the Spanish. Hawk had tested his authority by overruling the *paxa*. He must not be proven wrong.

Now that they had saved the white man from having his bones dry on the beach, the tribe was responsible for him. Sup would frown on the tribe if the man was now harmed or came to harm from others—unless Ryan offended the laws of Sup. It was a responsibility Hawk had thought on long and hard, then argued vehemently about with the *paxa*, before he had Badger give Ryan the water.

It is time to test the man's worth, and my judgment, Hawk thought as he crossed the distance to the hut. He stepped inside and nudged the sleeping man with his toe. Ryan was instantly awake, wary and watchful, ready for trouble. He quickly pulled on his boots and gained his feet. *It is a good sign*, Hawk thought. *A man who is alert, who does not complain, and who is this one's size could be useful to the tribe. He did not make trouble when Chahett did not come to his sleeping mat last night. Maybe he is wise enough to know that it is bad medicine to take a woman the night before a great hunt. A man needs all his strength and more. He needs good medicine. He needs the hand of Sup on his shoulder. Yes, this man seems to be different than most Anglos. My judgment was good*, Hawk thought, *at least so far.*

Hawk went from hut to hut and soon all the men had gathered around the fire. Each brought his spear and a carrying net with a gourd of water, jerked venison and fish, and a knife. Clint followed them to the horses and watched them ready the animals with carved wooden saddles over woven blankets and bridle them with headstalls only—no iron in the mouth to control the animal. Hawk saddled a mare and led her to Clint, who nodded his approval and mounted.

It felt strange at first, since Clint had not been in the saddle for over three years. The little mare, fresh to the morning, ducked her head and bucked, landing hard on all fours. Hawk watched with approval as the mare kicked and humped her back, and Clint patiently brought her to respect him.

Clint looked over his shoulder as they rode from camp and was pleased to see that Truhud stood watching them leave.

At least he would not have to watch his back.

In the evening shadows across the square from the cantina, two men talked quietly while they watched the guard at the door of the presidio.

As it did most afternoons, the breeze had risen, and the Mexican flag flapped in the wind. A little whirlwind of dust danced across the plaza, then swiveled and, carrying leaves with it, disappeared into an alleyway between two adobes.

"The bugger would have been better off if he had just told us what the lock hid," Sharpentier said. "The bastard cost me a quart of *pulque*, and still kept his trap locked tighter than that door."

"Has he passed out yet?" Skinner asked in a whisper.

"His head nodded a few times . . . there, his chin is on

his chest." Sharpentier stepped quietly from the darkness of a doorway to the wall of the presidio. He paused and bent to pick up a loosened cobblestone, then followed a side wall to where the guard slept, deep in a doorway.

Sharpentier brought the cobblestone down on the guard's head with a resounding thump. The man slumped forward, and the captain pulled the man's Bilboa sword from his scabbard and threw it into the nearby brush.

"That should quiet the bugger." Skinner laughed gruffly.

"I had to help him a wee bit," the captain said, looking behind to make sure no one had seen. "Drag the sogger away from the door."

As Skinner did so, Sharpentier used the bloodied stone on the lock. The blow echoed across the square. Again he struck it, and the old lock sprang open. Throwing the cobblestone away, he shoved the heavy door open.

Skinner followed him inside. The captain scratched a lucifer, which flared and filled the room with its pungent odor, covering that of the wet, musty room. The room lay long and narrow. Slotted boards lined the walls where muskets had once rested. Everything was covered with cobwebs. Beyond the muskets, a few long festooned lances leaned against the wall, and a dozen or so Bilboa swords reflected the light of the match. But the Spanish muskets were not to be found.

"She's empty," Skinner whispered harshly.

"No, there in the back." The captain moved forward. "Damn." Only one gallon-size keg, a powder canteen with *Hudson's Bay Company* stenciled on its side, rested forlornly in the corner. It was the total powder supply for the whole garrison.

"The fools," the captain muttered. He walked along the rear wall where four pyramidal piles of a hundred cannonballs rested on brass monkeys. "Enough ball for a bloody man-o-war and not enough powder to blow a pissant across the road."

"Let's get the hell out of here, Captain, before we're found out."

"The damndest thing," Sharpentier grumbled, following Skinner from the room. The guard moaned in the distance. "I've got a mind to bash his worthless head in," the captain said. But Skinner steered the captain toward the cantina.

The big Kanaka who stood in the shadows wanted to go help the Mexican guard. The captain of the sunken brig had hit him very hard, and even after half an hour the man did not move. The Kanaka stayed in the deep shadows and, as always, minded his own business. Besides, if he was found near the Mexican guard, he might be blamed for striking him. No, it would be best to stay out of sight and out of the way. Soon, another ship would be along, and he would be with some of his countrymen. He moved his huge round body, its soft flesh belying the strength of five men, deeper into the brush. He hoped that neither the God of the missionaries nor Pele would be unhappy with him. Like the men from the sunken brig, he was a stranger in a strange land. No, he would stay out of other people's business.

Clint Ryan watched with interest as the dozen Indians uncovered two thirty-foot pine and pitch canoes—*tomolos*, they called them—hidden in the brush above the beach. They loaded spears and coils of line aboard and carried the boats to the water. He pitched in to help and was surprised at the lightness of the boats. The pine was hand-split, lapped like long shingles, and well caulked with asphaltum, which was easily found along the California coast.

He thought he would soon be back at sea, which was fine with him, for it kept him away from the paxa and his men. But why were they launching boats? The heavy spears and line were not for fishing. They had to be hunting, hunting something big.

From the dock of the *Savannah* he had seen many swordfish dozing near the surface, their long dorsal fins flopping from side to side with the rise and fall of the swell. There were hundreds of ocean creatures that would require a spear or even the hard iron and heavy line of a whaling harpoon. He knew the Indians took sea otter, for they brought most of it into the ranchos. The *patrones* traded for them with the Indians before passing the skins on to the hide ships. Otter hides brought a hundred dollars each in China.

The men launched the boats through the crashing surf and began paddling madly to clear the swells. Before long, they were making good headway into the breeze. Two Indians paddled on each side of the boats, the bottoms of which were covered with piles of skins, woven line, and spears. A spotter, Clint figured, who was also a spearman or harpooner, rode in the bow, and the man guiding the boat with an oar tiller rode the rear.

In the distance, Clint judged twenty miles, lay the channel islands, and the boats were heading for them. If that was the destination, they were in for a day of hard paddling. What could they be searching for? He would find out soon enough.

Seven

After several hours of hard paddling, they neared the center of the channel. Clint could make out three distinct islands, still distant. Santa Cruz was the largest of the three, and he knew that it, like Santa Catalina, was often used to conceal cargo from the tax collectors at Monterey.

As he worked the bent hide-covered willow paddle, he kept a close eye for sails. Though his time with the Indians had not been particularly unpleasant, he was ready to find a ship. He wanted to return to the life he had known for the last twelve years. As a youth of seven, as soon as he arrived in Mystic from Ireland, he had been indentured to a tanner. His parents had gotten the fever while on board the ship, and his Scottish mother, Irish father, younger sister, and half the passengers and crew had been buried at sea.

The tanner who held his indenture had not been a kind man, often rewarding Clint for his hard work with kicks. But Clint learned well. At fifteen, when his indenture was up, he left to become a common sailor. Since then he had plied his trade over most of the world's oceans, on cod ships, brigs, barks, and full-rigged ships. Shanghaied aboard a British man-o-war, he had been a munitions helper for over a year, until he slipped the Brits in the Sandwich Islands and caught a Mystic-bound whaler home.

As the Indians neared the island's north end, a great gray whale surfaced and blew, and they stopped paddling to watch. Clint waited apprehensively for the order to paddle toward the great whale, anticipating what he knew would be a fruitless attempt with the paltry spears they carried. But the Indians merely rested and watched reverently while the great whale surfaced and then sounded.

They continued on, and so did his thoughts. Clint, like most sailors, was a respectable carpenter, sailmaker, cooper, and linesman in addition to his skills as a tanner. He had learned to navigate from a talkative Dutchman who was a skilled second mate and had learned a smattering of a half-dozen languages from the crews of more than a dozen ships. He could hold his own in Spanish, French, Dutch, German, and South Sea Pidgin, and even spoke a little Chinese.

Clint could read in English thanks to the Quaker first mate of a bark, a "friendship"—as ships where the men were well treated were known—that held regular after-hours reading classes for the crewmen. Clint read with a fervor everything he could get his hands on. He read Homer, Payne, Bacon, Shakespeare, the Bible, a half-dozen books on navigation, two dozen Almanacs, and a thousand newspapers from a hundred ports.

A school of several hundred porpoises surrounded the shingled canoes, diving, jumping the waves, racing time and each other, but the Indians ignored them also.

The tillerman changed course, and they began to circle the largest of the islands, Santa Cruz. Hawk, the bowman of Clint's boat, raised his hand and the paddlers stopped. Standing in the bow, he scanned the sea. He waved them on, and they rounded a headland where Clint was surprised to see ten more *tomolos* gathered.

Between the boats and the shore, a thousand creatures bobbed on the surface, Pilot whales, Clint recognized. The distinctive knotted melon-shaped heads and cold black bodies rose and fell quietly in a deep bay. At eighteen feet, the large males were almost as long as the boats, and a hundred times heavier. The cows were a few feet shorter, and the calves ranged in length from four feet up.

Well, Clint thought, *if this is what is to be, it's a damn sight better than going after the grays.* He could see a chance of taking the pilots.

Hawk instructed the other boat and, in conjunction with a long line of boats, began working the herd of whales as sheepdogs work their flock, paddling quickly, changing direction, herding. Hawk picked up two rocks the size of small cannonballs from within the pile of hides and, like the bowmen in the other boats, leaned far overboard, striking the stones together underwater. The whales roiled the water in front of the boats and soon swam shoulder to shoulder, a solid pulsing mass of gleaming black in a sea of foam and heaving swells.

Birds joined in the clamor, diving and working the smaller fish and sardines who scattered in front of the solid wall of whales. The birds screeched, reveling in the unexpected banquet. Even the whales cried and whistled like a pack of underwater hounds after an aquatic fox.

Only the men were silent.

Clint, his paddle digging deep as they pulled ever closer, wondered what would happen if the whales should turn on them. He imagined being in the water with a thousand black bodies, each outweighing him several hundred times. But like a good sailor, when the captain piped, he danced. He paddled until his shoulders ached and his mouth was cotton.

They worked the herd nearer and nearer the shore, and Clint realized they had no intention of harpooning the animals but were in hopes of beaching them. He had seen whales on the beach in many parts of the world. Sometimes the animals would inexplicably beach themselves. Even when guided to deep water by helpful bystanders, they had been known to return, beaching themselves again and again until the helpful watchers gave up in frustration.

A small inlet, not more than fifty paces across, lay behind a shallow wall of rocks. As the whales stacked up against the rocks, Clint wondered again why the animals did not turn on the boats—the warriors would have been no match for even one of the big males—but they did not. With a crush, several were forced over the rocks into the inlet. They left bloody trails where the rocks tore at their flesh, but quickly the surge washed the rocks clean. There had been no choice for the whales: either broach the rocks, or be crushed by the whales behind them. When a dozen had crossed the shallow reef, Hawk waved the boats away and, with the others, skirted the great herd. Most of the remaining animals turned and headed for deep water, but a few milled about outside the reef, their cries encouraging the escape of those trapped.

At Hawk's direction, his boat joined the others on a nearby white-sand beach. Clint heard Spanish being spoken by some of the other Indians, but he stayed with his group.

After an hour, with the sun low in the west, they rose and

walked to the lagoon. One of the largest of the trapped pilot whales had been stranded high on the rocks, almost out of the water, so the hunters started on him. Though they drove spears into the animal, he seemed resigned to his fate, almost thankful that his unnatural ordeal on the rocks had ended.

Quickly the men stripped away the fat, then the meat. While some butchered, others hauled the meat ashore and strung it high in the branches of nearby scrub oaks. Flocks of birds gathered to feed on the offal and steal the smaller scraps hung in the trees, but the Indians ignored them, and Clint could see why. There was plenty for men and birds alike, thousands and thousands of pounds of meat trapped in the lagoon, as much as they could haul back to the mainland in a hundred trips with the two boats. Small big-eared foxes of a variety Clint had never seen crept out of the undergrowth and worked shyly around the men, ignoring them, but wary of the bigger birds.

Then the men began capturing the whales still swimming in the shallow lagoon. Ropes of milkweed, nettle, and wild hemp were used to encircle the whales' tails and hold them while other Indians mounted them and drove their spears home. The whales humped and bucked, shaming the toughest bronc, and men were thrown easily from the backs of the animals. They did not go unscathed. The rocks and the rugged bottom got their share of flesh, and the men's blood mingled with that of the whales until soon the lagoon was muddied with blood.

Clint watched as gulls fought a tug-of-war over a long intestine, then he glanced to the sea beyond the reef and noticed a fin cutting the foam. He pointed it out to Hawk, who nodded but ignored the threat. The first shark was soon joined by others until more than twenty cruised the water. They did not attempt to breach the reef but were content to fight for the scraps and offal that washed out to them.

Clint rigged a block and tackle, using a scrub oak trunk as an anchor and a few Spanish words to instruct some of the men from other groups. Hawk watched with interest while Clint employed the slipshod rig to haul the whale carcasses up on the shoreside rocks, making the butchering job much easier. Hawk smiled at his newfound friend who, as he had expected, was proving himself. Sup had not been wrong.

By dark, the men were exhausted. They roasted oily pilot-whale meat over an open fire and slept on the beach.

Don Estoban Padilla, the *patrón* of Rancho del Robles Viejos and Señorita Juana's father, stood on the wide veranda of the hacienda, the *corredor*. It pleased him to hear the warbling of the morning birds, the lowing of cattle, and the playful whinnying of horses in the first yellow rays of sunshine. He had donned his brightly striped serape, which hung to midcalf front and back, to face the morning's chill.

Before him he could see a broad vista leading down to the sea a mile distant, but it represented only a small portion of the rancho that had been home to him all his life, and before that to his father, who had come to Alta California in 1792.

Estoban propped a booted foot against the porch rail and smiled as a vaquero demonstrated his reata skill. The *caballo*, a dun horse he had lassoed, made several gallant leaps across the corral, scattering a few cackling chickens in front of it, trying to shed its rider. The slender man stuck fast, the tails of the bandanna he had tied around his head flapping as the horse leapt and landed stiff-legged, then jumped again. He raked the sides of the horse with long-roweled spurs until the horse's ribs dripped blood.

Estoban nodded his head with enough energy to bounce his single graying queue that hung down below his shoulders in the fashion of the dons.

Finally the animal stood quietly, shivering until the vaquero commanded him to turn with a touch of the reins.

"Well done," Estoban proclaimed, then turned his head to the entryway of the house. "Maria!" he shouted into the shuttered window of the hacienda. "Bring me a cigarillo, *por favor.*"

Estoban studied the hillsides and the dark green live oaks and light green sycamores that dotted them. His father, Don Tiburcio Padilla, had come north as a *cholo*, a mission guard and Spanish soldier. The guards were recruited from those sentenced to jail in Mazatlán or Acapulco. Do your time in a miserable rat- and flea-infested jail, or do your time on the frontier, guarding the missions and protecting the padres. Tiburcio had been one of those who wisely chose Alta California.

His crimes, unlike most of the others, were political. An

educated man, Tiburcio soon rose above the other mission guards. After his sentence was up, though he could have chosen to return to Mazatlán, he refused. Instead, he stayed and distinguished himself as a builder. He was rewarded by the governor of California for his efforts and given a land grant.

The Chumash woman María stepped out of the hacienda and handed Don Estoban a long thin cigar, holding a lit tallow taper under it as he took a deep draw. He nodded to her, and she returned to her work sweeping the intricately woven Chinese carpets that covered the well-packed dirt floor of the big adobe casa. Most thought carpets unhealthy, but Don Estoban found them warm and pleasant to look at. He had never been one for convention. He sat on one of several white stools carved from the vertebrae of a great whale and shined to a high polish that lined the corredor.

Muñoz, the boy who helped old Alfonso in the *establo,* or barn, looked up to see his *patrón* watching and trotted over, pitchfork in hand.

"Do you wish me to saddle you a horse, *Patrón?*" the boy asked.

"No, Muñoz, today I must work on my ledgers. Give Diablo an extra handful of oats this morning. I worked him hard yesterday." The *patrón* kept five palomino Andalusian stallions for his personal use—the pride of his brood stock.

"*Sí,* señor," the boy said. Disappointed that he could not serve his *jefe* in a more direct way, he hurried back to the barn.

Rancho del Robles Viejos lay along the sea for over three leagues and rose two leagues into the mountains—forty-six thousand acres of prime grazing land. Ten thousand head of wild cattle hid in the rancho's ravines and brush, and one thousand head of horses ran free, wandering between adjoining ranchos. Annual rodeos were held to round up and brand the cattle.

For years the primary income of the rancho had been hides, horn, and tallow. Steers were butchered on the range where they were lassoed and spiked, then skinned and horned. *Arrobas*, hide bags, each holding seventeen pounds of tallow, were filled with the fine butterlike sidefat of animals that had spent their lives grazing contentedly on the gentle slopes of mist-watered hillsides overlooking the Pacific. The meat, so plentiful, was left for the carrion eaters.

But neither the hides nor the tallow brought what they

once had, and the Chumash, who for years had brought otter skins to the rancho to trade for iron, beans, and squash, now brought fewer and fewer because there were fewer and fewer Indians and otter.

Yes, times were changing, Estoban thought, and he must change with them. But change to what? Hides, horn, tallow, and otter skins had been a way of life since his father's time. The emancipation of the Indians fifteen years ago had changed things radically. After the revolution in Mexico, the government had decided that the church was too close to Mother Spain and decided to diminish her power severely in California. Under the guise of emancipation, Mexico City had dictated that the land and stock of the missions be returned to the Indians. It was done as ordered, and the mission system was destroyed. Worse, the Mexicans in California immediately cheated and bartered the Indians out of their land, and the governors took advantage of the situation.

After its fall, Mission San Juan Capistrano, the queen of the missions, and many acres surrounding were auctioned off by the governor and sold for seven hundred dollars to the governor's brother-in-law. Now Mexico was on the verge of war with the United States, and that too would change things. Mexico City was far removed from Alta California and seemed to care little for its problems. The petty rebellions inside Alta California had established a climate of distrust, and each don looked upon the other as a potential revolutionary.

Estoban settled his lean frame into a porch chair and watched as his vaqueros rode from the corral. He noted the latecomers who had just begun to stir in the distant *establo* or to lasso horses from the remuda, the herd, kept in the corral. Drawing deeply on his cigarillo, he studied the rolling slopes in the distance.

Wheat and corn had been grown successfully at some of the ranchos, and coastal vessels had carried it to Mexico, which had been successful in trading it. Maybe he would become a farmer. Somehow, that did not set well with him, even though they grew almost all they needed in the gardens and vineyards of the rancho. But to grow for someone else? To be a slave to the weather?

No, that was not the way of the vaquero.

Eight

The next day, the whale butchering continued until a hundred yards of oaks on the hillside overlooking the harbor were covered with strips of flesh and the meat and trees were covered with seabirds of a dozen varieties. Ravens, golden eagles, bald eagles, and a pair of condors had joined in the feast, and the cawing and screaming of the birds blended with the surging surf and the barking and whistling of the whales until finally the sounds were as one. Then the whales cried no more.

It was over, or so Clint thought.

They rested again, then walked inland and found a meadow of salt grass. The men harvested until they had a pile as tall as a man, then each carried huge bundles bound with rope back to the hillside. They spread the whale meat on the dry rocks above the ocean, then spread the salt grass on it. Some of the other Indians made huge packs of meat and started off on foot toward the interior of the island, where Clint presumed they lived. Hawk's party loaded all the meat the boats could safely carry and started back.

In the middle of the channel, after four hours of hard paddling, Clint spotted a ship in the distance. Within an hour, he could make out the sail pattern of a brig. He motioned to Hawk, who understood that he wanted to try to make contact with the ship, and Hawk changed course.

Maybe, just maybe, Clint thought, *I'll soon be back with my shipmates—if any of them still live*.

They paddled hard to intercept the ship, but the canoes rode deep in the water with the heavy load of meat and men. The brig sailed within a quarter mile of the boats, and Clint stood, shouted, and waved desperately. The crew of the *Charleston* waved back but sailed on.

Damn the soggers, Clint thought as he paddled, but resigned himself to his stay with the Indians. Soon. Soon, he would set out to Santa Barbara, even if he had to do it on foot.

The women met them at the beach. What meat could not be packed on the horses they carried in their large conical baskets and carrying nets.

Upon arriving in camp, Clint retreated to his hut and, tired from the long days of fighting the sun, wind, waves, and massive black whales, was quickly asleep. He awoke to the pounding of drums, the rattling of turtle shells, and the chanting of the tribe.

He joined the tribe at the fire, where a dance led by the *paxa* was already under way and the men were gorging themselves with roasted whale meat. They danced well into the night, celebrating the successful hunt, Clint presumed. After the dance, the men gathered around the fire and began passing a pipe. Other than an occasional pipe on a quiet night at sea, Clint seldom smoked, but he felt it would be impolite to refuse. He drew deeply on the pipe and winced at the bitterness of the tobacco. By the time the pipe had made the rounds of the men, he reached for it, saw two of it, and tried again to grasp it, but it kept going in and out of focus. The brave next to him helped him find his mouth, and he drew deeply.

It was morning when he came to. The others had retired to their huts, but he had slept where he sat, next to the now-dead fire. The boy who had befriended him sat near, waiting for Clint to awake.

"It is the *pestibaba* you smoked," José said with a knowing smile. "It is very strong. I should have told you to take very small puffs. I will take *tolache* when I take the vow, and it is much stronger. You call it jimson weed. It takes you to the spirit world and, if you are devout, brings you back."

"And if not?" Clint managed.

"If not, you go blind, or join the spirit world."

"No vow for me, thanks anyway," Clint said, managing a slight smile. Then his stomach cramped, and he doubled over. When it lessened, he was able to sit up. "I'm a little sick at my stomach." Clint rose to his feet unsteadily.

"Come, we will go into the woods and I will find the herb that will help you."

"Not this *tolache*?"

"No." The boy smiled. "This herb is only for the stomach."

Clint followed José deep into the scrub oak. Feeling dizzy, he called ahead to the boy, "I'm going to sit awhile and wait till this stuff wears off."

"You sit. I will return when I've found the *toknota*—fennel, I think the Spanish call it."

Clint reclined near a trickle of water so small it could barely be called a creek, and scooted back into the shade of the thick scrub of sandpaper oak under a heavier canopy of tall pepperwood laurel that seemed to favor the moist flat. He closed his eyes and waited for the dizziness to go away.

He must have dozed, he figured, for when he awoke, he heard voices and the low moaning of someone in pain. Another *pestibaba* victim? His eyes searched the direction of the moaning, downstream from where he sat in the shade. He moved a little to the side and spotted three women. One, a young girl, sat leaning against a tree, her belly swollen with child. She moaned quietly and clasped her belly with both hands. Her two companions were older women, probably midwives or the girl's relatives.

He watched self-consciously as the old women pulled the girl to her feet and helped her squat over a small depression they had scraped out in the sand. Moving would only call attention to him, so he remained in the shadows and watched. He wondered if it was proper, his observing this, but he was fascinated. What he was seeing was the most basic and exciting of life's processes.

From the corner of his eye he spotted a movement in the brush, then slunk back as the *paxa*, with a stone ax in one hand and a long spear in the other, stepped out from the shadows. Shaking the ax at the women in a threatening manner, he spoke in harsh tones. Then he turned and faded back into the shadows of the thick forest.

Clint sensed that the conflict between him and the *paxa* would come to a head if he were discovered watching this pagan spectacle, and the *paxa* was well armed. Even so, Clint could neither turn away nor leave.

The girl swayed back and forth, keening quietly, sitting on her haunches. The old women encouraged her and rubbed her back. Each midwife supported one arm. The girl moaned loudly, her face contorted. The women encouraged. She cried, and strained, and the old women still encouraged her with low tones and rubbed her back.

After this process was repeated several times, one of the old women spoke sharply, and the girl bore down, her face a mask of pain. Sweat beads glimmered on her forehead, and her hair clung with perspiration to the back of her neck.

One of the women ran a hand between the girl's legs and urged her to greater effort. The girl strained, and Clint stared in wonder as the wet dark head of the child appeared. The girl shifted her weight from side to side, holding her breath, straining so hard the vessels stood out in her sweat-soaked face and neck. She emitted a low moan, and the child slid from her.

Clint smiled, for under the coating of blood and mucus, the child appeared perfect. The birth, from what little he knew, had gone well.

The young girl sank to the ground and tried to reach for the child. One of the old women chastised her, shaking her head, and snatched the child up while the other cut the umbilical cord with an obsidian knife. They must want the girl to rid herself of the afterbirth first, Clint decided, as he had seen many a horse and cow do.

The girl cried out, a keening, penetrating scream that sent chills down Clint's backbone. *My God*, he thought, and pitied her. *Even with the miracle she had performed, what pain she must feel*.

One of the old women grasped the girl's shoulders tightly, pinning her to the ground while the other picked up the child and moved upstream, nearer to Clint. He sank deeper into the shadows. *She's going to wash the child in the stream*, he thought, watching closely.

Again Truhud entered the clearing. He snapped at the girl and yelled something to the old woman. The woman paused, looking down at the child for a second, her eyes filled with compassion. The *paxa* yelled a guttural command, and the old woman's look hardened with resolve. Before a shocked Clint could react, she grasped both the child's ankles in one hand and swung it up over her head, bringing it down hard, bashing its tiny head on a flat rock. At the same instant, an echoing animal scream from the girl shattered the stony silence.

Clint clamped his jaw shut to quell his angry yell and choked on his rising bile. His stomach roiled, and a rush of anger flooded him, but he did not move. He knew it was too late—far too late. The child was dead. Only the mother's whimpering wafted to Clint's stunned ears, but the sickening splatting sound still echoed in his mind.

Across the slight clearing, the old woman left the still child and returned to the other midwife and the girl. The *paxa* muttered something, then faded into the shadows. The old woman recovered a reed mat and returned to the child, rolling it up tightly in the mat. She glanced up from her work, and her gaze locked with Clint's. She had seen him, but she continued as if she had not. She paused and to Clint's surprise crossed herself, muttering something in what sounded like Latin. She left the other women and moved off into the brush, carrying the bundle under one arm as if it were a bundle of wood or laundry.

With a shudder, the girl uttered a final choking sobbing cry. Her arm extended toward the departing woman who carried her dead child, her fingers curled, clawlike, grasping. But neither it nor her whimpering did any good. The old woman disappeared into the underbrush. The girl sobbed quietly while the remaining old woman cleaned her with dry grass, then sat back patiently to await the afterbirth.

Clint sank back into the brush and tried to make some sense out of what he had seen. Somehow, he knew that Truhud was the cause of what had happened. A hatred filled him, consuming him until he wanted to run after the man and smash his head to pulp like the child's. Instead, he collected himself. He closed his eyes and stayed quiet until at least an hour had passed. When he opened them again, the girl and the old woman had gone.

He heard rattling in the brush and looked up to see José returning, his hands full of a gray-green herb. He handed it to Clint and started back toward the camp.

"Wait," Clint said. "While you were gone, some women came to that spot"—he pointed—"and one of them gave birth to a child . . . a beautiful, perfect child."

"It is good." José smiled.

"No, it was terrible. One of the old women killed the

child . . . bashed its head against one of the rocks . . ." He pointed.

"That is good also," the boy said, unconcerned.

Clint stared at him in horror.

"It was a firstborn," the boy explained.

"So? I am a firstborn," Clint stammered.

"Among the Chumash . . . the Chumash of the old way . . . the firstborn are killed. The rest of the children will be strong and tall if the firstborn is killed. He carries away the poison of the womb."

"That's crazy."

"It may be, señor, but it is our way."

"You didn't learn that 'way' at the mission?"

"No. The padres do not approve of many of our customs. But they have served us well. We do not approve of many of the mission ways. So we go back to the old way."

"Catholics do not murder children."

"No, but there was much sickness at the missions. Many of our people died from your pale-eye diseases. The padres often had us whipped—at least did not intervene when the *soldados* took up the lash."

"But to kill a child . . ."

"It is our way, Clint Ryan." The boy's eyes turned cold. "It is not for you to question."

Clint did not feel well enough to argue. The boy handed him the herb, and he chewed a mouthful slowly. His mind kept churning, thinking of the innocent child being dashed against the rock, its blood on the stone a mute monument to its passing. He wondered if his stomach would ever be at rest again.

But by the time they had reached camp, the herb had done its work. He went to the hut and sank down on the mat. Chahett appeared shortly after and quietly removed her clothes, but he ignored her and feigned sleep.

Then he heard the angry arguing outside the hut. He pulled on his boots and stuck his head out the opening.

Hawk stood with his back to the hut. In front of Hawk, each carrying a lance or war club, stood the *paxa* and three warriors, and they had blood in their eyes. Clint understood only one word of the heated exchange.

"*Anglo.*"

Nine

"**H**awk!" Clint said, his voice resonating with a deep strength he did not yet feel. Hawk turned to face him, and the *paxa* stepped up beside him.

"Is this argument over me?" Clint asked.

Hawk started to answer but caught himself and only nodded. The *paxa* shook his ax and took a step forward. His men moved to the side, flanking Clint. The guards who reclined on willow backrests nearby rose, and they too took positions hemming Clint in. He guessed that the boy or the old woman must have told the *paxa* of his witnessing the killing of the baby, causing his rage.

Clint had learned in a hundred ports, and almost as many confrontations aboard ship, that a good offense was the best defense. "If you want me dead, Truhud, maybe you would like to accomplish that feat yourself. Or are you man enough?"

Truhud's face went blank. Then he realized that he had been challenged. Clint figured he would be better off fighting one man than half the tribe. Clint spat on the ground between them. His lip curled in derision, and he continued. "You think you have the strength of Sup on your side—let's find out," he goaded. "Just you and me."

A slow smile crossed Hawk's face, and he snapped at Truhud in Chumash. The *paxa* glanced at his men, then his chin rose and his chest expanded. He was a big man, not as tall as Clint but heavily built, with powerful thighs, arms, and shoulders. With quiet deliberation, he spoke, his eyes never leaving Clint's. Clint did not understand his guttural Chumash, but the acceptance of the challenge was clear enough.

Hawk stepped between them and gave his back to the

53

paxa. With the life of the Anglo endangered, Hawk decided the time had come to break his vow. "He has accepted your challenge," he said. "You will fight in front of the whole tribe when the sun dips below the horizon."

"Weapons?"

"The choice of weapons is yours, in the Chumash way."

"To the death?" Clint asked.

"Or until one man kneels in submission and the other accepts. But he does not have to settle for anything but death, and I fear that Truhud will not."

"Good enough," Clint said.

"What weapons do you choose?"

"None," Clint said.

"None?" Hawk asked, not understanding.

"None. We will fight with our hands, in the New England way."

Hawk's look hardened. "Do not be fooled, Clint Ryan. The Chumash learn to wrestle as soon as they learn to walk. Truhud is a strong man and willing opponent. Use care, and remember—you fight for your life."

Clint looked at him for a long moment before he spoke. "When he kneels, I may spare him."

"I hope you have the choice," Hawk said. He laid a hand on Clint's shoulder, then turned away from the hut. "Rest," he called over his shoulder. "I will have Chahett bring you some food and water."

Clint lay on his deerskin robe, wondering if he had done the right thing. If he had kept his mouth shut, maybe Hawk might have prevailed again, but if not, he might now be laced with stone-headed axes. As it was, he would have to face only one man; Clint had rarely been bested at wrestling and had dropped many a man with a single punch. No, he decided, he was better off fighting Truhud than fighting many.

The big man who stayed in the shadows at the outskirts of the pueblo rubbed his growling stomach. It had been two days since he had eaten. He thought about going to the mission and entreating the padres for work or at least a meal, but his pride would not let him, at least not yet. He thought about going to the public house, and decided, yes, that was the thing to do. Ambling out of the scrub oak forest, he entered the little town.

It was only a few blocks down the winding main road to the spacious presidio.

He paused in front of the gates, and a ragtag guard with the round face, bulging eyes, and wide lips of a frog looked at him suspiciously and walked over.

"I came to see if I could work for food." He grinned widely.

The *cholo soldado* looked the huge man up and down and clutched his musket tightly. "Go away, Kanaka. We have no work here."

"My stomach, she rumbles like the wrath of Pele. I need to eat. I will be happy to work."

"I said we have no work here. Go back to your ship. In fact, go back to the Sandwich Islands." Taking a step backward, the guard lowered his chin till it doubled and glared out from under his leather helmet while he lowered the muzzle of the musket to the man's broad belly.

The Kanaka's smile faded. "I wish I *was* in the Sandwich Islands. There no man is turned away when his belly rumbles."

"Then go there."

He eyed the *cholo* for a moment and considered taking the musket away from him and breaking it over his froglike head but thought better of it. Instead, he ambled to the road and leaned on a hitching rail.

"I said, go," the *cholo* called out, his courage growing as the massive man retreated.

The Kanaka grinned, then humped his huge shoulders and brought a huge ham-size fist down on top of the four-inch rail. It snapped with a resounding crunch and collapsed in the road.

When the *cholo* jumped back in surprise, the Kanaka grinned even wider. The guard stepped inside the gate and slammed it shut. As the huge man lumbered away, he heard the *cholo* yelling for his fellow soldiers.

"Truhud awaits you at the communal fire," Hawk said. "Are you ready?"

"As ready as I'll ever be," Clint answered, and flashed Hawk a look of confidence that he did not really feel. He knew he was still not at his best, but he had to be good enough if he wanted to see the deck of a ship again. He pulled on his boots, took a drink of water from the gourd left by Chahett, and followed Hawk.

The whole tribe had gathered around the communal fire, forming a forty-foot circle with the fire at its center. The flames blazed, casting dancing shadows as the daylight faded. It was a particularly beautiful sunset, Clint noticed. Oranges and yellows striped the western sky.

Clint did not see Truhud at first. He was hidden among his followers on the far side of the fire. Clint pulled off his shirt, handed it to Hawk, and entered the clearing. The group of men on the far side parted, and Truhud stepped forward. He wore only a buckskin loincloth and was painted from head to toe. *I guess that's supposed to frighten me*, Clint thought as he surveyed the white arms and legs of the man and his black torso. Even his face, hands, and feet were painted. Only the palms of his hands were paint-free.

Clint took a deep breath and felt that rush of strength that came to him when he knew a confrontation was at hand. Truhud bent low in a wrestler's stance. Clint, barechested, wearing just trousers and boots, stepped within reach of the *paxa,* and the Chumash closed. They locked, arms entwined, and Clint attempted a hip throw. His hands slipped from the man's body, and he almost gave the Chumash his back—and the advantage. *Paint, hell,* Clint thought. *The son of a bitch has greased himself down. He'll be hard to throw if I can't hang on to him.*

Recovering quickly, Clint locked gazes with the *paxa,* who snarled. The Chumash charged in low, snatched one of Clint's legs, and dropped him to his back. The crowd roared. Clint spun to his side, hooked a toe behind the Chumash's ankle, and struck the same knee hard with his other booted foot. The Chumash too went down, and the crowd gasped in surprise.

Both men regained their feet. If he could not hang on to the slippery rattlesnake, he would change tactics. Dropping low, his hands at knee level, Clint awaited the man's charge.

Truhud too came in low, trying for a leg again. Clint's hard right uppercut caught him under the chin, snapping his head back and flinging blood over the crowd from an inch-wide cut. Truhud staggered back, but Clint went after him. A straight right and a left hook spun the man into the startled warriors. Truhud's men closed in front of him with crossed lances, blocking Clint from going for the kill.

Hawk shouted something from the other side of the circle, but the men made no move. Clint worked his way to the middle of the clearing without turning his back on the armed men.

In a moment, Truhud stepped into the clearing. Blood ran in a trickle from his nose, and his chin dripped, but his eyes were not defeated. He had the white-rimmed glare of a man who smells blood. He charged forward, once again coming in low, and sidestepped Clint's blow. They locked.

Being shorter, Truhud had some leverage and pinned both of Clint's arms. He set his feet forward and gave a mighty upward heave, rolling backward. Clint flew up and over the falling man, landing hard on his back as Truhud rolled on top of him.

Clint freed an arm and managed to roll to his belly. Truhud encircled Clint's throat with a powerful arm, got a chokehold, and began his death grip.

His wind cut off, Clint's vision faded. Then, with a surge of strength, Clint got a knee under him, locked Truhud's elbow and spun, taking the Chumash with him.

As Truhud slammed to his back, his grasp loosened. Clint scrambled to his feet and again they stood face to face.

Thinking he had the advantage, Truhud charged again. This time Clint met him with a hard jab, rocking the Indian back. Truhud tried to duck the next blow and rushed in low.

Clint brought up a knee with a sickening crunch and flipped Truhud to his back, blood spewing from his splattered nose.

Clint allowed him to gain his feet. The Chumash did not charge but stood, holding his nose, the blood flowing freely between his fingers.

Clint closed, connecting with a solid jab. Truhud staggered back, and Clint crossed with a left, then put everything he had into a straight right.

The Chumash fell like a pole into his crowd of supporters. Again they closed in front of him, and again, Clint stepped back to the center of the circle.

Clint took a deep breath as the men parted and Truhud staggered out with his supporters encouraging him. He stumbled forward, and Clint figured that one good blow would end it.

Clint stepped toward him, but with a flick of his wrist the

Chumash produced a stone knife he had concealed along the underside of his forearm. The black obsidian flashed, and a thin line of blood formed across Clint's chest as he reeled away.

Hawk yelled and jumped into the circle, but Clint waved him away. "I'll handle this," he said.

Shouts of derision rose up from the braves, directed at the *paxa*, and Truhud glanced from side to side to see who would dare challenge him.

Clint took advantage of the distraction and feigned attacking with his hands. The Chumash sliced with the knife, and Clint reared back avoiding the blow and driving a pointed boot deep into his enemy's crotch.

Truhud stumbled away, tried to maintain his crouched stance, but dropped to one knee. He dropped the knife, grabbed his crotch with both hands, and retched.

Clint stepped back and glanced over at Hawk. "Is that enough of a kneel?"

Hawk nodded. Clint stepped forward and picked up the obsidian knife. Truhud's men too took a forward step, lances in hand.

Clint flipped the knife over and grabbed it by the blade. With a powerful throw, he stuck it into a log in the center of the fire, where it echoed with a quivering thud. Almost immediately, its wooden handle burst into flame. Clint gave his back to the men and made his way out of the circle.

Chahett and a dozen others gathered around him, chattering their support as he walked to the hut.

All but Chahett left him to his privacy.

Ten

A moccasined foot nudged Clint awake just after sunup. He pulled on his boots and left the hut to find Hawk waiting with two saddled ponies.

Hawk handed Clint a set of reins, then swung easily into his own saddle. He pointed to the south. "Santa Barbara."

Clint mounted also, and the pony sidestepped, feeling the morning. The Chumash smiled as Clint found his seat, and they set out.

The *paxa* walked out of the communal hut and shook his fist as they passed. Clint admired the man's swollen nose and one closed eye, checked to make sure he did not have lance or bow nearby, then ignored him.

They climbed out of the canyon and topped a rise where the morning sun warmed his back. Clint was not completely himself yet, and the effects of the days in the sun were compounded by the bumps and scrapes of his fight, but his several nights' rest had worked wonders, and he was headed back to civilization. He could see the ocean in the distance and the outline of a ship on the horizon but could not make out her type, much less identify her.

They entered a dense forest of sandpaper oak and madrone. A dozen wild horses bolted from a thick stand of saplings, and he marveled at the strength of the mustangs as they wound their way up and out of the canyon.

A huge condor circled high above, its wings fixed, using the updrafts from the ocean air that warmed as it passed over land. Hawk reined up, and Clint drew alongside. Hawk handed him a gourd of water.

"*Gracias*," Clint said, but Hawk only nodded. They rode on.

They continued almost due south; the sun had risen on Clint's left and was dropping on his right. South was the way to Santa Barbara. Not true south, but their route would bring them to the shore of the Pacific, and it would lead them southeast to Santa Barbara. Like San Juan Capistrano and San Pedro, Santa Barbara had been selected as a port since it lay on a southerly shore, not exposed to the prevailing northwest winds.

That night, Hawk found a place by a small stream, and they hobbled the horses and shared some jerky he produced from his bedroll. Clint listened to the sound of the wind in the trees and the lonely cry of a wolf. His thoughts turned to the *Savannah* and her crew. He wondered how many, if any, he would find in Santa Barbara.

Clint awoke before dawn, soaked from the dew but feeling much better. They were saddled and on their way by the time the sun formed a silver line on the mountains to the east.

He could smell the sea before he heard it, hear it before he saw it. The beach lay wide and inviting. They dismounted, left the horses to graze in a grassy flat above the beach, and walked to the surf line, chasing the shore birds in front of them. Spotting their breathing holes as he watched Hawk do, he dug clams and ate them from the shell. Raucous gulls and a few graceful black-necked stilts fought for the remnants when the pair threw the shells aside. Clint sat and rested for a few minutes, watching curlews run their long saber-shaped bills into the sand to pluck fat worms.

Each of us has our own God-given talents, Clint thought in quiet reflection, *and each his own way*. He tried not to judge the backward direction the Chumash had chosen for themselves. They had been at the mission and seen what Clint thought were better ways. But the mission ways were not their ways. He and Hawk remounted, having eaten their fill, and continued down the beach.

They circled a large lagoon and paused at the edge of a meadow where a huge bear, its silver-tipped humpback to them, rocked on all fours, feeding on the naked carcass of a bullock—a bullock probably spiked by a vaquero, skinned, and left for the scavengers.

"*Oohoomahtee*," Hawk said quietly. "To you, the grizzly." Hawk exhibited his respect, reining away to give the bear a wide berth.

Clint watched in awe as the humpbacked bear tore huge chunks of meat from the animal and devoured them with grumbling roars that reverberated across the meadow and shook Clint's spine. The grizzly was the most fearsome animal Clint had ever come upon.

Giving the animal plenty of room to enjoy its feast without being disturbed, they rode on. By late afternoon they swung due east, and Clint thought he recognized the headland. They worked their way through sandpaper oaks, crested a hill, and below him the pueblo stretched, its tile and thatched roofs looking as beautiful to Clint as any fancified New England city.

Hawk reached over and took the reins of Clint's horse out of his hands.

"You're not going into Santa Barbara?" Clint asked.

Hawk shook his head, and Clint slipped from the saddle.

"Chahett told me to tell you she will miss you, like the moon would miss the sun."

"What does the name Chahett mean?"

"Bluebird," Hawk said. "Think of her when you see one."

"I will," Clint said, waving.

The tall Indian brought his fist across his chest, and Clint did likewise. Then the man spun the horse and urged him away, trailing the other horse behind.

"*Gracias, amigo*," Clint called, but the Indian did not turn back.

This man and his people had chosen to go with their own god. Clint wished them well, and even though he was convinced that their way, looking to the past, was wrong, it was their way.

But he must turn his mind to the present and his own kind. He strode toward Santa Barbara.

Hawk reined up on the last rise and looked back to watch the man called Ryan depart. He was a good man, he decided. Tall, strong, quiet, he would have been a welcome addition to the tribe. *But*, Hawk thought, *the Anglos have strange ways. And their ways are not our ways, just as the Spanish ways are not our ways. And Sup has punished us, taken most of our people to ride the sun to the afterworld, taken them with terrible diseases. But it is not this man's fault.* He watched Clint descend the hillside.

It is too bad he is afoot. I should have given him a horse. But horses were getting harder to come by, and the last time he had relieved the Santa Ines mission of one of the few they had left, the *cholos* had trailed him for a week. He had lost the Mexican pursuers but also lost a week he could have been hunting and filling the tribe's food baskets.

No, a horse was out of the question. Besides, the Anglos wanted boats, not horses. And this Anglo would soon be back aboard one of the great ships.

He would never be able to adopt the ways of the tribe. No Spaniard ever had. He would only be trouble.

Still, Hawk's heart was heavy to see him go.

And, he thought, chuckling, Chahett's was like a boulder.

Don Estoban Padilla, rose, stretched, and took the last puff on his cigarillo. He stepped off the veranda and ground the butt under his boot, his big-roweled spurs jingling as he moved. This day he would return to the work that was his true love—his life—working the cattle astride a beautiful Andalusian stallion.

The Indian women would have the cook fires going in the *cocina*, the kitchen, a separate adobe located to the rear, forty feet beyond the hacienda. This morning the fire would warm his old bones. The sea air felt good, but it could chill even in May.

Inocente, the slender vaquero who was the *segundo*, the second in command or foreman of Rancho del Robles Viejos, approached as Estoban rounded the corner toward the kitchen. The *patrón* noticed that his foreman wore *calzonevas*, leather pants for riding in the brush. A quirt hung strapped to his wrist. He planned a day's work on horseback—like most days on the rancho.

"*Buenos días, Jefe.*" Inocente called his *patrón* by the polite title *boss*. "It is a fine day."

"A fine day," Estoban repeated. "What do you have scheduled for this fine day?"

Inocente held the door for his *patrón*. "As we take our tea, I will inform you."

They filled mugs with black tea that had been steeping in the kitchen ever since the Indian woman had stoked the first fire of the morning and begun her work by the light of thin tapers. They laced the mugs with Barbados sugar cut from the cane that always rested in the center of the kitchen worktable and whitened it with fresh cream from a pitcher. Steaming mugs in hand, they headed outside to survey the rancho.

Luis Montalvo, a vaquero now too old to work the cattle, walked into the kitchen carrying a large haunch of beef from the *matanza*, the slaughterhouse, a windowless flat-roofed adobe also used as a smokehouse from time to time. It squatted a few paces beyond the kitchen. Luis nodded politely at the *patrón* and the *segundo* as they let him pass, then began chopping the beef for the cook.

"I noticed many Anglos in the pueblo yesterday," Inocente said, seemingly distressed.

"It is a sign of the times, *Segundo*. Yesterday, as I sat enjoying my cigar, I wondered how we could continue to thrive as my father did before me." Don Estoban took a sip of the tea and sighed. "Trade, Inocente, trade. Now that the hide, horn, and tallow have gone to ruin, we must find new ways, new products, and new markets. And unless we take to the sea ourselves, that means dealing with foreigners. Men of the sea." He smiled at his foreman. "Unless, of course, you wish me to set you to building a ship, amigo?"

"No, *Jefe*. I am of the land as you are. Even the short trip to Buenaventura on the coastal boat made my stomach spin like a steer bound tail to nose. If it is a choice between my taking to the sea or putting up with a few foreigners, I will take the Anglos and Kanakas."

The *patrón* nodded his agreement, albeit wearily.

"But, we must keep them in their place," Inocente added. "They are forward. Again I observed the rudeness of an Anglo only a few days ago. The *capitán* of the wrecked brig had the affront to stare as Juana and Tía Angelina passed in the carriage. I should have quirted him, *capitán* or not, but Juana—"

"She is young, Inocente, and does not understand the broader reason for keeping the Anglo in his place. I fear if we let them become too comfortable . . . Even now there are too many who settle in Alta California. Over the years, I have often warned the governors. It will come to no good, and eventually we will have to eject them all. But it is the *alcalde* and the *cholos*' job to keep the law—"

"They can keep the law," Inocente interrupted, "if they sober up long enough, and I can teach the *marineros* manners. These Anglos have a great need for lessons in common courtesy. I will see this Anglo again when Juana is not nearby, and he will learn to cut his eyes away and keep his tongue when a high-born señorita is within sight."

"These Anglos you speak of," the *patrón* said sagely, "have lost their ship and their livelihood. Idle hands have too much time with the mug, then do the devil's handiwork. But manners . . . that is a matter between you and the Anglo.

"I will remember that, *Jefe*. And when the Anglos taste the lash, they will remember."

Eleven

Clint could see the twin bell towers of the mission in the distance and the crumbling wall that had once surrounded the mission village. From his first short visit, before the wreck of the *Savannah*, he knew that the townspeople, since the mission village was mostly deserted, were taking the adobe brick from the wall for building projects of their own.

But still the mission itself stood proudly, surrounded by lush orchards. A vineyard stretched over a distant hill, its springtime vines verdant with new growth in the late morning sun.

As he picked his way down the hillside, Clint realized he had no money and nothing but his knife to trade—and that he must keep. The first house he passed was little more than a thatched-roof hovel that seemed held together by clinging bougainvillea. A small herd of goats, multicolored and bleating, grazed nearby, and a broken-down bay mule stood in a tiny corral at the rear. Two boys played outside its hide-covered doorway but stopped to laugh as Clint passed.

Clint walked around two rooting pigs, then paused under a spreading sycamore to look at himself in the reflection of a water trough. Though he had laundered them in the creek at the Chumash village, his striped shirt was torn and tattered and his duck pants were ripped to the knees. His leather boots were cracked and whitened with salt. He had not shaved since the wreck ten days before. His hair was tousled, and he carried the scratches and scrapes of the long journey.

Wetting and smoothing his hair, he glanced up and noticed a man watching him from the shade of an oak on a nearby hill—a huge man with a wide chest, immense thighs and arms, and a bulging belly. Clint waved at the big man, and the man smiled warmly and returned the wave but made no effort to rise and greet him. For a moment Clint wondered if the man was Mexican, but by the size of him, decided he was probably a Sandwich Islander. Another sailor. There would be more sailors in the pueblo, even though there were no ships in the harbor. Hide crews were almost always ashore, gathering hides, folding and storing them until they could be loaded on the brigs.

It would be good to be among his own kind again.

As he entered the town, people stopped and stared at him and his ragged clothes. He ignored them and strode on. He looked for any sign of the crew of the *Savannah*, but saw none. Finally, at the center of the town square, he saw the largest of the pueblo's buildings. It had to be the town hall, with officials who would know the fate of the *Savannah* crew.

He started for it, then noticed the cantina. If any of the crew of the *Savannah* had survived and made it to Santa Barbara, they would be in the cantina. He went in, his eyes adjusted to the darkness, and he caught the friendly odor of tobacco. He squinted and searched the room for a familiar face.

A broad-hipped barmaid approached him. "You wish a drink, Señor? *Aguardiente*? *Vino*? *Pulque*?"

"No, *gracias*. I seek other Anglos. *Marineros* from the brig *Savannah*."

"*Sí*, they were here, eight of them. They lost their ship on the rocks."

"I was with them. Where are they?"

"They sailed, Señor. The *Charleston* put in only yesterday, and they sailed with her. And it was a good thing. There was some mischief, and the *alcalde* was about to put them all in the *juzgado*."

Clint smiled but felt heartsick. It might be weeks before the *Charleston* or some other ship called at Santa Barbara again. He could be stranded here without a peso to his name until she returned. He decided to call on the public officials to see what, if anything, he could do while he waited. As he stepped through the doorway and started across the square, a fine caleche turned the corner, pulled by two beautiful matched grays and followed by three vaqueros on horseback.

The horses' hoofbeats rang on the cobblestones as they pranced.

The coach stopped in front of the *mercado* next to the cantina, where household goods and cloth were displayed behind barred unshuttered windows. From the caleche stepped the most beautiful girl Clint had ever seen. She was dressed in a crimson gown with a white lace *reboza*, a long scarf that signified she was unmarried, wrapped around her shoulders and head. She moved gracefully up to the tiled walk, followed by an older woman attired completely in black.

Clint could not help staring at her flawless cream complexion set off by chestnut hair as the girl approached. His eyes followed her, and she glanced his way. He reached for his hat, then, embarrassed, realized he did not have one.

"Good morning, ma'am," he said, "*Buenos días.*"

She eyed him over the top of her fan with dark flashing eyes.

He had just turned to walk away when a woven rawhide loop dropped over his head and snapped taut around his chest, catching one arm at his side, though he managed to free the other.

"*Vamos*, Anglo!" came the cry of a black-clad vaquero.

The reata bit flesh. He was jerked off his feet and slammed to the cobblestones. Pain shot through his back as the vaquero quirted his stallion to a gallop.

"No, Inocente!" the girl cried out.

Bouncing across the rough square, Clint fought to keep his head from crashing onto the paving stones as he rolled and struggled to free himself. The horse reached full gallop, and Clint careened out of the square and onto the dirt road. He spun and clawed at the loop with his free arm while the horse's hooves flung clods and dirt into his face.

Desperately, he swung his feet in front of him, fighting to free himself, but the reata slammed him head over heels facefirst into the dirt. The powerful stallion pounded on, joined by two others who flanked Clint—a dizzying confusion of flashing hooves on three sides of him.

He slammed into a horse trough and rolled. Pain shot through him. He spun the other way, got his arm up in front of his face, and crunched into a hitching post. Bone splintered, and he saw flashes of color and tasted copper, but he did not cry out. Through fading vision, he saw a tree stump coming.

Helpless, he met it with a resounding thump, and blackness enveloped him.

The riders dismounted and Inocente removed his reata from the man's quiet form. Seeing that the job had been done well, he remounted. They jerked their horses around and spurred them away without a glance at the still mound of scraped, bruised, and bleeding flesh. Their hoofbeats disappeared, and the road was quiet except for three red hens who wandered nearby, pecking, investigating the quiet form. One cackled a caution as the form moaned quietly, but continued to scratch away.

A mockingbird resumed mimicking the staccato chirps of a warbler, and Matthew Mataca Konokapali stepped hesitantly out of the shadows beneath the sandpaper oak, then shuffled his huge bulk slowly toward the prostrate figure. Uncertain for a moment, the Kanaka knelt and brushed the dirt from the broken man's face.

He lifted the injured man in beefy arms and as easily as he would have a child, carried him away with a great lumbering gait.

"It was uncalled-for, Father." Juana stomped her small foot on the Chinese carpet. "Absolutely uncalled-for. The man merely said good day. He was little more than a beggar, a wandering Anglo fool."

"Calm down, *niña*." Don Estoban smiled placatingly at his daughter. He had never seen her so angry. "It is not a thing for you to worry your pretty little head about. It is man's business. Isn't that right, Angelina?"

He looked to his sister-in-law, who stood staring out the distorted green-hued scene through the leaded bottle bottoms that made up the window. She turned and acknowledged his question with a harsh look but said nothing.

"It was insanity, Father," Juana continued. "Inocente is not to accompany me again. He is a madman."

"It is not your place to say who your father is to employ to look out for you, young lady." Estoban slapped his flat-crowned hat down on the long oak dining table. He stormed to a side cabinet, opened the door, and poured a shot of brandy into a crystal snifter. Angrily, he tried to replace the decanter's glass stopper but fumbled with it and finally dropped it. Fortunately, the hard-packed earth was covered with soft rugs, and the stopper bounced harmlessly. Estoban collected himself, bent effortlessly, and retrieved the stopper, carefully replacing it. When he turned to face his daughter, he was calm again. "As I said, it is not for you to worry about."

"It looked to me as if the man was dead, Papa. If so, his Christian burial is our responsibility. If not, we owe him comfort and a place to heal. And an apology and a reparation of some kind. Since he seemed to be afoot, a horse and saddle at the very least." A tear rolled down her cheek. She turned so as not to give her father the pleasure of seeing her wipe it away. "He was a harmless unarmed Anglo who merely wished me a good day."

"We owe the Anglos nothing." Estoban's voice rang out harshly in the sparsely furnished room. "Nothing. He was far too forward, and if he lives, he will know the meaning of humility." His voice softened. "You are tired, little Juana. Go to your room and rest. You will feel better by suppertime."

"If that man is dead, I will never feel better again." She sat on an intricately carved mahogany chest and dabbed at her eyes with a hanky, then looked up with renewed anger. "The Anglo is not the one who needs to learn humility. Inocente Ruiz is!"

"To your room, Juana. Relax and think of fiestas and fandangos and young men and your future. Do not think of Anglos." He turned and stared out the window. "Anglos," he said quietly, "are not a part of Alta California's future." But he did not believe his own words.

Choking down a sob, Juana spun on her heel and headed for her room.

"The foolishness of youth," Estoban said, more to himself than Angelina, who moved from the window to face him.

"She is young, my brother-in-law, but she is also right. What Inocente did was uncalled-for. The man did nothing to deserve more than a harsh word from your *segundo*."

Estoban snatched up his snifter and took a deep draw of the fiery liquid. "You, also, may retire to your room, Angelina."

"As you wish, Don Estoban, but that does not make a wrong into a right." She marched from the room.

Estoban stared after her. "I will never understand women," he muttered. He poured himself another drink, then called for María to bring him a cigar. He walked to the window of bottle bottoms and stared out. *I do hope the man lives*, he thought. *The loss of a life is an expensive price to pay for a lesson in manners. Perhaps a horse, if it makes Juana happy again, and if he lives.*

Clint awoke slowly, then wished he had not. Every bone and muscle in his body cried with pain. He forced his eyes open and found himself in a small dark room. A tiny shuttered window leaked light. One rough-plank chest huddled against the wall. He lay in a bed with leather webbing for a mattress. A carved wooden crucifix adorned the wall over his head. Sad-faced, Christ stared down at him. Clint stared back.

Now I know how you must have felt, he thought, and winced as he tried to get more comfortable. His mouth tasted of old blood, and each breath brought him the odor of herb poultices along with his blinding pain. Merely breathing was a gargantuan effort.

Feeling hot and uncomfortable, he managed to tug the blanket off with his right hand. His left arm was splinted. A multitude of abrasions were covered with herbs, wraps binding them.

"The bastard," he said aloud, remembering the vaquero who had roped and dragged him. Trying to rise, he moaned and collapsed back on the bed. His head swam and his body would not work.

I'm beginning to have a sincere dislike for sunny Alta California, he thought. He had had a thousand bruises and scrapes and as many confrontations in his ten years at sea, but never with the frequency, or the ferocity, of his less than four weeks in Alta California. And he had never before broken a bone. A broken bone could mean gangrene and sure death.

The door creaked open, and Clint focused suspicious eyes on the medium-size man silhouetted there. "You have come back to us," the man said, his voice low and mellifluous, his English flawless.

"I don't remember leaving. Who the hell are you?"

The man stepped into the room, and Clint flushed when he realized the clean-shaven man wore the gray *jerga* robes of a priest. His head was covered with a low-crowned, wide-brimmed hat, and his robe was fastened with a twisted rope, its ends hanging down the right side. A long rosary of polished wooden beads looped through the left side of the rope. He approached the bed on simple leather sandals.

"I'm sorry, Father . . . I didn't realize."

"I am Padre Javier. And you?"

"John Clinton Ryan."

"Ah, I suspected so. You are fortunate you came when you did."

Even in his pain, Clint managed a wry grin as he cast his eyes down over his bruised and broken body. "You call this fortunate?"

"More so than the greeting you would have received from your shipmates."

Clint furrowed his brows in confusion. "My shipmates?"

"The *capitán* . . . Señor Sharpentier."

"Yes. Captain Quade Sharpentier."

"He requested permission from the *alcalde* to hang you, Señor Ryan."

"What? What the hell for? Sorry, Father." Clint collected himself. "Why would Sharpentier bend a line around my neck?" He searched his mind. He had never much liked the man or respected his ability, though he could use a blade with the best of them. Still, Clint could think of no reason the man would want to hang him.

"He reported that the *Savannah* was lost due to your malfeasance."

"How the devil could I 'malfease' when I was asleep in my bunk?" His tone turned reflective. "Sounds as if Sharpentier is looking for a scapegoat."

"Maybe the fact you were in your bunk is precisely the reason he finds you at fault, my friend. He claimed you were the one on watch, or should have been."

Clint probed his mind for an answer. No one had called him to watch, and he had not been due to report to duty until several hours after the time of the wreck. Unless, of course, all hands were called or a man was injured or washed overboard. And that could have happened under the severe circumstances. Still, he could not have been at fault if he was not called.

"Was that the reason I was roped and dragged by one of California's capable vaqueros, the reason I'm in this cell?"

Now it was the priest's turn to smile. "I am sure Inocente Ruiz is a fine vaquero. Whether or not he is one of Alta

California's most capable is not for me to judge. He is certainly *not* one of our most pious, to that I can testify, for I seldom see him at mass." The priest waved his hand. "And this room is part of the mission, young man, not a cell."

"Sorry, Father." Clint felt a little sheepish for a moment. "Then why did Ruiz use me to drag the high spots out of your bumpy road?"

"It seems you offended Señorita Juana Padilla."

"Offended! How?" Clint tried to sit up, but his eyes blurred and he almost passed out. The padre reached to the floor at the foot of the bed and raised a tin cup of water to Clint's lips. Clint drank deeply.

"Thank you, Father." Clint lay back against his pillow. "Now, how did I offend this señorita?"

"I do not know. Perhaps you said something?"

"I offered 'buenos días' as I recall."

"Nothing more?"

"Not that I can recollect. I must admit, I gave her a long appreciative look. As I recall, she's one of the easiest women to look at that I've ever had the pleasure of bouncing away from." Clint tried to laugh but winced from the effort. Then his eyes hardened, and his jaw flexed for a moment before he spoke. "This vaquero, Inocente Ruiz. Will he return to finish the job?"

"I think his pride is fulfilled."

"He'll keep until my arm mends—then we'll see how large his stock of pride is when he's *facing* a man, not behind him."

"Vengeance is the Lord's, my son."

"But he must use the arm of man, Father." Clint smiled wryly. "Unless we're content to wait for a bolt of lightning."

"Turn the other cheek."

"If it's all the same to you, we'll debate the finer aspects of the Scripture when I'm a little clearer-headed."

"That will be a pleasure, young man. Then, of course, if you are truly clear-headed, you will accept things as they are and leave Señor Ruiz to the Lord."

Clint worked a muscle in his jaw, choosing to leave this discussion for another time, a time when he would bring Inocente Ruiz to task.

"And the arm? Will it work?" he asked.

"The break was clean, the skin not broken, and you were unconscious, so it was easily set."

"Thank God for that."

"And for all of His bountiful ways." The priest crossed himself. "You may thank Him, but you also owe a debt of gratitude to a huge Kanaka, a Sandwich Islander, who carried you all the way from the other side of the pueblo to the mission. I fed him. In fact, he ate a gallon of *atole*. Never have I seen such a man, or seen such an eater."

"His name?" Clint asked.

"I'm sorry, I was busy with you and don't remember. Later, if he's still here, you can find him easily. He's the largest man I have ever seen, as tall or taller than you and with the girth and strength of a bull."

Padre Javier rose and walked to the door. "This room is quite close to the blacksmith shop. I hope the noise is not too much. You are the guest of Dons Nicholas Den and Daniel Hill. Don Pío Pico, our illustrious governor," he said with a quiet vengeance, "has leased the mission to these Anglo gentlemen. There are only two of us priests here now."

"You padres no longer run the mission?"

"I am now only a parish priest, my son. My duties as a mission priest are a thing of the past. We are only here under the auspices of Señores Den and Hill. The bishop has taken Mission Santa Barbara as his home. So you see, no matter what Pío Pico proclaims, this is still a most holy place. More water?"

"No, thank you. And thank you for setting the arm . . . and allowing me to stay here."

"It is nothing, John Clinton Ryan. All part of God's work."

"But you are His tool, Father, so please accept my thanks."

"Accepted. Now sleep. I will waken you at supper time with a bowl of hot *pozole*."

Clint closed his eyes and was asleep before the padre slipped from the room. But he dreamed of a taut reata tight around his neck, flashing hooves, and a hawk-nosed vaquero who, no matter which way he turned, managed to stay behind him.

Twelve

Resting in the quiet room, his meals brought by the Chumash neophytes who still called the mission their home, gave Clint a chance to think at length about his situation. If Sharpentier believed him guilty of abandoning his post, he was in great trouble. A warrant would be issued for his arrest, a price put on his head, and he would be sought actively by all American sea captains and any other who wished to claim the reward. His dreams of a ship of his own would have to wait, not only until he was financially able but, more importantly, until he could clear his name.

Even though the captain was seeking a clearance from the Alta California government to hang him, Sharpentier might know he was innocent. The captain was no fool, but he was an opportunist and an unprincipled one. Sharpentier would have some serious charges to face when he returned to New England. A captain who had lost a ship would be harshly investigated, and if he did not have a damned fine excuse, an ironclad one, and someone else to place the blame on, there would be hell to pay. At best, he would never get another share as ship's captain. At worst, he could be hanged.

When the port crew worked topside, Mackie would have been the one to bring him any special summons to duty, but Mackie was the least dependable of the men on the *Savannah*. Clint had often wondered how the man had risen to second mate. But men change. Mackie might once have been a fine seaman and possibly even a good officer. Demon rum had ruined more than one man.

He wondered which of the men had survived. He hoped

Turk and Wishon had, for they had both become good friends. He knew that Sharpentier had. But which of the others?

And what was Clint to do if Sharpentier returned and truly meant to hang him?

He did not wish to be placed at odds with his shipmates, but he would not hang for another's malfeasance, as the priest had so aptly put it. No, he would fight the archangel himself when he knew he was right, and Sharpentier was about as far from a messenger of God as a man could be.

Clint lay quietly, his resolve firm. He would fight to the death before he would ride acorn's horse, the tall oak gallows!

He listened to every sound in the mission plaza outside his room, awaiting the footfalls of sailors carrying muskets and cutlass. Finally, exhausted, he fell into a fitful sleep.

It was four days and eight bowls of *pozole*—a stew of meat, oats, and vegetables—and mounds of the mission's dried fruit before Clint was able to leave the tiny room. Early in the morning he made his way out into the kitchen garden and sat on a stone bench, listening to the birds and watching the sunrise activities of the few remaining mission Indians.

The mission in better times had grown to a double quadrangle enclosing two large patios. There were the priests' quarters, a sacristy, and workshops surrounding the front patio; and more workshops—tannery, cobbler shop, coopery, grist mill, blacksmith shop, carpenter shop—and storerooms surrounding the rear patio. *Zanjas*, water ditches, interlaced the fields and vineyards, and culminated in an octagonal fountain in front of the mission that, second only to the bell towers, was the pride of the padres. In front of the fountain a long rectangular adobe basin, its sides lined with stones, served a more practical purpose—laundry. Women of the pueblo still gathered at the basin to beat their laundry clean and gossip.

Beyond the row of workshops that separated him from the main patio, Clint could see the twin towers of the main cathedral, each over seventy feet high and proudly containing bells cast in faraway Seville, Spain. Each morning they called the faithful to duty, and each mealtime they summoned them out of the fields with clear tones that swelled the heart. Chickens, goats, pigs, and sheep had the run of the rear courtyard, though they still managed to keep them out of the front and its hundreds of ornamental plants. Each tree in the rear had been nibbled, its underside as flat as an iron and as high as the goats could stand on their hind legs.

Padre Javier, a mug of tea in his hand, joined him. "I see you've decided to try your legs. I've brought you tea."

"The legs are a mite shaky, but the morning is fine." Clint took the tea and smiled silent thanks, then returned his attention to the working Indians he had been watching for almost an hour. "There are few to run such a large household."

"At one time we had several hundred neophytes, but some years ago the politicians in Monterey in their wisdom passed the emancipation, effectively breaking the back of the mission system. The Indians are no longer subject to the will or, unfortunately, the guidance of the church. Over the last sixteen years, they've wandered away and are mostly gone. Most of the other missions have fallen to ruin and been sold at ridiculous prices to friends or relatives of Governor Pío Pico, may his soul spend a thousand years . . ." He smiled at Clint. "But of course Christ teaches us to forgive."

"Why hasn't the bishop given this Pío Pico the bell, book, and candle?" Clint wondered why the governor had not been excommunicated.

"Times have changed for the church, particularly in Alta California. The bishop plays the politician these days, though I'd appreciate it if you didn't repeat my opinion. We parish priests have been advised in no uncertain terms to keep our political views to ourselves."

Clint changed the subject. "I'd like to test my legs some more, Father. Would you show me around the mission?"

"It would be my pleasure."

They spent an hour investigating the workrooms, each of which had room for a dozen workers, but no more than two manned each task. Two women sat in the weaving and spinning room where mission wool was turned to yarn, then woven into the rough gray *jerga* that the Indians and padres wore. They toured the blacksmith shop where iron was hammered into a hundred uses, manned only by a single smithy and his helper on the bellows, and the tannery, which was of particular interest to Clint. And finally they visited the large *dispensa* and cooperage, the storage room where the wide variety of goods formerly grown and manufactured by the mission were stored and where, in a small area, barrels were constructed for the storage. It was painfully bare of product, and no cooper was at work.

After watching Clint try to negotiate some stairs on his unsteady legs, the padre suggested they climb the hill behind the mission to see the vineyards and main gardens another day. Clint returned to his room and rested. Though every bone and muscle in his body still ached, he was pleased to know they still worked.

After another day's rest, Clint insisted on helping in the tannery. Since he could not do the heavy work one-handed, he did the fine finish work and soon found himself teaching the Indians New England currying techniques—the finishing of rough leather to fine. After several days in the tannery, he was concentrating on some particularly soft calfhide he had been currying with a sharp-edged oak sleeker when he was startled by a nearby voice.

"Do you have a home for that fine piece of leather?"

Clint looked up into the craggy face and dark eyes of a middle-aged vaquero, who reached out a callused hand to caress the calfskin.

"That is a fine job of tanning, amigo. Where did a *marinero* learn to tan?"

"I was not at sea until I was fifteen," Clint said. "I was apprenticed to a tanner before that."

"And the hide?"

"It's just part of what I do to earn my keep."

"So I may lay claim to it?"

Clint had not seen the craggy-faced man around the mission before. He had deep-set wise eyes that Clint would not have forgotten.

"If Padre Javier says you may claim it, then you'll get no argument from me."

The vaquero smiled silently and caressed the leather. "It will weave into the finest of reins and *romal*, a set to grace the proudest of stallions."

"You're the saddle maker?" Clint asked.

"I have made saddles, and take pride as a braider. I have braided many a rein and reata, but then most vaqueros have. I was once the head vaquero for the mission. Now I work for Don Nicholas Den. Where is your ship?"

"She was the *Savannah*."

Suddenly the realization came to Clint that he would no

longer have a home at sea. If Sharpentier laid the blame for the *Savannah*'s sinking on him, he might never get another sailing job, or worse. He would need the skills of land, this land, if he was to survive and avoid acorn's horse. He was a skilled tanner, but the hide business was failing. One thing he knew for sure—the more skills a man had, the easier his life would be.

The way this man carried himself, even more than his claim to being a *jefe*, made Clint believe that this was a true vaquero. Clint cleared his throat, drawing the man's attention.

"You may have this hide, and many more, amigo, if you'll teach me the skills of the vaquero."

This time the man's smile was wry. "The Anglos I have seen would do better to sail the roughest sea than try to sit an Andalusian stallion, or their hand with the *lazo*."

"I have ridden a few horses in my time, amigo," Clint said, taking offense at the man's superior attitude—though he had ridden little since he had been at sea, and his riding before had been limited to running errands and delivering for the tanner he had been indentured to.

The vaquero paused, appraising the Anglo whose arm hung useless in a sling. "If you will study the skills of the vaquero as diligently as you have obviously studied the skills of the tanner, then I will accept this—" he smiled again, "this challenge, Anglo. I am Ramón María Diego."

"I thought María was a woman's name," Clint said, then wished he had not when the man's features hardened.

"You will not think so when this María has taught you to *colear* the bull, throw him by the tail, or to bend low from your galloping stallion to impress the señoritas by plucking the head from a buried rooster with the *carrera del gallo* or to use the reata—if you are capable of learning, Anglo. Most likely, you will slink back to the tanner's vats and the stink of this place."

Feeling properly chastised, Clint rose, then extended his hand. "My name is John Clinton Ryan, Clint to my friends. And I will learn to ride and work cattle if you will teach me."

"We shall see, Señor Ryan, we shall see."

The man's refusal to call him by his first name did not go unnoticed as the vaquero accepted his hand with a callused steel grip. Clint looked into the vaquero's hard black eyes. He hoped his impulsive request had not been made to the wrong man.

"We will begin when you have four more hides for me. It

is a fair price for an impossible job. And when your broken wing is mended. You will need all your faculties to keep up with Ramón María Diego. *Adiós*."

The man spun on his heel. His viciously roweled spurs rang and his *calzonevas*, silver conchos flashing down the sides, snapped with dismissal as he strode from the tannery.

Thirteen

It was three weeks before Clint finished the five hides. About the same time, Padre Javier removed his splint, and he was able to begin working his arm. The splint had been off a week when Ramón Diego strode into the tannery.

"A man of his word," Clint said with a satisfied smile.

"When Ramón Diego says a thing, you can count on it, Anglo."

"Well, your hides are ready, and my arm is healed, and Ramón María Diego said he would teach me the ways of the vaquero."

"Some things only *Dios* can do, Anglo, but I will try, I will try. Remember, I am a mere mortal."

"It may not be as difficult as you think, señor."

"You are forward, Anglo, as all Anglos seem to be. And crow like the cock. When you learn to rope the goat, I will teach you to rope the bullock, and when you learn to rope the bullock, if you are able and have not lost all your fingers to the reata's bite, then I will teach you the game of wits."

"The game of wits?"

Ramón smiled wryly. "Or halfwits. Have you ever seen an *oso grande*, a grizzly?"

The image of the huge bear he had seen tearing great pieces of flesh from the skinned carcass flashed through his mind, and an uneasy feeling niggled at his spine.

"Yes, I've seen one."

"Well, my Anglo friend, wait until you see one forty feet away at the end of your reata. And at the end of three of your amigos' fine woven *lazos*. A thousand pounds of snarling fanged death only forty feet from the four of you. A creature

80

capable of beheading your horse with a sweep of his paw. And only your skill, and that of your *compadres*, stands between you and his claws. That is the true test of your skill with the *lazo* and of your amigos' faith in that skill."

Clint stared at the man, sure that he was kidding, but it was obvious from the hard set of his jaw that this man was not much of a teaser. Then he realized the man thought he would never reach that level of skill. The realization gnawed at his pride.

Clint said quietly, "If you ride to *lazo* the grizzly, I will ride with you, amigo."

"If you are invited, Anglo, then you will know you've become a true vaquero. That is almost as unlikely as the sun rising from the sea in the west. Right now, let's see if you can manage to sit a saddle." The vaquero gathered up his hides and sidled through the door, leaving Clint looking after him.

"Are you coming?" the vaquero shouted through the hide-covered doorway, and Clint hurriedly put away the buffer and sleeker he had been working with and followed.

North of Pueblo Los Angeles and the southerly convergence of the coastal range of mountains with the interior range is cradled a great valley. Deep in that interior valley, known as the Ton Tache, or Tules, for its many lakes and marshes lined with cattails, a tall, wide-chested, solidly built man, his torso bare, a loincloth covering his hips, his legs in leather leggin's over calf-high moccasins, knelt in a heavy growth of willows. A dozen tule elk grazed nearby. On the man's left hip rode a bag filled with two dozen foreshafts, some tipped with stone arrowheads, some merely fire-hardened. A few had tules woven in a bulb near the point. These bulbed foreshafts, when fitted onto the ends of one of the half-dozen arrowshafts he carried in a coyote-skin quiver on his back, were for waterfowl. When fired across the water, the bulbs would cause them to skip, maintaining an elevation just above the water, just high enough to break the back of a duck or goose.

But ducks and geese were the furthest things from his mind at the moment. Frozen in the shadows, he stood stark still as the elk grazed nearer. Ever so slowly, he pulled a lilac-root foreshaft with a two-inch striated obsidian point and fitted it into the hollow end of a two-foot oak arrowshaft. He admired the red hawk-feather fletching on the arrow and prayed silently to his brother the raptor to guide his arrow straight.

Just a few more steps, Brother Elk, the warrior silently prayed, *and you will be in range*. Just as he decided to begin the slow stealthful process of raising the laurel bow into position, the lead elk, a bull who would later in the year sport great four-foot horns, raised his nubbined head.

The big bull snorted his displeasure, and the others too raised their heads and tested the wind. Then, as one, they spun and bolted away. A pair of lanky gray wolves broke from the cover of a nearby stand of buckbrush and trotted halfheartedly after them but knew it was in vain. They left the trail, put their noses to the ground, and disappeared into the underbrush in search of an easier meal.

"Oh, Brother Wolf, you have deprived my tribe of a meal," Cha thought aloud, then threatened, "I will wear your hide to warm my shoulders before the cold comes again."

He left the cover of the willows and began his long trot back to the Ton Tache village. When he arrived, he paused only long enough to drink from a water gourd, then began his unpleasant chore—inspecting the dwindling stores of the band. He walked from room to room of the woven tule mat in the willow-frame greathouse, seventy paces long and only four wide. The whole band shared one structure, its rooms end to end along the lakeside. The branch stubs were left on the willow frame on which the tule-mat walls were hung and could be rapidly removed or rolled up in case of fire or flood.

Finely woven baskets—warp of willow and woof of sedgerood or redbud bark—held the roots, acorns or acorn flour, and wild buckwheat of the tribe. A few baskets were finer than the rest, holding the charms of each family. The finest of these sported a hundred mountain quail topknots woven into the topmost woofing, with a milkweed strand almost as thin as a human hair used to bind each fine feather upright.

More practical stone mortars and pestles, and flat *metates*—frying stones of steatite or granite—lined the walls of the hut. Willow hoops lay near each family's cooking fire, and cooking stones rested around its perimeter. Superheated in the fire, they were lowered into cooking baskets with the aid of the hoops.

As Cha moved among the women busy mending and grinding and gossiping, he checked each basket and haunch of hanging game. He swept shoulder-length black hair out of his worried eyes. A few elk had been taken in the spring and a few deer, but the primary food they had left was the bulb of the tule, so abundant on the lakeshore nearby and throughout the valley floor. But it was not enough. It was not yet summer, and already the land was drying up. It was time to ride the old trading trail to the sea and drive the horses home.

In his lifetime, Cha-ahm-sah, a Yokuts chieftain and shaman of the Ton Tache, had seen his people evolve from an acorn-gathering culture to one dependent upon the horse, not only as transportation but as their major food source.

Cha paused near a hut where children played a stick game. They had made miniature *atlatls*, or throwing darts, and practiced flinging dry cattail stalks. *It is good,* he thought, *for the children to learn skills early.*

He knelt by the fire of a woman who was busily heating rocks, picking them out of the fire with a hooped and sinew-bound willow and dipping them into a cooking basket full of *kawwah*, wild buckwheat. Her mush was almost done. She looked at him with interest but said nothing. Unlike the other men of the tribe, the chief could take more than one wife in his household. And it was better to share the chores with more than one, but she was old and knew he would take only young women to join his three wives.

As a boy, Cha had seen the Spanish *soldados* invade the valley and the tribes of the west side of the great Ton Tache valley driven across the mountains to the missions. He had escaped from just such a drive. Now, as they had been for several years, more than half the villages of the valley were vacant, their cooking fires and hollow cooking stones long cold.

But the Mexicans had brought his people an unexpected gift in return for those taken away. In those great roundups of Yokuts by the soldiers, horses had been lost to the wilderness. They bred, and the herds grew, and the People captured them. The tribe not only learned their value as transportation but learned the value of horsemeat. Now that meat, not acorns, was the staple of the tribe. Great herds had once roamed the valley, but they had been decimated by the People, bears, wolves, and pumas. Now only a few bands could be found, and they were wary of men and stayed well out of bow range.

But the missions and the ranchos of the coast still had horses, thousands of them.

If he did not take his warriors to the coast again, the cooking fires of the Tache village would be cold forevermore. In years past, the ducks, geese, and sandhill cranes covered the surface of the lake near Tache, the greatest of the Yokuts villages, and had been plentiful. Now the birds that marked the lake's surface were only coots, and the bald eagles got more of them than the People managed. After several years of drought, the duck and goose crop had not been good, and the lake had shrunk to less than half its former size. The great tribal house had been moved a half-dozen times to stay near the lake's edge. The men of the village had to spend days hidden under their reed floats, paddling around the huge shallow lake, to slip under the water to capture even one goose by its legs. In years past, a dozen ducks and geese a day would have been no problem.

The village was tired of eating roots and was beginning to look at their riding stock with hungry eyes. It was not a good thing, for the riding horses were needed for the hunt and were the lifeblood of the village.

Yes, he decided, he would call the People together after Father Sun had made his run across the sky. A hundred Yokuts warriors would ride, and a thousand horses would be driven back to the valley. Enough to replenish the canyons of the nearby hills. Enough to guarantee the survival of the tribe for years to come.

It would be different this time, for this time the Yokuts had the firesticks. A dozen muskets and the shot and powder to feed them. A Mexican force of *cholo soldados*, soldiers from Mission San José, had been careless, and the ones that were not killed by the attacking party of Yokuts had fled north, leaving all their stores behind. Thanks to some of the Yokuts who had lived at the mission, the People had learned the fine points of the old flintlocks.

The *cholos*, who had killed so many of Cha's men in years past, would be in for a great surprise. This time their musket fire would be answered in kind. No longer would the Yokuts have to get within bow range.

It has been decided, Cha thought, and nodded solemnly.

He saw two of his men arrive, each with a throwing stick and a pair of *homokes*, jackrabbits, draped over their shoulders, a thong lacing their hocks together. They also had a dozen *till*, quail, in carrying nets hung from their broad shoulders. These hunters had gone far to find their game. The *till* had the high topknots of the mountain quail found miles from the Tache camp.

Some of the People will have meat tonight, Cha thought, *but not all.*

Not nearly all.

But the cooking baskets and roasting racks would be heavy with horsemeat when they returned from the land of the leatherchests if they could avoid the Mexican *soldados*, or, if they could not, if the musket balls would penetrate their heavy leather armor.

"I have heard that the *marinero* lives, Tía, and is residing at the mission." Juana, who was stitching a band of leather around the hem of an old skirt, looked across the table at her aunt.

Her aunt chose to ignore the reference to the Anglo. "Juana, what you are doing is foolishness. Leather is not becoming to a señorita. You should be sewing something for the coming procession, the fandango, and rodeo. You will need to look your finest for the fiesta of Corpus Christi." Angelina shook her head at the girl's attempt to protect her hems.

"This is not for riding down Calle Principal, Tía, only for riding on the rancho. The hems of my skirts are all soiled now. No one but the vaqueros will see. Now, tell me what you've heard of the *marinero*."

"He has healed, and he is learning the way of the vaquero. Ramón Diego is allowing him to ride from the remuda to Don Nicholas Den."

"And he is learning?"

"Better than most Anglos, so I hear." Tía Angelina looked up from her mending. "You have an unusual interest in this Anglo, Juana. Your father would not approve."

"He was a very rough-looking man, Tía, but there was something about him."

"True, he was dressed in rags," her tía agreed, "but he was tall, with the hair of those of the north of Spain, and he had the eyes of an angel."

"Tía!" Juana exclaimed, laughing. "I am surprised at you."

"This old woman is not cold and in her grave, Juana." Tía

Angelina laid her sewing on the table. "But you must listen, *querida*"—she used the term of endearment with her niece— "the *gente de razón* would not approve of your worrying about this Anglo, eyes of an angel or not."

"Would you be shocked, Tía," Juana said with a slight smile, "if I told you I cared little about the upper class of Santa Barbara? The *gente de razón* sometimes remind me of cocks that crow in the yard and hens that peck and peck at one of their sister's bloodspots until their poor sister is dead."

"No, my niece," Angelina said with a deep sigh, "I would not be shocked." She appraised her beautiful young charge, and her eyes grew distant, as if she were thinking of a time long past. "You have the look of a wild mare about you sometimes," she murmured. Then her voice strengthened. "But I would be surprised if you were so foolish as to tell anyone other than your *dueña* such things."

"Then you would also not be shocked to know that I intend to give this Anglo a horse and saddle, and if Inocente does not apologize to him, I will do so myself."

"And your father will see that you see nothing more than the inside of your room for a year, *querida*. Do not let the tail of the whip bloody your own back while trying to lash the mule."

"Father will listen to me."

"As you shout from your locked room, Juana. As you shout from your room."

Fourteen

Juana stood on the wide *corredor* of the hacienda. Tía Angelina stood ramrod straight behind her, and her mother, Doña Isabel, her back as ridged as the whalebone stool she sat on, watched with indignation. Across the wide yard, her father, Inocente, and the old *vaquero del establo* Alfonso, whose duty was to keep the barn and watch over the brood stock and family's personal animals, walked from the spacious building leading a graceful palomino mare.

"I do not approve of this," Doña Isabel murmured to her sister Angelina.

"It is her birthday, Isabel. Times are changing. Besides"— she bent low so Juana could not hear—"it will get her mind off the young men."

"But for a young woman to ride so much—you know the risk."

"She will tire of it soon enough." Angelina smiled knowingly.

Juana stepped down from the wide porch when her father and Inocente arrived. Alfonso stood back, sombrero in hand, gray hair flowing in waves to his shoulders, smiling with toothless but sincere pleasure. Her father, usually somber, wore a wide smile too.

"She is beautiful, Father. Thank you."

"Inocente is seeing to your saddle, *niña*. It is his gift." She had been riding on a worn saddle with flattened padding used by her aunt when she was a girl.

"And thank you also, Inocente."

The vaquero cut his eyes away from Juana's. He wondered why he could never look this girl in the eye and felt his face flush. He cleared his throat. "It will be finished soon, Señorita. I am sorry it is not ready now, but we wanted it perfect." The sidesaddle had not been finished fine enough to suit Inocente; he had taken it back to the saddle maker and ordered it redone. Only the finest for little Juana.

Alfonso took a tentative step forward, a proud pleasure in his old eyes. "And I have groomed her, Señorita Juana. See how her coat gleams? I have even oiled and polished her hooves for you."

"She is lovely, Alfonso. Thank you."

Inocente stepped back as Juana walked around the mare. And while she admired the animal, Inocente admired her from the corner of his eye. Again he felt his neck redden. This girl was only a few years younger than he, but she was a Padilla. He knew he should not have thoughts of the *jefe's* daughter, but too many times this last year he had let his mind wander to what could be. He silently chastised himself. He was a mere mestizo, while she was of the *jefe's* family. A daughter of a don. A Castilian. He forced his attention to the mare.

At fifteen hands, the palomino was not particularly tall, but neither was Juana. Inocente had begged Don Estoban to select an even smaller horse, an older and gentler one. But the old don felt he was already conceding by allowing any of his family to ride a mare. A vaquero would not be seen astride anything other than a stallion, and the Californio did not believe in gelding his stallions. Inocente had at least influenced the selection to that extent. The mare was the gentlest of animals.

". . . and Inocente has taken great pains with her," Estoban was saying. "She will be a fine riding horse." He turned to the women on the porch. "Don't you think so, Mama?"

Doña Isabel rose from her seat and gave her back to her husband as she entered the front door of the hacienda. "You know what I think of Juana riding. The carriage is the proper place for a daughter of mine." Her voice and her long flowing black skirts disappeared with her.

Juana glanced at her retreating mother, but the closing door cut off any chance for rebuttal. Juana turned to her father and smiled with love in her eyes. "She is the most beautiful mare I've ever seen, Father." She ran her fingers through the mare's mane, combing its thick strands and smoothing it against the graceful golden neck. The mare softly nuzzled Juana's arm, nickering quietly.

"Please, Inocente, be very careful with her." Juana's beautiful doe eyes pleaded. "I do not believe in the quirt. Train her with gentleness."

"With care, little Juana," he managed, though it was hard to make his tongue work.

"Thank you, Inocente. You surprise me. I didn't think you had a gentle side."

"She will be trained well, whatever it takes." Embarrassed with his display of what he considered weakness and vanity, he strode away toward the barn.

"Trained well, Inocente," Juana called after him, "but with love. Always with love." Juana stood on her tiptoes and brushed her father's cheek with her own. His smile reflected her happiness.

"And I will take very good care of her, Señorita Juana," Alfonso said, his hat still clutched in his gnarled hands.

"I know you will, Alfonso. I can always count on you."

Satisfied, he pulled on his sombrero, and followed in Inocente's footsteps.

Juana stood beside her father. "You know, Papa, we should do something for the *marinero*."

"What *marinero*?"

"Come inside now, Juana," Tía Angelina called impatiently, trying to avoid the confrontation she knew was coming. "It is time to get ready for supper."

"What *marinero*?" Don Estoban asked again, but his eyes had narrowed.

"I told you, Father. The man Inocente roped and dragged halfway around the pueblo. I understand the Anglo received a broken arm. He could have died from that terrible dragging. Inocente owes him an apology."

Estoban's face reddened for a moment. "It is your birthday, Juana. Your day. Do not spoil it with thoughts of some worthless *marinero*. Go with your aunt."

Juana spun on her heel, and started toward the hacienda, then turned back at the top of the steps. "The mare is beautiful, Father. Thank you. I wish you would reconsider about the Anglo."

"Go help your tía," he said firmly, and she turned and hurried inside.

* * *

"Take the loop and *lazo* that *grulla*." Ramón motioned to the band of horses in the far corner of the corral.

"'*Grulla*'?" Clint did not understand the word.

"The light dun-colored stallion," the vaquero explained.

Clint took the leather reata from the corral post, shook out a loop, and moved across the corral. A line was already second nature to him. Still, on the first toss he missed. Patiently, he retrieved the loop, separated the stallion from the others, and this time deftly dropped the loop over the horse's head. The stallion placidly followed him across the corral.

"Put these on." Ramón handed him a pair of spurs with rowels at least three inches across. Clint strapped them over his worn, salt-stained boots.

"Now the bridle." Ramón motioned to the Spanish bit that lay across the saddle he had had Clint carry from the barn.

Clint picked it up, made sure the chin strap was unfastened, and reached up to slip it over the horse's ears with one hand, inserting the bit with the other. The animal flipped his head and pulled back. Clint had to drop the bit and take up the slack in the reata to control him.

"He is a Spanish horse, Anglo," Ramón said patiently. "A fine Andalusian stallion. He understands the *se ensilla, como en Castilla*. The reins over his neck first. He senses the control, with the reins in place."

This time, Clint draped the reins over the horse's neck as Ramon suggested, and the horse stood quietly and took the bit.

"*Bueno*, Anglo. Now for the saddle."

Clint thoroughly brushed the horse's back, then carefully fitted a hair-filled *jerga* saddle blanket. Only then did he pick up the high-cantled Spanish saddle and swing it into place, making sure it was well up against the big stallion's withers. Reaching under the animal, he retrieved the woven horsehair cinch, then ran the latigo two loops through the cinch ring and jerked the latigo up tightly.

He turned and looked expectantly at Ramón.

"Are you prepared to mount, Anglo?"

Without answering, Clint put a foot into the *tapadero* and found the round wooden stirrup.

"No, no, no," Ramón chastised. "You have forgotten the *paso de la muerte*, the step of death."

"What the hell is that?" Clint removed his foot.

"How do you know the horse's flesh is not crimped or pinched by the cinch, the latigo, or the saddle? Mount a stallion pinched by the latigo, and he will promptly show his displeasure—and rightfully so." Ramon took the reins and led the horse in a tight circle to the left, then to the right.

"Now," he said, returning the reins to Clint, "if you are fortunate, he is ready."

"The *paso de la muerte?*" Clint repeated, and smiled.

"*Sí*, Anglo, it is your death we are attempting to prevent, not the stallion's. Mount."

Clint swung easily into the saddle.

"We train our young horses with a *bosal*, without a bit."

"A '*bosal*'?"

"A nosepiece. When the reins of the *jacima*, of which the *bosal* is a part, are pulled, the nosepiece tightens gently across the nostrils, cutting off the stallion's wind. Soon he learns not to pull against the rein. Only after he is broken do we allow the iron in his mouth. The bit you are using now is a *barroyecca*. It will tear that animal's tongue from his head if you are careless—or cruel. So treat him with respect, and with a rein as tender as if it were in the mouth of your beloved. I promise such respect will be repaid."

Even though Clint looked rather comical in ragged duck pants and striped shirt, Ramón watched with approval. "You sit the saddle well, Anglo. And you seem comfortable with the reata. If we are fortunate, and you are not thrown on your *cabeza*, this may only take a few years." Ramón did not smile, but his eyes glinted with humor.

"Then we best get with it." Clint's smile was faint, but he sensed Ramón's pleasure as the man turned and headed for the barn and his own saddle. *Perhaps I did pick the right man*, Clint thought. *Perhaps exactly the right man*.

As Ramón walked away, another man leaned on the top rail of the corral, his shoulders ax-handle wide and his belly wider—and all supported by thighs the size of oak trunks. His features were broad and full, his ample head of hair black as coal, and his skin bean-brown, but he was not a Mexican.

Clint figured that this huge man must be the Kanaka who had helped him, the man he had seen when he first entered the pueblo. Reining his horse over, he extended his hand to the smiling man. Though Clint's hand was not small, it was lost in the ham-size hand of the Kanaka.

"I'm Clint Ryan, and you must be the man who brought me to the mission."

The big man smiled like a delighted child. "You were not so heavy."

"I owe you more than thanks. You saved my life."

"Then I am glad you were not so heavy."

"Somehow, I don't think many men would be too heavy for you to tote. You're a Kanaka?"

"Yes, and a sailorman, like you."

"And what is your name?"

"I am Matthew Mataca Konokapali. A name as big as me," he said, spreading his massive arms wide and laughing at his own joke.

"Matthew Mataca Kona—Konokapali. Nice to meet you. You don't mind if I call you Matt?"

"It is my missionary given name. You said my Sandwich Island name well, for a Bostoner. It is good to meet you, Mr. Clint Ryan."

"If I call you Matt, it would please me if you called me Clint."

"Clint it is."

Clint was marveling at the size of the man when Ramón rode out of the barn and called to him.

"It is time, Anglo, to see if you can use that 'line,' as you call it."

Clint said to the big Kanaka, "I've a few *reales* from working at the mission for Don Nicholas Den. If you're here when we return, I'll stand you to a mug. It's the least I can do, friend."

"I will wait." The big man lumbered into the shade of the barn.

Quade Sharpentier stood in the bow of the *Charleston*. Usually he was contented with the wind in his face, a port behind him where they had completed some successful trading, and a port in front where there was more trading to be done. But not now, for this was not his ship. He was a passenger, an interloper in another man's charge. They had sailed as far as Drake's Bay, just north of the entrance to the great San Francisco harbor. They had also stopped at the old town of Yerba Buena, now being called San Francisco by most captains, and the trading had been good. They would make one stop at Punta Ano Nuevo and, if the winds were favorable, Monterey and Port San Luis Obispo. After that, Sharpentier would have another chance to see if the deserter, John Clinton Ryan, had turned up in Santa Barbara.

The rumor, heard by Sharpentier in a cantina in Yerba Buena, was that a new Anglo had arrived in Santa Barbara, a light-haired man who wore the clothes of a seaman. It could only be Clint Ryan, Sharpentier thought, and his jaws clamped. The Turk had been right—the bastard had lived.

Skinner walked up beside him and leaned his heavy bulk against the forward rail. "It seems a long voyage, Captain."

"It'll be longer if I have to return to Boston without stretching Ryan's neck. That and only that will be a fitting end to the sinking of the *Savannah*. The *Charleston*'s holds are near full. We'll be heading back to Boston before the month's out. If I'm to satisfy the owners, I must have Ryan's head."

"And the *alcalde*?"

"If what I heard in Yerba Buena is right, it may be of no consequence what the *alcalde* thinks. He may soon be just another greaser. Another of California's small rebellions has taken place. There is a flag flying over Sonoma, a flag with a five-pointed star and a bear. Don Vallejo has been taken prisoner, and the Anglos and many of the Mexicans claim independence from Mexico. There has been no official word, but they say the dragoons in Texas are marching into Mexico.

"California, from the sea to the Rocky Mountains, may soon be a territory of the United States." The angry captain of the *Savannah* ran a hand into his salt-and-pepper beard and scratched his chin. "If only I had a ship, we could play a part in this." Sharpentier turned his back to the wind and attempted to light a cigar. "But Captain Armstrong is a company man. Not a man of destiny." The wind took the flame from the match.

"If the rebels prevail," he said, giving up on the cigar, "or if this rumor of war in Texas is true, it will be Anglo law, not Mexican law, that rules . . . not that it matters. We'll hang Ryan on sight if we see him, even if my upcoming business with Consul Larkin is not successful."

"What business is that?"

"Private business. Not your concern, but you think on this. We can take Ryan if we wish. The *Charleston* carries a dozen Hawkens long guns and two dozen of the finest Aston handguns. Not to speak of the midship six-pounder and the swivel two-pounder on the stern. Even if they try to protect him, the Mexicans would drop under our firepower."

"Will Captain Armstrong back you up?" Skinner asked.

"If he doesn't, I'll have you bump him over the rail in the night," Sharpentier said with a facetious grin. Then his look hardened along with his tone. "In fact"—Sharpentier's eyes narrowed—"that's not a bad thought, mate. We would have ship and crew, and be back in business. And if I stepped in and solved the problem of the *Charleston*'s lack of a captain, and returned a full cargo to Boston . . ."

Skinner's face twisted with a grim smile as he shaded his eyes with his hand and studied the horizon. "Seems a bit of a storm is coming, rough weather ahead, Captain. And I've noticed Armstrong has the habit of pacing the windward rail each night."

Quade Sharpentier, a captain without a ship, laid a hand on his first mate's broad shoulder. "Let's go below where I can enjoy this long nine, and I'll stand you to a mug of grog. The man about to make me a captain again deserves at least that."

Skinner's small eyes became slits. "And a piece of the captain's share of the profits? That's the least you should do for a mate who'll testify to Ryan being away from his duty station, as well as assure your prompt and efficient assumption of duty on this leaky tub."

Sharpentier stopped short, surprised by the thickset man's request. He scratched his beard. *By God, I've underestimated him*, Sharpentier thought. *Maybe there is a brain in that thick skull.*

"Ten percent of the captain's share could be had," he said quietly, noticing a seaman who had come forward to tend a jib halyard, "by a man who helped return me to captain. And another ten if that man were to find and stretch the neck of Ryan, then testify to his malfeasance."

"Let's go below . . . partner," Skinner said, and walked on ahead, not following deferentially as he normally would.

Sharpentier hesitated and looked after him for a moment. *The bastard's already taking his partnership a bit too seriously. When I'm captain again, with a cat-o-nine-tails in hand and a full crew to back me up, I'll bring the big ox back into line. He'll agree I promised no share, or he too will do the hangman's jig.*

Fifteen

Cha-ahm-sah reined up and turned his mount off the old trading trail. He and his men had been three days picking their way southwest through the marshes and tules of the valley. By nightfall they would be into the coastal mountains, where the great condor lived. Clouds hung low over the coastal mountains, and gusts of wind roiled the dust and raised small whitecaps on the lake the Spanish called Buena Vista.

Cha urged the mustang down to the lake to let him drink. Two regal white egrets left their ankle-deep hunting stance and began the slow, beating run that would take them into the air. Tadpoles fled from the disturbance as their grandfather croaked from a nearby stand of tules. Then his white belly plopped on the water, signaling his retreat into the safety of the quiet lake.

Eyeing a willow stake and woven-tule fish corral a few yards out in the shallow water, Cha thought about setting his men to raiding the supply of fish he knew would have been herded there by the Yokuts tribe across the lake, but he did not.

The edge of hunger made a warrior ferocious.

Nearly one hundred men rode behind Cha. They were the Yokuts warriors of two great Ton Tache villages. Full-chested powerful men, all carried bows, a few carried iron hatchets and iron-tipped lances festooned with silk flags that had been taken from the *cholos;* and ten carefully selected men, including Cha, carried the iron firesticks taken from the San José Mission patrol almost a year before. Those without iron weapons carried stone axes and knives, and stone-tipped lances.

95

A few skilled men carried *atlatls*, throwing sticks with stone-weighted bottoms. Special darts, constructed much like arrows but with thicker shafts, were flung by the *atlatls* with great velocity and accuracy. All the warriors, even those with the firesticks, carried bows, either short, powerful, juniper bows; long, graceful laurel or baywood bows; and at least a dozen war arrows each. Made in one piece, with a stone head fixed in place, the war arrows differed from the fletched but unheaded shafts that could be fitted with a variety of heads for hunting. These single-piece heavy-headed arrows were only for killing men. The bows of the great warriors were stored in lion's-tail bow covers until they neared the coast, then nettle fiber or sinew bowstrings would be strung and the bows readied for action.

The weapons were not the only sign that these men were on a man-killing mission. Each man wore his most powerful medicine. Elk, bear, and lion teeth adorned the necks and biceps of the men. Paint on both men and animals also declared their intent. Black, white, and ocher were the predominant colors, but highlights of blue and splotches of red, mostly feathers, glimmered in the sunlight.

This time the cholos *will run in fear of the men of Ton Tache*, Cha thought with satisfaction. Dismounting, Cha dropped to his hands, dipped low, and took a deep drink from the lake. Removing his drinking gourd from the back of his hand-carved saddle, he knelt to fill it while the other men lined the lakeside.

Far away, well beyond bowshot, four tule elk slipped from the reeds near the lake and trotted, their heads tilted so the horns lay flat on their backs. They crashed through a patch of willows, then up into the dry, sage-colored foothills.

We could chase them, Cha thought, *and probably bring down one or two with the number of men we have, but what good would one or two elk be? One small meal for this war party*. And he wanted to keep them keen and moving—with the edge of hunger.

No, a hundred horses, maybe a thousand, that was Cha's reason for crossing these mountains and facing the guns of the *cholos* and vaqueros. This time it would be different.

He remounted and reverently rubbed the stock of the musket stored in the doeskin wrapper that passed under his leg. On one side of the carved wooden saddle hung a horn containing the black-fire magic that drove the lead ball from the firestick, and beside it hung a leather bag with ball and patch.

Strong medicine, firestick medicine. A thousand horses.

He motioned silently, and the men remounted and strung out behind him as he whipped the mustang into a lope. Far away across the lake he could see the smoke of another Yokuts village, Too-Lahm-Nee, whose fish corral he had decided not to raid. The Too-Lahm-Nee band was over four hundred strong, with almost as many warriors as rode with him, but he would not seek their assistance. He had enough men.

Soon he would be in the land of the Chumash, his enemy. Many times the Chumash had ridden with the Mexicans to round up the Yokuts of the western side of the valley, and now many of Cha's people were among those forced to live at the missions. Many had died from the Spanish diseases or had been mixed with Mexican or Chumash blood until they could no longer be called Yokuts, the People. Maybe he would free a few Yokuts, if he could find any.

But nothing was as important as the horses.

As they climbed higher into the hills, the weather quieted, but the clouds hung low and dark.

In normal times he would have avoided this trail, for it passed the spot where the ancient ones, the giants who had roamed the before world, had come to die. Bones, hard as rocks and as long as his horse, had been found, and some believed the great giants who roamed the skies and caused the thunder with their footfalls still lived in the thick black pools. The men grew quiet as they neared, for no one wished to disturb the spirits.

Cha reined the mustang around the first of many great black pools that seeped from a rock formation at the base of a nearby hill. What the Spanish called *brea* was useful to line baskets for carrying water, but it fouled the ponds nearby and could trap even a horse. Along the border of the pit, bleached bones lay in the gleaming black and lined its banks. Creatures large and small had been lured in by the hope of easy prey—other trapped animals and birds. Eyeless sockets stared at the riders, some in skulls still feathered and furred but as lifeless as the barren branches of dead brush rising out of the muck.

A mist hung in the air over the wide expanse, almost

covering a barren cottonwood on the far side that had given up the spark of life with the onslaught of heavy black goo but still served as a roosting site for three turkey vultures. The odor of death permeated the place, and the dank air made the odor cling to men and animals. Even the dragonflies did not disturb the evil pool's surface on this damp day. Only one spot was the center of concentric ripples. Cha reined up and watched a still-living coyote, stuck up to its belly, making a desperate lunge for freedom when he spotted the men. But it was to no avail, and the clinging ooze sucked him back. The dead quail that had enticed the coyote into the mire was only five feet from him. Even the clever *kiyoo*, the coyote, brother to the Yokuts, could not outsmart the home of the giants.

They cleared the black pools, to the lamenting howl of the dying coyote, and Cha urged the mustang into an easy lope away from this death place. His hundred warriors stretched out for a quarter of a mile behind him. There were still two days of hard riding before they reached the first of the horses at Mission Santa Ines where they might have to face the leatherchests.

Captain Armstrong paced the windward rail of the *Charleston* as the sun dropped below the horizon. The night was clear, the wind quartering aft. With the sails set and trimmed, he had allowed the crew to go below to chow. Peterson, whom the captain hoped to groom as a second mate, stood a turn at the wheel.

Armstrong relaxed against the taffrail, watching the man at the helm adjust a couple of points as the wind shifted. He dug a clay pipe out of his coat and packed it with tobacco. Protecting it with his cupped hand, he struck a lucifer and drew until the tobacco took. Glancing forward, he noticed Skinner, one of his newly acquired crewmen off the shipwreck, step out of the fo'c'sle and wondered why the man was not at supper with the rest of the crew.

As Skinner made his way aft, Armstrong studied the man's ambling gait and furrowed his brows. He did not like having to displace his first mate to make room in his quarters for Captain Sharpentier, but rank was rank. He knew that Skinner hated bunking in the fo'c'sle as much as his own first mate did, but such was life at sea.

Armstrong did not like Skinner. He found him a man who

ruled by the back of his hand and the muscle in his arm rather than by example. And though he would never admit it in front of his men, he thought little of Sharpentier. He had not been surprised when the *Savannah* had gone aground.

He *had* been surprised when they laid the blame on Clint Ryan. He had known Ryan since his own cod days on the East Coast and found him to be competent and willing. More than likely, the blame belonged with Sharpentier.

Armstrong glanced up as Skinner mounted the quarterdeck. He nodded at Peterson and stepped farther aft to stand beside the captain.

"A good night for a quiet smoke," Skinner said.

"Aye," Armstrong answered, not anxious to strike up a conversation. The sky was darkening fast, and soon it would be the blackest part of the night, for the moon was not yet up.

"I heard a grinding noise from the rudder gear this afternoon," Skinner said, moving farther aft and cocking his head to listen. Armstrong followed.

"I hear nothing."

"Sounded as if the rudder hinge points are dry of grease. A bad place to neglect, Cap'n."

"There's a gearbox on my rudder points, man, and they are packed solid with greased hemp."

"There, don't ye hear that?" Skinner leaned far out over the stern. He backed away and pointed to the spot. Armstrong took the bait and stepped forward. Grasping a tarred mizzenmast stay, he leaned out.

He caught the flash of the belaying pin just in time to strengthen his grasp on the stay. The pin slammed against his head, smashed his ear, and dimmed his vision. He swung his other hand back and grabbed the stay with both hands. The pin cracked across his mouth, shattering teeth, but still he hung on, fighting to keep from losing consciousness.

"Ye bastard!" he spat, sending blood and teeth flying, desperately grasping the stay, desperately trying to keep from going overboard.

At the helm, Peterson glanced over his shoulder just in time to see Skinner slam the heavy pin against Armstrong's knuckles, breaking his fingers and knocking his left hand free. Then he struck at the right. By the time he had cracked it the second time, breaking a finger but still not knocking it loose, Peterson was on him. But the smaller man was no match for

Skinner, who with a heave tossed the helmsman over his shoulder. Peterson crashed into the tenuously clinging Armstrong, and both men cartwheeled into the sea.

Their cries echoed across the water as they bobbed to the surface in the luminescence of the wake, but Skinner knew they would not be heard by the men in the galley below.

"Damn stubborn," Skinner mumbled, stepping over to realign the wheel and tie it fast with the tail of the mizzenmast halyard. As soon as he was satisfied that it was sound, he glanced into the darkness aft of the ship, gave a slight farewell wave, and made his way back to the fo'c'sle. He wanted to be asleep in his bunk when the rest of the crew came on board from supper and found the captain and helmsman missing.

Lying on his cramped bunk for the last time, he thought smugly that with the sunrise he would be in the first mate's cabin and Sharpentier in the captain's—where they rightly belonged.

Ramón unsaddled the big roan he had been riding, then unbridled him, rubbed him down, and turned him out. He watched Clint do the same to a skunk-striped dun stallion.

"Come, Anglo," Ramon said, "I will spend a *real* of my hard-earned wages to buy you a mug of *aguardiente.*"

It had been two weeks of dawn-to-dusk riding and working the cattle, and throwing a thousand loops with the reata. Clint now wore the *jerga* of a mission Indian and a pair of boots given him by Padre Javier as payment for Clint's work in the tannery. He carried one of Ramón's fine woven reatas everywhere he went, constantly coiling and uncoiling, roping and retrieving.

He loved the familiar feel of the reata in his hands. It reminded him of bending lines shipboard.

Though dressed far better than the rags he had been wearing when he arrived, Clint was not dressed nearly as stylishly as Ramón. The vaquero sported leather *calzonevas,* the Californio equivalent of chaps, with silver conchos for buttons down the sides, usually unfastened halfway up the leg. More practical than chaps, they were worn without an underlayer of trousers in the summer, and over woolen *jerga* trousers when it turned cold. The flared bottoms accommodated tall boots, usually well oiled but now dusty from the long day in the saddle. The vaquero's dyed wool shirt was red, and he wore a multicolored bandanna tied around his head. Over it rested a flat-brimmed black felt hat with a woven rawhide chin tie. Most of the time the hat rode on his back. In winter he wore a waist-length jacket embroidered with darker thread to match the wool pants under the *calzonevas*.

A quirt, or *romal*, of multicolored leather hung from his waist, fitted through a leather belt that held only the quirt and his gleaming-steel bone-handled knife.

When afoot, Ramón carried his coiled reata over his shoulder, never willing to let the braided well-tallowed sixty-foot leather line far from his sight. The supple tool was his most prized possession.

Huge spurs with three-inch rowels jangled as he walked, as did those Clint wore. A vaquero would never mount the half-wild stallions they were sometimes forced to ride without the vicious spurs.

When they reached the cantina, Matt Mataca Konokapali, the huge Kanaka, was lounging under a nearby oak. Clint waved him over to the hide-covered doorway. Each day since they had met, Matt had joined them for a drink, but only one. Never would the huge Kanaka take the second.

A young boy sat on his haunches by the cantina door. As was the custom, each man allowed the boy to remove his spurs and return them to his saddle horn or drape them across the hitching rail. As was expected, Ramón gave him two coppers and received a *"gracias"* in return.

Clint pushed aside a black and white cowhide door covering, and they entered. Several other vaqueros and a few townspeople occupied the place, pushing up to the rough-plank bar and filling many of the sturdy wooden tables. Tobacco smoke hung beneath the ceiling from pipes and cigars, and wisps of black smoke rose from whale-oil lamps backed by tin sconces that lined the adobe walls. A black and white spotted shoat named Gordo begged for handouts and was occasionally accommodated by amused patrons or kicked by those who were not. Ramón sat at a vacant table and waved at the barmaid, who without being asked brought them three mugs of *aguardiente*.

"You have done well, Anglo," Ramón said quietly to Clint after taking a deep draw.

Matt smiled and sat silently as he usually did.

"*Gracias*, Ramón," Clint said seriously. He had learned

that compliments from the vaquero were hard-earned. In fact, this was the first one he had received.

"*Salud*." Ramón clinked mugs with him.

"The way of the vaquero is far different from the way I learned to handle stock in New England," Clint said.

"To the vaquero the horse is everything." Ramón sipped his drink. "A man without a horse is no man at all. A man who cannot use the reata is no man at all."

"You've been a good teacher, Ramón."

"You still have much to learn, Anglo."

They drank in silence for a while. Clint knew only too well how much he had to learn. He had watched Ramón do things with the reata that he would have believed impossible. Once, the vaquero had roped a bullock at full speed, the loop forming a figure eight and catching both horns and one foreleg. With a dally on the tall pommel, the bullock then tumbled head over heels in a cloud of dust, and Ramón had commented quietly, "He was a mean one, or I would not have been so rough with him."

As Clint watched his new friend drink, he thought of how the man rode. It was almost a surprise to see him dismount at the end of a day's work, for he seemed a part of the horse during the day. In his years at sea and the strange ports he had visited, Clint had seen Berbers and Mongols and Argentine gauchos ride, but none surpassed the skill of these Californios.

"Clint, you have the touch," Ramón said, for the first time using Clint's first name. "Never have I seen a man take to the reata as you have. Certainly never an Anglo. I hope you will stay with it."

Clint felt the heat on the back of his neck and his face. It was more than a compliment, coming from this man. "I will stay with it as long as you're willing to teach me," he said.

"*Bueno*," Ramón said. "But we will take it slowly. A wise man does not build the gate until he's constructed the corral. More *aguardiente*!" he called to the girl. He turned back to Clint. "In one week, we celebrate the procession of Corpus Christi. Then it is fandango and fiesta time. After the celebration, we will ride against the other ranchos, and all will know who the finest vaqueros are."

"I'll enjoy watching that," Clint said as the girl arrived with the filled mugs.

"'Watching'? You will ride by my side, amigo, so you must

be ready. I would not like to be embarrassed by my student."

Clint looked at him in surprise, then smiled. "*Salud, amigo.*" They clinked mugs.

"I should not have this," Matt said softly, eyeing the second drink that now sat in front of him. Gordo the pig had tracked the barmaid to the table and nudged Matt's thick leg with his snout. Matt considered giving the animal the mug, but Clint interrupted the thought.

"Hell's fire, man, it's a celebration!" Clint slapped him on the back with dust-raising enthusiasm. "You've got to drink to the rodeo."

Matt looked at him skeptically, but upended his first mug, then reached for the second. Gordo squealed his displeasure, then wandered away. Both Ramón and Clint extended their mugs, and the three of them toasted.

"*Salud.*"

"Bring us more!" Ramón ordered loudly.

The robust serving maid walked away swinging her broad hips. Clint eyed her appreciatively and offered a toast: "To both ends of the busk."

"Wait, wait, amigos," Ramón said. "I wish to know what I drink to."

"The busk, mate," Clint said, and he and Matt laughed. "'Tis a sailor's toast. The busks are the whalebone stays the ladies wear in their corsets. We sailors favor the parts at 'both ends.'"

"I can drink to that, amigos."

By the end of the first hour, they had consumed several mugs, and the usually stoic Matt Konokapali rocked back and forth in his chair, joining Clint in singing sea chanteys in English with a booming voice.

> *Where there ain't no snow,*
> *And the winds don't blow,*
> *What d'you think we had for supper?*
> *Possum tails and a donkey's crupper.*
> *If whiskey was a river and I could swim,*
> *I'd take a jump and dive right in.*

Though Ramón understood little of the songs, he kept time, enthusiastically thumping his mug on the table. Gordo, who had begged more than his share, lay at Matt's feet, occasionally contributing a snort to the tune.

Matt's brown face was blotched with red, but his smile shone as usual. Each time a mug was set in front of him, he downed it in a single gulp, laughed and reached for another, then struck up another song.

Four *cholo* guards sat at a table across the room where they had been since Matt, Clint, and Ramón had entered the cantina. They had warily watched Clint and his friends for the last hour. Finally, the largest of the four got up and crossed the room, stopping next to Matt, who sang loudest. The man cocked a booted foot back and kicked Gordo with a resounding thump. The shoat ran squealing to the door.

Clint stopped singing and glared up at the man.

The *cholo*, a large man in his own right, spoke from under a full handlebar mustache. He bent near Matt, eyeing him up and down. "You are loud, *gordo*, and you are disturbing our conversation."

"What? I don't understand, do you call me Gordo the pig, or *gordo*, as in fat?" Matt asked drunkenly, but his eyes took on a cunning cast. Being called fat did not particularly bother him, but he preferred to think of himself as regal, like the ancient kings and queens of the Sandwich Islands who weighed over four hundred pounds, just as he did.

"You are loud, and *borracho*. Your gringo songs are not entertaining. We wish to drink in peace. Why don't you and your friends drink outside." His three *compadres* walked up behind him.

Matt appraised the man and his three friends but never stopped smiling. "He thinks I'm fat—and drunk." Matt guffawed and slapped a tree-trunk thigh. "He's right, you know."

But Ramón saw no humor in the *cholo*'s manner. "These are friends of mine." Ramón rose slowly and faced the much larger guard across the table.

"You should choose your friends with more care, Ramón Diego," the man said.

Clint also rose, his eyes glinting like blue ice, but said nothing. Several other vaqueros and townspeople came to their feet and backed off, sensing that a conflict was brewing.

"Oh, I do choose carefully," Ramón said, returning the *cholo*'s arrogant smile. "If I chose carelessly, I would have sat with you, Enrique."

The big guard's smile faded.

"I think outside is good," Matt mumbled, still sitting, still smiling.

Enrique said, "Your friend shows much wisdom, even if he looks the oaf and is *gordo* and *borracho*."

Clint felt the heat rising in his neck, but still he said nothing. He figured it was Ramón's show. Clint was a guest in this land, and these were men Ramón knew.

But Matthew Mataca Konokapali must have decided it was time to move on. He slammed down his mug and exploded out of the chair. He charged into the men, harvesting all four of them like sheaves of wheat.

El toro, Clint thought, *just as Padre Javier said*.

With biceps the size of most men's waists and powerful oak-stump legs churning beneath him like a ship's pump, Matt drove into the men, shoving them ahead of him toward the door. Gordo scrambled out of the way, his hooves flailing on the slippery plank floor.

Though someone had closed the two-inch-thick door behind its hide cover, it did not even slow the powerful Kanaka and his six-hundred-pound burden. The hide ripped away, and the door splintered off its hinges, crashing over the porch and into the road.

Clint and Ramón charged out behind, willing to help their friend, but their assistance was not needed. One man was on his knees gasping for breath, the second and third lay in the road, not moving. Enrique clawed for the knife in his waistband, but Matt had him by the throat with one hand. With an expression of bliss still on his face, Matt brought the other ham-size fist down on the guard's head, driving him to his knees, his eyes rolling up into his senseless head. Matt released him, and he dropped like a fallen timber.

Matt smiled at Clint and Ramón. "More *aguardiente*."

"My door!" Teodoro, the barkeep, screamed from behind Clint and Ramón. They turned to see the cantina owner and a crowd of very quiet vaqueros and townspeople staring in astonishment. "You've ruined my door!" the owner wailed.

"I will pay for it," Ramón said.

Gordo made his way between the legs of the watching crowd to sniff at the fallen guards.

"If I leave them here, maybe the pig will eat them," Matt said, then turned to Ramón. "Since it is now your door, I will borrow it." He reached down and picked up two *cholos* by their belts. He carried them to the door and unceremoniously dropped them on it, then returned for the other two. One was struggling to his feet.

"You must join your friends." Matt brought his balled fist down on the man's head with a thunk. The guard went down as if he had been struck with a bung mallet. Matt picked him up like a rag doll and deposited him on top of the others. Like a mother caring for her brood, he covered them with the hide ripped from the doorway, then hoisted one end of the laden door and began dragging them away. "I will take them home," he said.

"It's a half mile to the presidio," Clint said.

"Don't steal my drink," Matt said, and continued effortlessly dragging the door and the pile of *cholos* away, leaving a deep wide groove in the dirt road. Gordo trotted along behind, seemingly interested in the turn of events and possibly planning to snack on any item that tumbled from the makeshift travois.

Matt's voice rang out across the dusty road.

> If whiskey was a river and I could swim,
> I'd take a jump and dive right in.
> We dug his grave with a silver spade,
> And lowered him down with a golden chain.
> Who's been here since I've been gone?
> A nice little gal with booties on.
> There once was a farmer in Sussex did dwell,
> Now he is dead and he's gone to hell.

Teodoro called after him, "I need my door!" but he made no effort to chase the big man.

"I think I could use another drink," Ramón said with a baleful glance at the disappearing Kanaka.

"And I," Clint agreed.

"Not in this cantina," Teodoro said, then looked sheepish. "I'm afraid your loco friend will come back."

"We will go to Paco's Cantina," Ramón said with righteous indignation, and handed the man a fistful of coins. Clint and Ramón straightened their clothes and walked proudly, if drunkenly, away.

"If this is not enough, I will call upon you, Ramón!" Teodoro yelled behind them.

"Tell Matthew Mataca Konokapali where we have gone," Clint said.

"I will be closed!" Teodoro hurried back inside to figure out how to close without a door.

When Matt did not return, Clint figured he had gone off somewhere to sleep off the gallon of *aguardiente* he had consumed.

Sixteen

The next morning, Padre Javier shook Clint awake.

"*Buenos días*," Clint managed. He certainly did not feel that it was a good morning. As he tried to focus his eyes, he remembered what he had learned long ago: Wild oats make a poor breakfast.

"Your friend Matthew has had some trouble with the mission guards."

Clint sat up rubbing his eyes, his mouth tasting as if he had kissed Gordo good-night. "I know, Father," he mumbled as he stretched. "I was there."

"You know he is in the stocks?"

"The stocks?" Clint threw off his blanket and rose. "Where?"

"At the presidio. I understand he arrived with four unconscious guards. When they questioned him, he said only that he was going back to the cantina to meet some friends."

"And?" Clint asked, stepping into his breeches.

"And several of the guards disagreed. He fought at least six of them into submission. It was only when they called out to some passing vaqueros for help and they were able to use their reatas on him that he was subdued. Like roping the grizzly, they said later."

"Is he all right?" Clint tucked his shirttail in.

"He is better than most of the *cholos* he fought with, or the vaquero who injured his leg when the Kanaka sat back against the reata and pulled his horse down on top of him."

"But Matt's all right?"

"As well as can be expected in the stocks. I have not seen

the stocks used in Santa Barbara for years." Padre Javier shook his head.

"What can we do?" Clint pulled on his boots.

"There is nothing to do, I'm afraid. It is said he will be released from the stocks in a week. But then he faces six months in the *juzgado*."

"Six months? I need to see him."

"No! I will relay any message. The *cholos* are not so happy with Anglos right now."

"All right, you talk to him. But see if you can arrange for his release. Ramón will vouch for him. I'll get him a job aboard ship, or something."

"I see. You have good relations with ship captains now?" The priest smiled indulgently and shook his head. "I will talk to the *alcalde*, but he has never changed his mind about a punishment yet."

For the first time, Juana mounted the mare she had named Florito, little flower, and sat tentatively in the saddle.

Her father sat a tall palomino stallion, Sol Diablo, one of California's finest Andalusians, which he rode regularly, one of twenty beautiful palominos that were kept in the barn as brood stock. Inocente mounted his tall roan and reined up beside the girl.

"And the saddle, Juana, it is comfortable?"

"It is wonderful, Inocente. So soft I could ride all day."

"We shall see, daughter," Estoban said. Behind them Angelina climbed into the shiny black caleche, and her Indian driver took whip in hand.

Estoban watched his daughter ride, sitting straight in the saddle. The turtle-shell comb high above her chestnut hair held a lace mantilla, the emblem of a wealthy Californio lady. *She is a beautiful sight*, he thought. *A daughter to make a man proud*.

"You have done well, daughter," Estoban said.

"I would not miss this trip, Father. It is said the last ship brought five bolts of the best silk, and the fandango will be here soon."

Halfway through the journey they spotted five vaqueros working a small herd of cattle out of a thick grove of buckeye trees on a gentle hillside. One bullock broke from the herd and pounded toward the road. A tall vaquero, dressed more like an

Indian in mission *jerga*, spurred his horse after the large calf. Before the animal could reach the road, the vaquero's reata snaked out and caught the young animal, its perfect loop finding both horns. He took his dally and reined the horse to a sliding stop. Dust rose as the calf fought and tried to shed himself of the restraint. Finally, it bowed its neck and stood stiff-legged against the reata, only a few feet from the passing caleche.

The vaquero made no move to drag the bullock back to the herd. Instead, he sat motionless, watching with cold hard eyes.

Riding beside Juana, Inocente suddenly jerked his horse to a stop.

The vaquero, just over a reata's length away, slowly pushed his bandanna from his head, exposing his sandy hair. His blue eyes did not move from those of the *segundo*.

Juana looked at the man over her turtle-shell fan. This was the *marinero* who had been dragged and almost killed by Inocente, this vaquero who had just caught a bullock with the skill of one of the best. Then she noticed the angry stare passing between the men.

"Inocente!" she said harshly. "We must hurry."

The tall, dark-skinned vaquero cut his eyes to her for only a moment, then looked back at the gringo vaquero. The man had not turned away. His blue eyes burned across the distance between them.

"Another time, Anglo." Inocente's voice rang across the silence.

"Inocente!" Juana called more loudly than her *dueña* would approve. Her father reined up and turned back to see what she was shouting about.

"Any time," Clint said quietly to Inocente, but they all heard.

"To the pueblo!" Estoban shouted to Inocente.

"I will be at Teodoro's Cantina tomorrow night, Anglo," Inocente said in a low voice, "if you desire another lesson in manners." The tall thin vaquero jerked his horse around and left in a cloud of dust.

Frowning and still suffering from his hangover, Ramón rode up beside Clint, who watched the Padillas and their *segundo* ride away.

"You know Don Estoban?" Ramón asked.

"No, but I know the feel of that vaquero's reata."

"Inocente. He is not a bad man, but he is a very bad enemy."

"Not bad?" Clint looked skeptically at Ramón. "He roped me from behind and broke my arm. He dragged me until I was almost dead. He'll wish he was bad when I finish with him."

"He is no coward," Ramón cautioned. "His blade and his musket have sent more than one man to meet his maker."

"Good," Clint said coldly. "Then I'll have nothing on my conscience when I send him to join them."

Clint nudged his horse away, dragging the bullock behind. Astride the big roan, Ramón watched him for a moment. This was a side of the Anglo he had not seen. He believed the Anglo meant exactly what he said.

But Inocente was his friend, just as Clint Ryan was his friend. This was a thing he did not wish to see happen.

That night, Clint slept soundly. He and Ramón had not made their usual visit to the cantina.

Padre Javier had reported that he had been unsuccessful at convincing the *alcalde* to go easy on Matt and had convinced Clint to stay away from the presidio, at least until the *cholos* had recovered from their injuries.

Clint snapped alert, straining his ears for what had awakened him. He could see thorough the cracks in the shutters that it was still very dark outside.

There was a strange soft pounding at the door. Taking his knife in hand, he moved silently across the room, then jerked the door open. Matt Konokapali looked much like the crucifix over Clint's bed, except for the grin. His head and hands still stuck through the thick timbers of the stock. Its base stuck out in front of him seven feet. That earth-covered appendage, gently rocking back and forth, had been pounding on the door.

"My God, man. How did you get here?" Clint stared in astonishment.

"I don't like being stuck in the presidio in this thing. I jus' kept working it back and forth until it loosed up. It took a long time to get the hole big enough. Then I pulled it out and backed up all the way here. Took most of the night."

"Wait here," Clint ordered, and left for the blacksmith's shop next door. He returned with a hammer and chisel, quickly knocked off the brass lock, and helped Matt out of the stock.

Matt rubbed his chafed and bleeding neck and wrists.

"What time it it?" Clint asked.

"Almost dawn."

"You've got to get the hell out of here."

"Aye," Matt said, and turned to leave.

"Wait," Clint said. "We've got to get rid of this thing." He picked up the light end of the massive stock, and marveled at the fact that the man had been able to drag it over half a mile. Following along behind Matt, who effortlessly carried the heavy end, they hurried out of the mission yard and up the hill through the vineyards.

Finally, when Clint felt almost ready to drop, Matt stopped.

"Is this far enough?"

"Far . . . enough," Clint gasped.

They pulled the stock into the vineyards and covered it with vines.

"I go now."

"Where?"

"Away."

"You've got to have somewhere to go." Clint pondered a moment. "I know a place." He pulled Matt to a clearing, and in the moonlight drew a map in the dirt. He explained where he wanted Matt to go and what he wanted him to say when he got there. The huge man waved and disappeared into the darkness of the scrub oaks.

The *alcalde* would want to know who had helped his prisoner escape, so Clint made sure he would not find out. He ran for the corral and saddled a horse. Cutting a bough from an evergreen tree, he rode the horse into the mission yard. Just as it was getting light enough to see, he dragged the bough behind him to wipe out the distinct trail of the stock. He sat on the horse and eyed the rest of the track that led on to the presidio. It pointed to the mission, but nothing could be proven. He laughed to himself. The footprints looked as if someone had dragged something *to* the presidio since Matt had walked backward.

After cleaning up as much of the trail as he dared in the time he had, he cast aside the bough and returned to the mission just as the sun fully crested the mountains and kissed the adobe with golden morning light.

By the time the sun reached its zenith, Clint and Ramón had worked a small band of cattle into a clearing where a team of spikers and skinners waited.

Clint spoke to no one, not even Ramón, about his planned confrontation with Inocente. He wanted no one to interfere with what he must do. He felt good, even with little sleep, and he was healed and ready to repay the beating he had received. Instinctively he knew that if he was to make a new life in this land, he must have the respect of its people. He had been aboard enough ships, worked with enough hard men, to know that no one respected a man who would not stand up for himself. And all but a fool would respect a man who did, even if he lost.

Clint threw his loop, capturing another bullock, and had begun dragging it to a spiker when he saw a fast-moving rider approaching from the distance. He delivered the bullock, waited until his loop was returned, then rode a few yards up the trail to meet the man. To his surprise, it was Padre Javier.

With his robes flapping in the breeze and his sandaled feet in the stirrups, he was a rather amusing sight, but when he reined to a sliding stop, Clint realized he was in dead earnest.

"You must ride into the hills for a few days," he said.

"Why, Father?"

"The *Charleston* has returned, and with her Captain Sharpentier and some of your old shipmates."

"Now is as good a time as any to prove my innocence to Sharpentier. Captain Armstrong of the *Charleston* is a fair man. I served under him when he was first mate on a cod ship. I've decided I don't want to return to sea, but still, proving my innocence is important."

"It seems Captain Armstrong was lost at sea, along with his helmsman. A very strange incident, so it is said— overboard on a quiet night in a calm sea. The ship is now under the command of Sharpentier, and he has a warrant issued by Thomas Larkin, the American consul in Monterey. The *alcalde* is compelled to honor it. You must not return."

Ramón had remained silent until now. "We need to check the high country for stock, and now is as good a time as any."

"I don't like the thought of running," Clint said.

Ramón's eyes hardened. "Do you like the thought of

swinging at the end of a rope while the ravens pluck at your eyes?"

"Sharpentier has thirty men and the *alcalde* another forty or fifty," the priest added. "Go! There will be much trouble if you return while the *Charleston* is in port, and we wish no trouble in Santa Barbara. Go, my son, if only because I ask it of you."

Clint regarded him for a long moment, then decided he could not affront this man who had done so much for him. "If you wish," he said, and reined the horse around.

He and Ramón headed away from Pueblo Santa Barbara at a trail-eating gallop.

Seventeen

Cha avoided the remnants of two Chumash villages as he and his band climbed higher and higher into the dry lee side of the coastal mountains. He did not fear them, for the Yokuts could have crushed them easily, but he wanted no chance of runners going ahead and betraying his coming. A party of a hundred armed Ton Tache Yokuts riders would attract great attention and excitement.

As a condor circled effortlessly high above, Cha reined up under a huge digger pine and took a deep breath of cool sea air. In the far distance, still two days' ride through the rugged mountains, he could see the ocean for the first time since they had left the Ton Tache. With his men reining up beside him, he dismounted among the melon-sized digger cones that lay scattered in profusion. He took a long draw from his drinking gourd, then filled his palm and wet his mustang's mouth. They had been most of the day without water, but he knew that on the coastal side they would find more and more as they worked their way lower and lower.

Sah-ma-not, Cha's *winatun*, or subchief, nudged his horse near Cha and dismounted to gaze into the sunset. "Sup has painted well tonight," he commented as the sky changed from lemon to orange and the streaks of clouds lit with fire. "Do we ride to the small place of the leatherchests and settle for a few horses, or to the place of thousands?" Sahma asked.

"We have fared our journey well, Sahma. We are strong. I will watch the sun find his sleeping place and look for a sign."

Now it was time for Cha to make a decision. If he headed into the sun, he would come upon the valley the Spanish called Santa Ines; if he continued with the setting sun to his

115

right, he would come to Santa Barbara. He moved to a gold, green, and blue lichen-covered rock and sat. Santa Barbara would mean more horses but also more leatherchests.

The falling sun drenched the distant clouds in a darkening array of colors, and still Cha pondered quietly. By the time the sea had swallowed Father Sun in a leisurely gulp and the sky above gloried in the capture with a display that dulled the lichen's, he had made up his mind.

The men had dismounted, removed their carved wooden saddles with their scant supplies and sleeping robes tied on the back, and turned out the horses. Some of the more industrious of the braves began to make a huge pile of digger pinecones, leaning dry branches against the pile to roast out the nuts, but Cha stopped them. It would not do to have a noticeable fire this close to the coast. They settled for acorn-mash cakes and the dried meat or fish that each of them carried, then rolled in their sleeping robes and awaited the dawn.

"We're not very well prepared for a few days in the mountains," Clint grumbled as he paced Ramón's steady lope.

"Rancho del Robles Viejos is just over the rise. My father works there . . . and we know Don Estoban and his *segundo* are in the pueblo and not at home. We can get a few provisions there."

Clint clamped his teeth as he realized that Ramón was purposely avoiding any contact with Inocente Ruiz. For the first time since Padre Javier had come with his warning, Clint thought of his appointment with Inocente at Teodoro's Cantina. His fists balled, and the muscles in his shoulders bunched. The man would think him a coward when he did not show up.

He felt like turning around and galloping back to the pueblo, but it was not that simple. Padre Javier had asked a personal favor of him. Though his confrontation with Ruiz was a matter of pride, Padre Javier had helped save his life, and he owed him. *Hell,* he thought, *I'm damned if I do and damned if I don't. Inocente will wait, and who gives a damn what he thinks,* he decided as they crested a small rise and saw the rancho's impressive buildings ahead. *Now, this is the way to live.*

Clint surveyed the hacienda and forced his mind from Inocente Ruiz. The hacienda faced the ocean in the distance;

the barn and a large corral were within easy walking distance in one direction and the kitchen building, the *cocina*, sat within spitting distance from the rear of the red-tile-roofed adobe house. A flat-roofed *matanza*, or slaughterhouse, huddled a few feet beyond. The whitewashed adobes reflected the western sky and shimmered with a golden glow.

A thin wisp of smoke betrayed the last of the supper fire, and the aroma teased Clint. A herd of horses stood in knee-deep lush green grass in a meadow between the house and the sea, and huge mottled sycamores lined the meadow and framed the pastoral scene.

They dismounted, and Ramón called out to his father. The old man appeared at the barn door. His eyes, in a craggy face of undeterminable age, lit up at the sight of his son, and the smile that followed revealed a mouth with few remaining teeth. He was a man who looked as if he had ridden the world and soaked up its knowledge.

At the sight of his father, Ramón removed his hat. Clint followed suit.

"Clint Ryan, this is my father, Alfonso María Diego."

The old vaquero pushed his flat hat back to reveal a mane of steel-gray hair that flowed to his shoulders. He extended a knotted hand, and Clint shook it, impressed with its strength and hard callused texture. He watched as Ramón related recent news to his father. The son listened attentively when the old man spoke. When the old man rolled a smoke, which Ramón lit for him, and offered one to them, Ramón politely declined. Though Ramón must have been easily twenty years Clint's senior, he would not smoke in front of his father.

Alfonso instructed an Indian boy, Muñoz, to grain, water, and rub down the lathered horses.

The men talked as they walked to the kitchen, and Ramón told his father of Clint's run-in with Inocente Ruiz.

After they were seated in the *cocina* and had a plate of leftover beef, beans, and squash steaming in front of them, and a cup of coffee that would raise a blood blister on a leather boot, Alfonso turned to Clint. "You must not think too badly of Inocente. You are a stranger and don't understand our ways. A California don and his vaqueros place their women above all else." He smiled mischievously. "Except possibly their Andalusian stallions."

Clint listened intently but said nothing.

"To meet the eyes of a California señora or señorita to whom you have not been introduced," Alfonso continued, "is not considered polite, even if you are a Californio. To stare is an insult. To speak is considered an affront of the worst kind."

Clint did not reply, even when the old vaquero paused to give him the opportunity.

"If you do not repeat the offense, I am sure the matter is settled."

Clint mopped the last of his plate with a tortilla, then sat back in the seat and shoved the empty plate away. "I don't mean to be rude, Señor Diego. As you say, I am a stranger. I had only seen a Californio señorita from a distance before Señorita Padilla walked in front of me in the pueblo. She was looking directly at me, and where I come from, it would have been rude *not* to speak. I meant no offense when I addressed her, as any gentleman would do on the streets of Mystic or Boston or New York."

Clint rose from his seat and walked to the window. "Where I come from, we cut strangers a little slack. I was unaware of my mistake, and if it had been pointed out to me, I would have offered an apology." Clint turned away from the window to face the two vaqueros. "Inocente Ruiz and I have an appointment—face-to-face this time. I intend to teach him some tolerance if I have to do it with my knuckles, the heel of my boot, or, if he prefers, with the blade of my knife. If he wishes the blade, then God will judge him. And that's no brag, just fact. It's a foolish man who writes a draft with his mouth that his abilities can't cash."

"Inocente's skill with the blade is renowned," Alfonso warned.

A loaf of bread rested on a table across the room; behind it a thick hardwood cutting board leaned against the wall— eight paces away. Almost before Alfonso had finished his statement, Clint's blade appeared in his hand and flashed across the room, pinning the loaf to the cutting board with a quivering thump.

Alfonso's and Ramón's eyes widened.

"And mine," Clint offered quietly, "has come from a thousand ports in a hundred countries, full of hard, skilled men who fancy themselves and their abilities. Men who will face a man, not attack him from the rear."

"He will not back down," Alfonso said.

"Nor will I. I learned long ago that no one respects a man with retreat in his heart."

There was a long silence.

Finally, Alfonso rose. "Well, mi amigo, you are a friend of Ramón's, and that is enough for me. I will get you two some blankets and some coffee, tortillas, and frijoles, then you must be on your way."

"Tonight?" Ramón asked.

"Yes, tonight, I am afraid. Don Estoban may return even yet, and it would be best if you were gone."

"As you wish, mi padre," Ramón said. Only when they were mounted and riding away did Ramón return his hat to his head. In the darkness they walked the horses, not risking a faster pace on a trail that was not much more than *carreta* tracks.

"It is obvious you think a great deal of your father, Ramón. I respect that. I never had much chance to know mine, nor my mother."

"Alfonso Diego was once the finest horseman I've ever known. He is seventy now, and prides himself only on what he teaches the young men. He can only do that now by telling what he once demonstrated. He still rides, but is cautious."

"The bones become brittle, and he is wise to respect that."

"He will have a home with Don Padilla for as long as he lives, and I pray that is a long time. He loves his horses, and he reveres Señorita Juana as he would a granddaughter. I was glad you explained to him."

"And I'm glad you heard it. I hope you understand."

They rode until they were off the rancho, then made a dry camp at the first open spot with good grass, hobbling the horses. To the accompaniment of the mournful songs of a lone wolf and an owl, they rolled in their blankets.

Clint took a long time to fall asleep, tired as he was. He knew that somewhere Inocente Ruiz was believing him a coward, and the thought gnawed at him like a gut full of maggots. With the thought that he would soon have the opportunity to right that mistaken belief, he finally drifted off.

Don Francisco, the *alcalde*, had avoided seeing Captain Quade Sharpentier on the day he returned, but the man was obstinate. He had heard from his clerk that the man possessed

a warrant issued by the American consul Thomas Larkin, and
he knew that he must at least acknowledge it if not actively
pursue its intent. He held no grudge against the *marinero*
Ryan and cared little about the problems of the Anglos. He had
no wish for a hanging in Pueblo Santa Barbara. It was such a
messy business.

But the captain was persistent and again this morning
awaited him in the anteroom. The *alcalde* took a long look out
the window to the center court, the plaza, and the presidio
soldados lounging about. A few festooned lances with flapping
silk banners rested against the walls of the presidio, and the
guards' heavy leather breastplates and helmets had been
removed and draped across the hitching rail or rested on a
trickling fountain's low wall. He shook his head, irritated with
his *capitán del guardia* for the laxness of his men, but he had
no time to chastise them. He had to deal with the Anglo.

Don Francisco turned away from the window and sat
down at his broad carved desk. He might as well get this over
with. Picking up a small bell at the edge of his desk, he rang
for his clerk, who immediately stuck his head in the door.
"Send *Capitán* Sharpentier in."

This time the captain was dressed in a full-dress uniform
almost as resplendent as the *alcalde*'s. His gold buttons
gleamed, and gold-embroidered epaulets sparkled when he
walked forward and snapped his heels smartly in front of the
alcalde's desk. Don Francisco Acaya rose politely, motioned to
a chair, then returned to his own as a sealed document was
placed in front of him. He ran a thumbnail through its red wax
seal.

"It is a warrant, *Alcalde*," Sharpentier said, his tone
officious and terse.

"Ah, a warrant. And for whom?"

"John Clinton Ryan, as you well know. Do you know his
whereabouts?"

"The last I heard, he was in residence at the mission." He
unfolded and read the parchment.

"Then we will go there."

"As you wish . . . but the *marinero* Ryan, if you find
him, you must promise he will be hung from your yardarm, far
at sea."

"And his body offered to the sharks." Sharpentier smiled
for the first time since he had entered the *alcalde*'s office.

"Unless he tries to flee. Then we must do what we must do."

"Captain Sharpentier," Don Francisco stated evenly, "we want no trouble on the shores of California." He walked around his desk. "I want your word that you will take your trouble and your punishment back aboard your ship."

"Our yardarms will serve just as well as your oaks, *Alcalde*." His lip curled into what pretended to be a smile. "We would not wish to offend your sensibilities."

"Then I and a few of my *soldados* will accompany you to the mission to make sure you fulfill your promise. We would not want you or your men to get . . . overly enthused."

"As you wish, *Alcalde*. I only want to obey the law." The captain did not miss the *alcalde*'s dubious glance.

With Aston musket and cutlass in hand, Quade, Skinner, and eight men accompanied the *cholos*. The *alcalde* brought his *capitán* and sixteen *soldados*, each with lance and musket. The *marineros*, except for Sharpentier, walked, and the *soldados* rode in full leather regalia, hard double-thick leather chest guards and leather *calzonevas*. Leather fenders attached to saddles from foreshoulder to hip point for the horses' protection, and each *soldado* carried a festooned eight-foot lance. Dust billowed behind as they trotted into the mission courtyard where they were met by Padre Javier.

"You have a man here, Padre," the *alcalde* said after dismounting with surprising grace for a man of his girth. "The Anglo, John Clinton Ryan."

Padre Javier nervously fumbled with the string of wooden beads that hung from his waist. "He has been here."

"But he is no longer?" the *alcalde* looked relieved.

"No, *Alcalde*, he has left."

Sharpentier, who had been listening, leaped from his horse. "We will search the place, just in case."

"No, Captain, you will take the word of the Padre," the *alcalde* said with finality.

"Which room was his?" Sharpentier pressed.

"It was there." The Padre pointed to a door across the courtyard. "And I don't mind if they look," he said quickly to the *alcalde*, not wanting a confrontation in the mission courtyard.

Sharpentier, with Skinner lumbering behind, strode across the yard and entered the room. Padre Javier and the *alcalde* followed but stayed outside as they searched. In a moment the captain stormed out.

"Nothing. Not a damned thing." He clamped his jaw, staring at the ground for a moment. Then he spotted something, bent, and picked up a tarnished chunk of metal. He turned it over in his hand as he walked to the Padre. "Did you have him locked up?"

"Why, no." Padre Javier reached for the small broken object.

The *alcalde* grabbed it out of the captain's hand. "It is the lock from the stocks. But how could it be here?"

The padre shrugged his shoulders, a carved wooden crucifix cradled in his hands.

"I want to search the rest of the mission and grounds," Sharpentier said.

"No." The *alcalde's* tone was adamant. "We have already violated the sanctity of this place enough. You and your men may search elsewhere if you wish."

Sharpentier gave the *alcalde* a long hard look, then turned and reluctantly mounted his horse. He reined it away, and his men followed on foot.

The *alcalde* turned to Padre Javier. "How *did* my lock get here, Fray Javier?"

Eighteen

The padre shrugged again, for he did not know from direct observance. He had heard from his neophytes about the Kanaka's arrival, had carefully avoided lying then, and would do so now. He did not have to reveal all he knew unless specifically asked.

"The Anglo, Ryan, was he a friend of the Kanaka?"

"He knew him, I think, but everyone knows everyone in Pueblo Santa Barbara."

"But everyone does not have the lock from my stock lying on the ground outside his door."

"It means nothing."

"Maybe not to you, Padre."

The *alcalde* sent his men on a search for the stocks, and within a few minutes they found the drag marks leading up through the vineyards. In the brush beyond, they found the stock itself.

The *alcalde* returned to the mission while four *soldados*, laboring and puffing, dragged the stock down the hill to where it could be loaded upon a *carreta* and returned to the presidio.

The *alcalde* again confronted Padre Javier. "When and if you see Señor Ryan again, I wish to speak with him. The warrant from the Anglos is one thing, but helping my prisoner escape is another altogether."

"As you wish, Don Francisco." Padre Javier nodded as the *alcalde* walked away.

The padre expelled an exasperated sigh. This Anglo, John Clinton Ryan, seemed to have a way of getting in trouble's path.

* * *

Padre Javier busied himself with the preparations for the coming fiesta and celebration of Corpus Christi. It was one of the most revered functions of the church during the year, and one of the most well attended. Both the faithful and not-so-faithful would come from miles around. The representation of the body of Christ paraded through the streets had special appeal to the Indians and the Californios, and seemed to rally them around the church. It was important, particularly at this time when the church's influence was low, to keep up the ceremony of the church and her traditions.

Yes, Javier decided, *it is important that this be the finest celebration of Christ ever in the pueblo.*

Entering the private sanctuary behind the main church, the padre opened a deep wide leather trunk and began to remove the vestments that he would wear in the parade and at the mass following. He smiled at the thought of the cannon fire saluting the body of Christ, the men and women all dressed in their finest, the banners that would fly, and the hundreds of *gente de razón* and neophytes who would march in solemn regard for the Savior.

Yes, it would be a wonderful day.

Alfonso stood inside the barn at Rancho del Robles Viejos. His nearby room was little more than a walled-in stall, but it was all he needed, and he was near his beloved stallions. In front of him, one end of a rein was attached to a nail. For a length of two feet it was braided; then, where the old vaquero worked, it frayed into a half-dozen loose strands of fine rawhide. The *trenzador*, braider—and Alfonso was one of the best—was concentrating and did not hear Inocente approach.

"I understand Ramón was here last night."

Alfonso jumped, startled at the voice. "Yes, he stopped on his way north."

"And he was not alone?"

The old man raised his head and centered his gaze on the hawklike eyes of the head vaquero of Rancho del Robles Viejos. "No, Inocente, he was not alone."

"I was to meet this Anglo at Teodoro's. He was foolish enough to insult—"

"There was no mention of a meeting . . . and that is better forgotten, amigo."

"Forgotten?" Inocente's voice hardened. "Only the day

before yesterday, he again stared at her as if she were on display in the pueblo *mercado*. Had he kept our appointment—were he not a coward—he would have gotten far worse last night than the first time he affronted a Padilla."

"These old eyes have judged many horses and many men, Inocente, and I don't believe this man to be a coward. I do know you are much too quick to judge. It is a failing of youth."

"Maybe your old eyes are too old, *viejo*. He did not show up at the appointed place. He is a coward."

Alfonso frowned. "A cougar is seldom where you think he will be, amigo. But that does not mean his claws are not sharp, his movement swift. I spoke with this Anglo, and he did not understand our ways. He meant no offense to Señorita Juana."

One of Estoban's stallions neighed and stomped in his stall. Inocente slapped his quirt on his thigh. "If he returns, tell him Inocente Ruiz waited for him. Tell him I still wait." The slapping quirt echoed a constant rhythm. "Have these horses been exercised today?"

"Of course, *segundo*. Has this old man ever forgotten?"

Inocente turned on his heel and strode from the barn.

Clint leaned forward in the saddle and followed Ramón up a steep, rocky path. The high mountains formed a dramatic backdrop to Ramón's erect figure in the saddle. The horses labored, and their hooves clattered a staccato beat as they set tnemselves, clambered up a few steps, and set again. The animals were well lathered by the time they crested the rocky escarpment and were again in the shadowed glade of the heavy forest.

Ramón, a few yards ahead, slipped from the saddle and put his finger to his lips before Clint could speak. The vaquero loosened his lead rope from the saddle and tied the horse to a scrub oak, then quietly moved forward to crouch behind a granite outcropping. With his eyes barely above the edge, he peered into the next canyon.

Clint tied off his sorrel mustang and followed, careful not to make the slightest noise. As he looked over the ridge, he was surprised to see a large group of Indians lounging near a trickle of water in the shade of some canyon sycamores.

Ramón carefully backed away from the outcropping, and Clint followed.

When they got back to the horses, Ramón moved near

and whispered, "Yokuts, from the interior valley. They are far from home, painted, and well armed. They must be a raiding party."

"What are they after?"

"They've come many times before. They seek horses, and whatever else they can steal. Years ago, they took some women also. It was months before we got them back. We killed a score or more, but it cost us the lives of five good vaqueros. We must warn the ranchos."

Clint mounted and followed Ramón, who retraced his path, quietly walking the animals until they reached the bottom of the rocky trail, then galloping.

They came to a narrow gorge where the trail dropped away steeply deep into a larger ravine. Ramón never hesitated, driving his horse forward. Clint pounded after, a few paces behind, then jerked the rein as Ramón's horse almost lost its footing.

The horse recovered and reared—and Clint realized why. Ramón lashed out with his *romal* and caught a surprised Yokuts brave with a stinging blow across the face.

The brave, temporarily blinded, jerked rein so hard that his horse backed into the one behind and both animals reared violently.

Ramón spun his horse. *"Vamos!"* he shouted.

At the sight of four Yokuts, all armed with musket, bow, and lance, Clint turned his animal and gave him the spurs.

They were well ahead of the scouting party, clattering up out of the ravine, by the time the Yokuts braves collected themselves and gave chase. When they reached the top of the narrow trail, Clint reined off to the side behind a jutting outcrop. He had his reata in hand and was shaking out a loop when Ramón raced by.

"Keep going!" Clint yelled. "I'll slow them down."

Unable to join him in the narrow space, Ramón spurred his horse up the trail. Clint sat his nervous mount, fingering the loop and listening to the sound of approaching hooves.

The Yokuts were bunched tightly as they passed Clint's hiding place. Clint's wide loop snaked out and caught both of the lead riders. He dallied the reata and rode into the trail behind the last brave, driving his animal back down the cleft behind the Indians.

The snap of the braided leather line almost jerked his

horse off its feet and cut deeply into Clint's thigh, but the game animal dug in, and both braves flew from the saddle directly into the path of the two who followed. Indians and horses collided, and the mustangs cried out and stumbled, throwing their riders onto the rocky trail in a cloud of dust.

Clint dragged the two painted riders through the tangled mass of screaming horses, men, and rocks until his sorrel mustang turned and backed stiff-legged, as if he had a bullock at the end of his reata.

On the trail above, Ramón saw the second pair of braves trying to regain their mounts and weapons. He spurred his horse viciously and galloped back down the trail, swinging his *romal* with deadly accuracy. As the braves tried to climb up the sides of the narrow canyon, he drove their horses in front of him until they were forced to trample the Indians Clint had caught in his loop.

"Leave the reata and ride!" Ramón shouted, scraping past Clint at a run.

Clint cast off his dally, spun his horse, and raced off down the trail. They rode for twenty minutes until they were high on the side of a ravine with a good view of their backtrail. Then they slowed the panting horses to a walk.

"You learn well, amigo," said Ramón.

"I was lucky."

"Did you see that one of those men carried a musket?"

"I didn't have much time to check out their tack or their weapons. Didn't get their names either. They didn't seem to want to visit much."

"It is the first time the Yokuts have been armed."

"And now they've got a damn fine reata." Clint felt more than a little disgruntled at the loss.

"I will get you another, amigo."

Ramón and Clint turned their tired mounts back toward Rancho del Robles Viejos and Pueblo Santa Barbara. But their ears remained tuned to their backtrail, and their eyes scanned the trail ahead for an ambush.

Quade Sharpentier sat in a dark corner of Teodoro's Cantina and downed the last of a mug of *aguardiente*. He banged the table for another. He had searched the pueblo and found no trace of John Clinton Ryan. The Californio attitude of *poco tiempo* and *mañana*—too little time, let's do it

tomorrow—set him on edge. He was beginning to believe that
shrugging one's shoulders was the national pastime of Alta
California.

The captain smoothed his gray-streaked beard and realized it needed a trim. He wished he were in Boston, but
Boston would only mean an inquiry. Only hanging Clint Ryan
would bring an end to the matter of the sinking of the
Savannah. Sharpentier understood men of commerce well
enough to know that if he sent correspondence ahead report-
ing that he had already punished the sogger responsible, that
he had assumed command of another company ship without a
captain, and more importantly that the ship was returning with
a highly profitable cargo, all would be forgotten.

Even though he had not yet found and silenced his
scapegoat, he had made giant strides since the loss of the
Savannah.

Thanks to Skinner's brute strength, Captain Armstrong
had taken a dive off the quarterdeck into Davy Jones's locker,
followed by his helmsman, which was fine with Sharpentier.
Sharpentier had another ship and a crew—albeit one that
questioned their captain's sudden death.

Sharpentier rose from his table and crossed the room to
where three of the crew of the *Charleston* sat. They quieted as
he approached.

"Well, men, are you about ready to get back to line and
canvas?" he asked, trying his best to appear friendly.

Goetz, a dusky-complected square-headed man whom
Sharpentier figured to be a German, did not return his smile.
"There be too many in the fo'c'sle, Cap'n," he grumbled. "Ye
should cull a few and leave them ashore to work the hide
fields."

"With full pay, o'course," Sharpentier said sarcastically,
waving the *camerera* over. "Bring these men a round," he
instructed her, then watched her full-fleshed rump straining
against the skirt.

"If they do a full day's work," the German said.

"Maybe you would like to be one who was left here to find
work amongst the greasers?" Sharpentier snapped.

The German looked away. "I signed with Cap'n Armstrong, Boston to California and back to Boston. I do my work,
and I'll complete the voyage."

"Then you'll not complain about conditions beyond any

man's control. Captain Armstrong met with an unfortunate accident, and as a captain of the line I have assumed his responsibilities. The next man I hear complaining like a yellow cur will find himself ashore and looking for a way back to New England."

Goetz kept his eyes fixed on the table, but his face noticeably reddened, and his knuckles, grasping his empty mug, whitened. The barmaid returned with fresh drinks. Sharpentier kept his hard eyes on the German, but the man did not look up or reply.

Sharpentier spun on his heel and returned to his own table without paying the girl. The German mumbled something that Sharpentier could not hear, dug into his pocket, and tossed some coins on the table.

Rumors of Captain Armstrong's murder and of the cloven-hoofed being aboard, as the sailors referred to any evildoers, had run rampant through the brig. If it had not been for the brace of Aston pistols that Sharpentier and Skinner had worn when a representative came to raise the crew's objections, Sharpentier might be hanging from the same yardarm he had planned for Ryan.

While Sharpentier stood with Astons drawn, Skinner had banged two men's heads together, pulled a dagger, and offered to make capons of gamecocks. Their crowing had abruptly ceased. The pistols and the threat were enough to quell any thoughts of mutiny.

Unfortunately for Quade Sharpentier, Armstrong had been a well-liked and respected man. And a crew with too much time on their hands had little better to do than grouse and complain and worry about what had happened. Yes, he had best get them back to the hard labor of sailing. A quick trip.

Usually, a ship did not call on the same port in any two-month period, so Sharpentier decided to catch them off guard. By the time he returned in less than a week, the crew would be resigned to his command, the fiesta of Corpus Christi would be well under way, the *aguardiente* would be flowing, and no one would know of their coming. He would make a short trip to Buenaventura, then return and, if the weather held, anchor off the point out of sight of the town, away from prying eyes.

If Ryan was in the area, he would be at the fiesta, as would all of Pueblo Santa Barbara and the surrounding ranchos.

Yes, he and the crew would slip back into town unnoticed, only this time every man would be armed with cutlass and musket.

Juana and Tía Angelina finished packing Juana's small valise. The family would stay at the home of friends in the pueblo and would be well rested when the celebration of Corpus Christi began in the morning. Then four days of fiesta and fandango, eating and dancing.

"I wish Papa would allow me to ride Florita to the fiesta, Tía."

"You are a lady, Juana. It would not be fitting. Besides, the only riders in the procession will be lancers."

"I hate to leave my little Florita here." Juana smiled at her aunt's skeptical glance. "She will miss me."

"You are such a soft heart. She will love having a few days' rest instead of you riding her all over the rancho every day. It will give Alfonso a chance to fatten her up."

In all the preparation, Juana quickly forgot about her little palomino mare. She held a lace dress in front of her and smiled at her reflection in the polished metal mirror. "I am so excited, Tía."

"Inocente will think you look beautiful."

"Inocente?" Juana stared at her image in the mirror, a blank expression on her face. She turned to her aunt. "Inocente thinks I am still a little girl."

"How can you have such perfect eyesight, and not see?"

Juana twirled, and the gown swirled around her. She waited a long moment before she spoke. "I admire Inocente in many ways . . . but he has always treated me like he treats Mama or you. I don't think he thinks of me . . . You know what I mean, Tía."

"He is only five years older than you, Juana."

Again she did not speak for a moment. "He will notice me in this gown." She laughed lightly and began to fit the gown over her head. From beneath its folds, her voice seemed to gain confidence. "I hope Inocente notices no other."

"And I, little niece, and I."

* * *

At the first sound of water in over five hours of hard brush-busting riding, Ramón and Clint dismounted and let the horses drink.

Before they could drink their fill, Ramón pulled their heads up. "It would not do to let them bloat themselves," the vaquero said.

"Will we ride straight through?" Clint asked.

"Yes. We must have time to warn the ranchos and the pueblo. After we alert Don Estoban and my father, you can ride to the Juarez and Alverado Rancho while I ride on into the pueblo. That way, there is no chance you will run into the crew of the *Charleston* or this Captain Sharpentier."

"If you need me to ride into town, I will. It's time I solved that problem."

"You have plenty to do, amigo. Then we will meet back at Rancho del Robles Viejos."

"How long before we reach the rancho?"

"By dawn, if our horses don't give out." Ramón swung into the saddle. The country had flattened out and the trail improved, so he spurred the horse into a gallop. He was twenty yards ahead by the time Clint followed.

Clint's horse pulled up lame with the lights of the rancho in sight. He dismounted, unsaddled and unbridled the sorrel mustang, and let him limp off into the pasture while Ramón rode on ahead.

Clint realized how bone-tired he was as he swung the saddle over his shoulder and centered dust-filled eyes on the oil lamps of the rancho. He stretched and worked the kinks out of his shoulders, ran his kerchief over his teeth and under his eyes, and trudged forward. Before he had walked a hundred yards, Muñoz, the Chumash Indian boy who worked with Alfonso, loped up, leading another mount behind his own. Clint saddled while Muñoz caught the lame horse, and they rode on in.

As he approached the rancho, Clint again thought of Inocente and wondered about the reception he would receive. At best, it would be cold. At worst, it could be deadly.

When he entered the main house, Inocente was nowhere to be seen. Ramón and Alfonso stood in a long wide main room in front of a small fire dwarfed by a huge fireplace.

"They are all in town," said Ramón, handing Clint a cup of coffee that smelled as if it had been on the stove all night. "The fiesta begins today."

"I cannot leave you here alone, Papa," Ramón said to his father.

"That is as it is. All of the young men and women are at the fiesta. And you cannot stay, nor can Señor Clint. As you have said, you must ride on to the pueblo. I have Muñoz, and old Rafael, and Luis."

"Two old men and a boy," Ramón spat.

"Careful with your tongue, *muchacho*."

As exhausted as he was, Clint could not help but smile. Alfonso was a tough old *vinagron*. Ramón flinched but said no more.

"We have muskets," the old man continued, "and there is no reason for those loco Indians to know the vaqueros are away, if even they come near here."

"Then we ride," said Ramón.

The stable boy Muñoz entered the front door. "I have saddled two of Señor Padilla's finest," he said.

Clint and Ramón drank down the last of the coffee and headed across the *corredor* to the horses. Clint mounted a seventeen-hand palomino and marveled at the size and strength of the animal. Never had he sat such a horse. It almost made him forget how weary he was. The golden horse pranced from side to side, and powerful muscles in its neck, withers, and shoulders knotted and relaxed.

"He is called Diablo del Sol," the old man said with pride, noting Clint's expression, "the Sun Devil. He is one of the patrón's favorites, so ride him with care."

"I will return him safely, Alfonso."

"*Bueno*." The old man patted Clint on the thigh, then turned to his son and did the same. Words were not necessary.

Nineteen

Riding to warn the other ranchos turned out to be no easy task. Even though both haciendas lay near the ocean, the trails were poorly marked, and shortly after Clint aroused the few members of the Juarez Rancho who were present, the fog crept over the long, gently sloping land that lay between the mountains and the sea. On his way to the Alverados' hacienda, he had to pick his way carefully, and many times he lost the trail and had to backtrack.

It was growing lighter by the time Clint reached an adobe wall and followed it to a gate. The Alverado Rancho too was watched by only a few old men and women, their faces creviced like peach pits. Clint arrived just as the morning meal was being served and sat gratefully to coffee and chocolate rolled in tortillas.

The old people sent him on his way with a muslin sack full of tortillas stuffed with beef and stewed chiles. Had he not been worried about the Yokuts, he would have fallen asleep in the saddle as the surefooted palomino kept up a steady trail-eating walk back to Rancho del Robles Viejos.

Padre Javier rose well before first light, as did the kitchen help and two of his most faithful altar boys. The priest went directly to the chapel, dressed in his simple *jerga* robes, and knelt to pray. It was to be a special day for him. The bishop was too ill with croup and high fever to participate, and if the truth were known, too old and weak. So Padre Javier would for the first time have the honor of bearing the monstrance containing the Blessed Sacrament representing the body of Christ out of the church through the streets of the pueblo—the Corpus

Christi procession. The finest vestments of the church would be displayed. The honor and the responsibility both elated and worried him.

He and his altar boys took a light breakfast of corn tortillas and fruit, then returned to the rectory to begin the ritual of dressing. He removed his simple *jerga* and stood wearing only a linen habit and sandals. Spread on his bed were an array of beautifully embroidered linens and silks, some with gold thread. With ritual silence and pomp, the boys helped him don the linen amice, folded around his shoulders and over his chest and tied in place around the waist with string. The alb, a sacklike tunic of white linen, came next. With long narrow sleeves and a hole for his head, it was secured around his waist by a band. It hung low and just cleared the ground. Four rectangular patches, richly embroidered, graced the front and back of the alb just over the hem and each sleeve. The bottom hem was edged with two inches of Portuguese lace.

The maniple was next. A narrow strip of silk a yard long and five inches in width, tapering to three at the ends, was draped over his left forearm. It had two ties to secure it to the arm to prevent accidental dropping. The maniple was finely embroidered with three crosses. Then the stole, a nine-foot linen strip, tapered from its six-inch ends to its four-inch middle, was draped across his neck, crossed over his breast, and fastened in place by the ends of the girdle. Like the maniple, it was embroidered with a cross, but this one rode at the back of his neck.

Last, both boys raised the chasuble, holding it high so the padre could step forward and allow it to be lowered over his head, a cloak of silk with a regal purple lining and a five-inch matching stripe, or pilar, down the chasuble's center front and back. The pilar was heavily laced with gold thread.

Though he was dressed properly for the mass he would conduct before the procession, an even more intricate garment lay across the foot of his bed. Before the procession began, he would remove the maniple and chasuble and don the cope. A semicircular cape ten feet across, five feet deep, and lined with red silk, it was adorned with even more gold on a band, an orphrey, eleven inches wide. When worn, it rose above the shoulder line, almost creating a hood.

The padre was ready for mass, and upon its completion he

would bear the representation of the body of Christ through the streets.

Taking the opportunity to rest while the scouts were out, Cha and the rest of his band enjoyed the shade of a grove of pepperwood laurel near a trickle of water. The chief of the Yokuts knelt holding a laurel branch over a small fire, the white meat of a rattler sizzling in its fork. As he removed it, his four scouts rode into camp, beaten and bruised.

He fingered some of the hot meat into his mouth, then handed the rest to another brave and walked over to the men who were helping the most injured brave from his mount.

"Leatherchests?" he asked, examining the man's dislocated shoulder.

"No, cattle riders," Mulul, another subchief and the leader of the scouts, answered.

"There must have been many."

"No." Mulul cut his eyes away from Cha's inquisitive gaze. "Only two, but they surprised us, and the leather-that-captures pulled these two from the saddle."

"Lie on the ground," Cha instructed the injured man. Placing a foot in the man's armpit, with both hands firmly on the man's wrist, Cha jerked the arm and got the shoulder back into place. The man slumped, out cold without saying a word or uttering a moan.

Cha turned his attention back to his subchief. "This time, Mulul, do not be surprised. Take five men and go in search of these cattle riders. Do not allow them to reach the camp of the leatherchests."

Mulul and his men left the wounded braves to mend by the trickle of water, and Cha and the rest of the band moved on at a lope. Cha intended to find horses and have them on the trail back to the Ton Tache before the sun found its resting place in the sea again.

Mulul and his men caught up with the main body of men before nightfall. "The cattle riders are too far ahead," was all the subchief had to offer. The look he received from Cha told him what his chief thought of this information.

Cha waved Sahma up to ride beside him. "Work your way back and tell all the subchiefs to be on the lookout for the leatherchests. I have decided that we will settle for only a hundred horses. We must strike and return to the Ton Tache before the cattle riders have a chance to bring the leather-chests down upon us."

They rode long into the night. By the time a glimmer of light came to the west and began to make the sister stars disappear, Cha and his band had reined up under wide-branched oaks whose limbs dripped with moss. They looked down to a distant flat at a group of Mexican buildings, and as father sun crept over the mountains to greet the day, Cha made out at least a hundred horses in the pasture between the buildings and the sea. The herd would have to be enough since they had lost the element of surprise. But finding them was not possessing them.

He divided his band into three groups, keeping only ten men, but four of these besides himself had the firesticks.

Sahma led one of the other groups, and Mulul led the third. As the other two groups made their way into ravines where they could pass unseen on either side of the buildings, Cha and his small band worked their way through an oak grove directly toward them.

Juana and her family spent the early morning dressing in their finest for the morning mass and the procession that would follow. They were staying at the home of Don Julio Camacho, and the Camachos would accompany them to the church. Isidora Camacho, Juana's dearest friend, and Juana would participate in the procession. Juana had arrived the day before in time to help in the building of the *enramadas*, a shrine of white muslin with the image of the family's favorite saint set above a red cloth covered with flowers and candles. It rested in the street, just in front of the beautiful ivy-covered Camacho hacienda. In front of all the haciendas up and down the street other shrines covered in linen or boughs glowed with lighted candles.

"Hurry, little Juana, or we will be late." Her tía, dressed in her finest black lace gown, entered the room where Isidora and Juana dressed. She picked Juana's turtle-shell comb and mantilla off the bed and adjusted its white lace, then walked over and placed it on her head.

"Be careful not to muss my hair," Juana scolded.

"You have a week of celebration to impress the vaqueros, Juana," Isidora teased.

After the Corpus Christi, the fiesta would begin. The

feasting would go on for a full week, each don hosting parties at his hacienda. Those vaqueros of low family standing, not invited to the haciendas, would celebrate with gambling and drinking in the *establos*, and a dozen cockfights would be under way in the barns and corrals at any one time. Thursday, the bullfight would take place. Friday, the great bull-and-bear fight would be held in the plaza. On Thursday, the bull, unlike the same event in Mexico or Spain, would be spared the sword. The fighter would work only to bring him to his knees in exhaustion. If the bull fought well, he would not be used in Friday's event where the fight was to the death.

Finally, on Saturday came the fandango, where the bands that had been wandering from event to event and house to house would gather as one great orchestra and the dancing would last all night. The week would climax with mass on the following Sunday morning where the challenge would be to stay awake. Afterward, each exhausted family would stagger home.

Juana did not think much of Dora's teasing about so serious a subject as impressing the young men of the pueblo. "You are spoken for, Dora," Juana said impatiently as she tucked a tendril of chestnut hair into its exact position. "I am not."

"And you will never be if you do not stand still and allow me to do this properly," her aunt chastised.

The sound of a knock echoed through the bedroom, and Don Estoban's voice rang through the door. "We will be late, *niñas*. Hurry."

With a final glance in the polished metal mirror over the dresser, the women hurried out of the room to join the rest of the household's ladies, already seated in Don Estoban's caleche. The men would follow on their stallions, which pranced proudly, seemingly aware of the fine glittering silver conchos on their black leather tack.

Satisfied they had enough time, Don Estoban and Don Julio Camacho led the families at a slow walk to church to begin Santa Barbara's finest and most holy week.

Juana, in the caleche's rear-facing seat, watched the vaqueros who followed. She had never stopped to realize how handsome Inocente was. He led the men. Tall and straight in the saddle, he rode with head held high. She smiled, but he merely nodded.

She was unable to catch his glance again.

* * *

Alfonso and Muñoz were in the barn, for the horses were Alfonso's responsibility and he would die before he saw them harmed. With musket in hand, he walked from stall to stall where only the best of the Padilla stock was kept and talked in low tones to the animals. When he reached Florita's stall, he slipped a chunk of sugar—an expensive treat—from his pocket and fed it to the gentle mare.

Two other old vaqueros, Luis and Rafael, were in the main hacienda with a few old women who were caring for the very young children, who had also been left behind.

Some distance away, Cha paused amid a stand of thick willows. A slow-moving stream cooled his horse's hooves while he peered through the branches and carefully studied the buildings beyond. It was too quiet. Vaqueros should be in the corral, and smoke should be billowing in preparation for the morning meal.

Yes, something was wrong.

He and his men were to be a diversion, attracting the vaqueros while Sahma and the bulk of the men drove away the horses from the pasture between the hacienda and the sea. he gave his men time to get in position, then, with some trepidation, whipped his horse up and out of the streambed. His small band galloped behind.

"They come!" Muñoz shouted from his vantage point at the far end of the barn.

Alfonso ran to the door nearest the hacienda. "They come from the north. Get the women and children down!" Then he ran to join Muñoz.

The band of Yokuts was still over a hundred yards away. Alfonso counted ten. Only ten. Surely they would not attack the hacienda with only ten warriors.

In his many years, Alfonso had observed some strange behavior from the Indian tribes, so he cautioned Muñoz not to fire. Maybe this band was just a group of young bucks showing their bravery by an intimidating gallop within musket range of the house. Maybe, just maybe, they would ride on. Alfonso glanced at the boy. Fear tortured his young eyes, but he tracked the approaching Indians with his musket.

The Yokuts swung their mounts, keeping a hundred-yard distance as they circled the hacienda and its outbuildings.

* * *

All of central California's wealthiest families were present in the church, dressed in their finest. Padre Javier nervously began the mass.

Flushed with excitement, Juana and Isidora held fans before their faces and glanced around, catching the eyes of several handsome young men. Poked by the fan of her *dueña*, she returned her attention to the padre and the mass, but her thoughts were of fiesta, fandango, and rodeo.

Don Estoban closed his eyes in solemn prayer. At least he hoped he looked to be in solemn prayer as he dozed. His chin dipped to his chest, and he grunted as his señora elbowed his ribs soundly.

Juana giggled and received another poke from her *dueña's* folded fan.

Yes, something is very strange here, Cha thought, hunkering low in the saddle. Vaqueros should have been pouring from the barn and kitchen, saddling and spurring their mounts to ride after the few men he used as bait. And firesticks should have been seen in every window of the hacienda.

He knew the value of the horse house. Only the best animals were kept there, the fastest and most beautiful.

Where were the vaqueros?

Muñoz ducked lower behind the *carreta* he knelt beside as the Indians again approached, the pounding of their horses' hooves a threat that rattled his backbone. The heathens were painted red and black, carrying shields and lances, and, to his horror, muskets. He had never heard of Yokuts being armed with muskets before. Sweat rolled down his neck, and his tongue rasped against his teeth, dry as cornhusks. Closer— they were coming closer. Were they going to come straight at him?

He tried to swallow, but the spittle would not come. *Por Dios,* he wished the other vaqueros were here.

"Don't fire," Alfonso cautioned from his position at the far end of the barn, "unless they turn toward us."

One of the Indians' horses stumbled and almost lost its rider. In recovering, not more than forty yards away, he turned to face Muñoz. The boy gasped at the terrible apparition and tightened his grip on the musket. It bucked in his hands. He had fired.

The ball went high, but the shot was a signal to Alfonso, Luis, and Rafael. Almost as an echo, their muskets roared, then all were reloading. One Yokuts horse stumbled and fell, a ball in his chest, and his rider rolled in the dust. But the brave came quickly to his feet and swung up behind another.

Cha reined away, carefully eyeing the buildings over his shoulder as he rode to the cover of the creekbed and clattered and splashed on through. He pulled up and counted his men. No one hit. The loss of a horse was all. Still, no riders followed. He had counted not more than four or five muzzle blasts from the buildings. Could the vaqueros all be gone? Could only a few be guarding the hacienda and the barn full of the finest horses?

He rode to the far side of the creek and up a little rise. In the distance he could see his men pushing the large herd of horses out of the pasture.

"Sahma," he called, waving the subchief over. "Tell Mulul to take the youngest of the men and drive the horses straight back to the Ton Tache. Do not wait for any of us. Bring the rest of the men, the most experienced fighters, back here."

Sahma nodded and gave heels to his mount.

Cha sent eight of his braves to the far side of the buildings, with instructions to take up positions there, then waited patiently, studying the hacienda and thinking.

Twenty

The mass complete, the parishioners hurried from the church, some to their homes lining the streets, some to preselected spots along the route, some to take up their positions in the procession.

There was a flurry of activity outside as Padre Javier returned to the rectory with his two select altar boys. For the first time, he stepped into the cope. *Vanity is a mortal sin*, he reminded himself, but still he swelled with pride.

They returned to the altar and with great care he cradled the monstrance in his hands, leaning the transparent box, or pyx, against his chest. Gilded in gold, the frame of the box glimmered, reflecting the church's many candles. Crystal and gold adorned the monstrance, but nothing was so important to the procession as its contents—the Blessed Sacrament representing the holy body of Christ.

Surprised by the weight of the robes and the monstrance, Padre Javier almost stumbled as he began his slow but steady walk down the aisle and out the doors of the church. Along the walkway leading to the road, hundreds of faithful stood watching, some carrying long poles topped by church banners and pennons of white, scarlet, or purple, with figures of Christ, the Virgin, saints, or sacred symbols.

He waited for the assembly of the procession to get in order.

Cha's blood ran hot. The hacienda seemed all but abandoned. He had never been inside a grand house of the Mexicans, but he had seen enough of the horses that were kept in the Mexicans' horse houses to know their value as the fastest and strongest. *Now I will see how the Mexican lives*, he decided, *and help myself to his horses, his finery, and his women*.

The rest of his band galloped up, and he quickly signed his plan. Twenty men to each side of the buildings, then a simple charge.

The heat of battle surging through them and boiling their blood, the braves rode to their positions on each of three sides of the buildings. The first group, who had been sent on ahead, still waited on the fourth side, their mounts nervously prancing.

The hacienda was surrounded.

They awaited Cha's signal.

The choir, accompanied by the faithful, rose in song with *"El Alabado."* An altar boy in a red cossack and white surplice, or frock, strode out, beginning the procession. He carried a large cross, and on either side of him and slightly behind, another altar boy carried a tall golden candlestick. He was followed by the aristocratic Californio women and girls, including Juana and Isidora, almost all dressed in lace. They walked two abreast, singing and carrying candles, their faces and heads covered by intricate lace mantillas, some staked with jeweled combs. Behind them Chumash women, the more simple *rebozos* covering their heads, fell into line, and behind them came men and boys of the *gente de razón*, some carrying church banners, hats in hands or hanging down their backs. The Chumash men, bareheaded and barefoot in simple *jerga*, also carried a number of beautiful banners and followed the men of the *gente de razón*. Then little girls, two by two, led twelve men bearing lighted candles in tall silver candlesticks, representing the twelve Apostles. Next came small girls of aristocratic parentage, including a six-year-old Camacho girl, Margarita. Like the other girls, she carried a Chumash basket filled with flower petals and scattered them as she walked. Finally, in all his splendor, the faithful stretched before him for a quarter mile, Padre Javier fell into line.

Four of the pueblo's most prominent citizens carried a canopy of fine white silk fringed in gold over the priest. On each side marched a dozen *soldados* in full leather armor and helmet, each with Bilboa sword drawn and laid on his shoulders—the guards of the Scared Host. In front of Padre

Javier, two neophytes swung silver censers before the monstrance, anointing the air with incense. Two more carried silver incense boats, and a finely robed deacon held each corner of the priest's trailing cape.

The procession made its way into the street, and as the Corpus Christi neared, the observers dropped to their knees and crossed themselves.

They passed the first shrine, and as he would at each, Padre Javier paused and blessed the shrine as the participants' voices rose with the hymn *"Tantum Ergo."*

The padre could not help it. His chest filled with pride.

In the large presidio office, Ramón argued with the *alcalde*. He had arrived in the pueblo during the mass and had been waiting until the man returned to the presidio so he could report the news of the Yokuts. It had taken him the better part of two hours to gain his audience with the *alcalde*, and he was angry. He had managed in the meantime to inform a number of the less pious vaqueros who had not attended mass, and some had already ridden for their homes. But most judged the danger to be small and the coming fiesta much more important. He had also traded mounts, taking one of the Camachos' fresh horses in place of his winded animal.

When he finally managed to speak to the *alcalde*, the procession was nearing, and he was given little attention.

"I told you, Don Francisco," Ramón said with restrained fury, "I saw them myself. There were over a hundred, and they were armed and painted for war. By now, they could be at any of the northern ranchos, which are all easy targets with the men away."

"I have sent my clerk to the barracks and alerted the kitchen help. A patrol will mount as soon as they've completed the procession and eaten."

"Eaten! *Madre de Dios*, man, there are a hundred or more Yokuts riding on the ranchos, and your men are to wait until the Corpus Christi is over, then eat?"

The *alcalde*'s eyes narrowed. "You have brought the news of this trouble, Ramón Diego. Now I will handle the matter as I see fit. These men may have many hours in the saddle ahead of them. They will serve much better if they are favored in the eyes of the Lord and are fed."

He turned his attention back to the procession as the lead

cross bearer reached the road in front of the presidio. "You would better serve," he said, looking back over his shoulder, "if you would continue to arouse the pueblo and alert each family as best you can."

Frustrated, Ramón marched from the office, mounted, and rode the two blocks to the Camacho hacienda. Inocente, who had returned directly from mass and had been among those warned by Ramón, was mounted, holding the reins to Estoban's big palomino and awaiting his *patrón* in front of the tall, vine-covered wall of the pueblo hacienda.

"Is he ready?" Ramón shouted, jerking his horse to a sliding halt.

"He is dressing."

Ramón paused and stared at the shrine so carefully constructed by Juana and Isidora. He crossed himself and closed his eyes for a second, then spun his mount. "I'm going on ahead."

"Ride like never before, Ramón," Inocente said. "We will be right behind you."

Without an answer, Ramón, who had been in the saddle for most of twenty-four hours, quirted the fresh mount he had borrowed and galloped away toward Rancho del Robles Viejos.

As he eyed the dozens of Yokuts riders, Alfonso's toothless mouth fell open. He scrambled across the barn to the boy and said in a reassuring voice, "Open the stalls. Let the horses run free. Then you hide, *muchacho*."

There was little hope for himself, but at least the boy might be saved. As Muñoz ran from stall to stall releasing the horses, Alfonso saddled his old gray stallion. He had ridden many other stallions over the years but none finer than Gatogris, the Gray Cat, as he had called the horse for the eighteen years he had ridden him. When young, the stallion had been as quick as a puma. The old vaquero swung his leg over the dappled rump and settled into the familiar saddle, his musket in one hand, his reata in the other. *I will not die standing in the mud,* he thought. *I will die like a vaquero, mounted, riding face-to-face with the devil. I will see if the savage can match a vaquero at his own game.*

To the ringing sound of eighty galloping horses, Alfonso spurred Gatogris out of the barn and spun toward the closest band of screaming savages. The old stallion, as proud as its rider, pranced and sidestepped while Alfonso studied the approaching horde. Like one of Cortez's own, the gray bowed his neck and snorted as he took the light touch of the spur. Alfonso bent low in the saddle, driving the game Andalusian toward the oncoming braves.

He could hear the muskets of Luis and Rafael bark behind him, a salute to what he knew would be his final moments in the saddle. They would not have time to reload before the Indians fell on them. Ahead of him, twenty braves—lances, axes, and muskets raised—shouted into the wind, their lathered ponies pounding forward.

Alfonso and the braves closed. He raised his musket in one hand and fired as he saw the puffs of smoke from their guns and felt the slap of wind as balls whistled by. A stab of pain, and he was flung to one side, out of the path of a whistling feathered lance. A glance at his bloodied sleeve told him a ball had torn through the fleshy part of his arm. He threw the musket, sailing end over end, at the approaching Yokuts, and one was slammed from the saddle.

With an echoing thud, the proud old stallion drove into the band of Indians. Dust billowed. Alfonso, two Indians, and horses tumbled to the ground. The old vaquero regained his seat, and Gatogris was on his feet before the other braves could collect themselves to bring axes and lances to bear.

In seconds, Alfonso had his spinning reata in hand, and his loop snaked out. He caught a short, stout brave around the neck. A turn around the pommel, and he spurred the stallion away, jerking the surprised Indian from the saddle. The Indian was dead weight, his eyes bulging, his neck broken, before he hit the ground.

Alfonso's stallion dug in his heels and charged, still dragging the Indian behind since the old vaquero, blood streaming down his arm, was unwilling to abandon his precious reata.

Four braves, their horses not fettered by a dragging load as Gatogris was, quickly closed on Alfonso. With whoops of victory, they buried their lanceheads in his back. He pitched forward in the saddle, clung for a moment, then fell and rolled on the rough ground, snapping the shafts and tearing apart his chest cavity. A brave with fire in his eyes and an ax in his grasp leapt from his carved wooden saddle and straddled the old man.

With fading eyes, Alfonso saw the enemy over him and with final defiance, spat foamy blood in the warrior's face. The warrior backhanded the blood away, screamed the death cry of his ancestors, and smashed the ax into the old man's skull. Blood turned the flowing mane of gray hair crimson.

The brave grunted in satisfaction and freed his bloodied ax. Even though the Mexican was an ancient one, killing this brave man who was an expert with the leather-that-captures would be a tale for the campfires.

Gatogris lay nearby, a lead ball buried deep in his muscular chest. Kicking, trying to regain his feet, he bubbled blood in a pink froth, marking his dappled coat, then stilled.

The braves regrouped to join the others who had gained entrance into the grand house.

With the procession complete and the monstrance re-turned to the altar, Padre Javier disrobed and stored the vestments, then dressed in his *jerga* garment with its simple wooden rosary. He knew he should be feeling elated. The Corpus Christi had gone perfectly. Almost two thousand had lined the roads of Pueblo Santa Barbara to pay homage. But he was strangely reticent about celebrating. A tingle of dread niggled the deepest part of his insides. Something was amiss, but he could not put his finger on it.

He knew he was expected at the presidio, where the first of many fiestas had already begun. He hurried out, his altar boys following close behind.

He guessed he was just letting down from the excitement of the day. Still, he could not shake the feeling.

Even with a fresh horse, it was two hours of hard riding before Ramón neared the rancho. He caught a movement out of the corner of his eye and reined up, then realized that Clint too galloped through the scurb oak toward the Padilla haci-enda. He spurred his horse, and the trails converged. Clint reined up ahead of him.

"Did you see the smoke?" Clint asked.

"Smoke?"

"As I crested the rise back there . . . a hell of a lot of smoke coming from the rancho."

Without another word, Ramón spurred the stallion, lead-ing the way.

They entered the clearing, and Ramón jerked rein, setting the stallion back on his haunches in a sliding halt.

Searing flames licked over the scorched adobe walls of the hacienda and barn; their red-tiled roofs had already collapsed. Only the *cocina* and the *matanza* remained unscathed. No one could be seen.

Ramón nudged his mount forward at a slow walk. "Alfonso," he called, his eyes searching. "Alfonso Diego."

But he received no answer. Reining up near a window of the hacienda, its leaded windows melted away, its shutters blackened with fire, Ramón looked inside and recognized the remains of Luis. His charred corpse sat in firing position, still clutching a blackened musket. The heat of the smoldering building drove Ramón back. He reined from the grisly scene and nudged his horse toward the barn, but it too stood in ruins.

Clint checked the other windows of the house, then followed. "Another man is at the side window," Clint said, "but he has a burnt peg leg . . . it's not Alfonso."

"It is Rafael," Ramón offered. Ramón studied the barn, then stood in his stirrups to look out over the pasture beyond.

"*Madre de Dios*," he swore, and urged his horse into a lope. Clint stayed close behind.

They passed the butchered carcass of an Indian pony, its forequarters intact but its hindquarters and loins hurriedly stripped away. Ramón slowed his horse to a walk and reined up.

Alfonso, two stone lanceheads protruding through his chest, his head smashed, lay near his old stallion.

Setting his jaw, Ramón dismounted and walked slowly to the stallion. With a flick of his knife, he cut the *látigo* and loosened the saddle. He removed and unfolded the blanket and walked over to cover his father. Kneeling beside him, he slowly crossed himself. His breathing seemed to catch several times, but he shed no tears.

Clint's mouth rasped dry, and his shoulders bunched in taut anger. He had not known the old man well, but he respected him and his son. He wished he could say something but sensed that nothing he could say would soothe Ramón's grief.

Ramón rose and stared up at Clint, his eyes flat and cold. "For this, a thousand Yokuts will die."

Ramón walked back to the fallen gray stallion, undallied his father's reata, and followed it to its end. A rueful smile played at the corners of his mouth as he shooed a raven away from the stout brave sprawled in the earth, his neck at an odd angle, his eyes plucked away by the scavenger. "*Salud*, Alfonso Diego," he said quietly.

He removed the loop, and coiled the reata as he returned to Clint. He handed the finely braided coil of leather to him. "I told you I would get you another. He wove the finest. No man was his equal as *trenzador*. He would want a good *lazodor* to have it."

Clint said nothing. He did not want to fight the burning knot in his throat.

Ramón remounted. "Let us see if we can find any living," Ramón said, and headed back toward the smoking shell of the hacienda. His ears rang, and his mouth was as dry as the ashes of yesterday's fire. His stomach knotted in revolt at what he had seen, and he tasted bile. He did not hear them coming, for his mind was years away, in the time his father had put him astride his first pony. Then the sound of hoofbeats jolted him from his thoughts. Estoban Padilla, Inocente, and twenty vaqueros rounded the burned-out remains.

Clint and Ramón loped over to the men staring in grim fascination at the carnage. As they joined them, the heavy door to the *matanza* creaked open, and Muñoz peeked out. He saw the vaqueros and fell to his knees in prayer. Behind him, the women and little children sank to their knees in joyous weeping.

"Has anyone been hurt?" Don Estoban asked as he dismounted.

Muñoz crossed himself a final time and rose. "Alfonso told me to hide, so I gathered the women and children in the *matanza* and barred the door. We could hear them on the roof, but they left before they tried very hard to enter." Muñoz glanced around, and when he saw the empty pasture and the house stripped of belongings, he knew why. They had what they had come for. His voice lowered and rang with dread. "Luis, Rafael, and Alfonso are not with us."

"They are dead," Ramón said coldly. "And I ride to avenge them. Who rides with me?"

The vaqueros' voices rose as one.

Twenty-one

Clint stepped forward, ready to mount and ride out with the vaqueros.

Inocente Ruiz locked eyes with him but spoke to Ramón. "My vaqueros and I will ride with you, Ramón, but we will not ride with this Anglo."

Clint remained silent, but his cold, chipped-ice eyes spoke for him. Again he felt it was Ramón's play.

"It is not your fight," Ramón said quietly, turning to him.

"I want to ride with you, Ramón."

"It is not your fight. It is ours." He reached over and placed a hand on Clint's shoulder. "And I need twenty more than I need one."

"Then I will hunt on my own," Clint said, breaking his hard gaze from Inocente's.

Don Estoban Padilla stepped forward. "For each man who returns one head of my brood stock"—his voiced rose, and he shook his fists—"a thousand *reales!*"

"I ride for blood," Ramón whispered.

"Then we ride!" Inocente yelled, spinning his horse and thundering away.

Ramón hesitated and touched the brim of his flat hat. "I am sorry, amigo, but this is the best way. *Por favor,* see that my father's body is taken to the mission."

"As you wish, amigo," Clint answered, but Ramón was already five long strides away, joining his *compadres*. Clint's chest burned with frustration as he watched the group of determined vaqueros gallop away.

Don Estoban looked beaten and weary. He glanced at the

remnants of his home, then at the barn. "Two lifetimes of work," he muttered.

A lone *carreta* rested near the corral, and an ox grazed in the pasture, unbothered by the carnage surrounding it.

His eyes distant and flat, Estoban glanced at Clint. "You may take the *carreta* and the boy. Have Muñoz return quickly. I will need him here. Inform the pueblo of what has happened, and tell the *alcalde* that my vaqueros have ridden in pursuit." Estoban motioned to the old women, who wept quietly. "Find something to wrap the bodies in. You will have much time to mourn after we see what we can salvage from this mess."

Clint remounted as soon as he had helped with the grisly job of wrapping the bodies in blankets and loading them in the *carreta*. Muñoz took the driver's seat of the cart and cracked a whip over the ox's wide horns, but the animal merely flicked his ears.

Just as he began another pass with the whip, the carriage—carrying Juana, Tía Angelina, and Juana's mother, Doña Isabel—entered the yard. Their Indian driver reined up, but the women remained sitting, stunned and silent, until Doña Isabel broke down in tears and buried her face in her hands. Juana jumped from the carriage and ran toward the barn. "Florita! She was not in the fire?"

"No, daughter," Estonban answered. "Not in the fire, but gone, as all the horses are. The Yokuts drove them out."

"But . . . but . . ." Juana could not bear the terrible thought; then she stared up at her father. "They will butcher my little palomino."

"You should not worry about a horse at a time like this," Estoban snapped, and Juana's attention turned to the *carreta* with its bundled load.

"Not ours? Not our people?" she whispered, and her eyes flooded with tears.

"Alfonso, Luis, and Rafael."

Juana swayed against the *carreta*, the tears in her eyes spilling down her cheeks. She dropped to her knees and prayed. Tía Angelina joined her.

"We do no good here," Clint muttered to Muñoz, and urged the stallion around. After several echoing cracks of the whip, Clint led the *carreta* away at a slow walk, its creaking wheels a sad accompaniment to the women's prayers.

By the time they reached the mission, it was the middle

of the afternoon. Clint had been frustrated by the slow pace of the *carreta*, but he had promised Ramón, and it was the least he could do.

He would give almost anything for one of the *Charleston*'s Aston pistols or Hawkens muskets and one of her fine sabers. He was mounted as well as any man, if only he were armed as well. *Wishing is fool's work*, he decided. While his stallion plodded behind the cart, Clint let his head fall to his chest. He slept in the saddle, the stallion clomping along slowly.

Sometime later, he was awakened by a cry from Muñoz. Knowing they were near the pueblo and wary of a meeting with Captain Sharpentier, Clint snapped instantly alert.

Padre Javier met them at the mission gates, sadly crossing himself as he saw the first of the carnage that he had feared would come. Finally he knew what had been bothering him. He did not believe in premonition, but more and more as he grew older, he accepted things he did not understand.

"Take them to the laundry room. It is where we prepare the bodies for burial."

Clint slid out of the saddle and extended his hand to the padre. "Should I be on the lookout for Sharpentier?" he asked.

"He left days ago. I don't think the *Charleston* will return for more than a month, probably two."

Clint loosened the horse's cinch and handed the braided reins to an Indian boy. Having been assured that the *Charleston* had sailed, he dropped to the grass and left the padre to his grim business. It was almost an hour before the padre returned and handed him a mug of coffee.

Clint rubbed his tired eyes and climbed to his feet. "Padre Javier, I must ride to avenge the death of my friend's father."

"Vengeance is the Lord's, my son," said the padre.

"I know, but if you'll find me a musket, I'll ride and give the Lord a hand."

Padre Javier paused uncertainly for a moment, then his look hardened. "Come with me."

The padre strode away, and Clint hurried to keep up. Padre Javier turned into a wide gated courtyard filled with flowering frangipani and rose bushes.

"Where are we?" Clint asked.

"The hacienda of Don Nicholas Den."

The priest pounded at a massive carved mahogany door.

An Indian answered and led them inside to fine hand-rubbed plank floors, the first Clint had seen in Alta California.

The man who entered the room to meet them was slender and wiry, light-haired, blue-eyed, and square-jawed, and unlike the Mexicans, wore full muttonchop sideburns.

The priest introduced them, and Clint was surprised to hear an Irish accent in the Spanish greeting.

"County Kilkenny?" Clint asked, as he shook hands.

"Why, yes, lad, and yourself?" The don smiled widely.

"The same, but I remember it little."

"Ryan, Ryan," Don Nicholas said, pondering. "I knew some Ryans, and fine folk they were. Aye, Ireland's a grand place, green as an emerald and twice as lovely." Don Nicholas walked to a sideboard and reached into one of the cubbyholes. "You wouldn't mind sharing a wee bit of the tears of St. Patrick with a fellow Irishman?"

Clint did not dissuade his host from pouring a dollop for each of the three of them.

"To old Ireland," Don Nicholas toasted, and the three men drank.

The smooth whiskey was elixir to Clint after the Mexican *aguardiente* he had been drinking. "It's been a long time . . . too long," he said.

"Now, Padre." Don Nicholas turned to his gray-robed guest. "What brings you here?"

"Our young Irish friend here wishes to ride in pursuit of the Yokuts raiders—"

"He would take up our fight?" The don let his gaze drift to Clint, who was content to let the padre do his talking.

"He has his own reasons."

The don shrewdly appraised Clint. "I've heard that you're a wanted man, Señor Ryan."

"I've heard that too, Don Nicholas. But they seek the wrong man. The first mate is a thick-headed ox of a Welshman, and the captain is the son—bastard son, I would suppose—of a bloody Englishman. I fear they find an Irish hide as good as any upon which to place the blame."

"Some things never change. 'Tis an answer suiting a son of Kilkenny." Don Nicholas brought the bottle out again.

"I need the loan of a musket," Clint said, and related the story of the raid on the Padillas' rancho.

Don Nicholas surveyed him up and down. "So the Celt

wants blood. I don't have a musket to spare, my friend, but I might have a Druid charm or two that will suit you as well." He motioned for the two men to bring their glasses and led them to the rear of the spacious house. Clint wondered what good an ancient Celtic charm would do against a band of heathens but followed.

The Irish don entered his private quarters and paused in front of a tall locked chest. He produced a ring of jangling keys from his pocket. Opening the chest, he reached among a rack of long guns and handed one to Clint, the likes of which Clint had never seen.

"By the saints, this is a piece." Clint rubbed the blued weapon's walnut stock in appreciation.

"And this is a piece to match." The don handed him a handgun. Both pieces had revolving cylinders, or breeches. "Eight shots for the pistol and ten for the ring-lever rifle. Both are thirty-six caliber. Small ball, but very accurate, built by Samuel Colt for the Texas Navy."

The don gathered powder flasks and shot from the cabinet. "And you, sir, will be a veritable one-man army with both pieces at your disposal. I was fortunate to buy them off an ex-officer of the republic of Texas, a man of dubious background, I would guess, who came to the shores of Santa Barbara a little short of cash. He owned three of each model. I understand there were one hundred eighty of the rifles manufactured for the Texas Navy and about the same number of hand guns for the Texas Rangers. He would only sell the two of each I own."

"And you would lend me these?" Clint asked.

"Only if you promise to teach those thieving heathens a lesson. Old Alfonso Diego was a good friend of mine. He taught me much about cattle and horses when I first landed on the shores of California. And his son, Ramón, speaks highly of you."

"I will return these as I found them."

"And return with your skin. I would hate to think of a Celt's hide decorating the hovel of some heathen, or of the savage with a Druid charm at his disposal."

With the rifle slipped securely into a saddle scabbard that rode under his leg and the pistol in a saddle holster on the right side of the horn, Clint felt prepared. He had his knife at his belt and his reata tied to the saddle.

Clint, Don Nicholas Den, and the padre took dinner at the Den hacienda—roast hen, poached fish, potatoes, and a variety of fruits and wines with each dish. It was the finest meal Clint could remember, and he was hard put to take his leave after it was finished. But leave he must, for the others would be far in front of him, and he had a stop to make on the way.

Don Nicholas had loaned him not only the firearms, but a second horse—a fine tall red roan almost the equal of the palomino. With two horses, he could move much faster. He also left with a bedroll, a goatgut of water, and several pounds of jerked meat.

He rode well into the night, slept for not more than two hours, and rode on. As dawn blushed the sky over the mountains to the west, he came upon the place he sought.

Hawk and his Chumash band were up and moving about when he rode into the camp. At first, Hawk did not recognize him, now that he was dressed in a decent *jerga* and the flat-crowned hat and fine leather boots of the vaquero, riding two of the finest horses in the country, but when he did, he welcomed Clint with open arms.

As did Matthew Mataca Konokapali.

"You sent me to a good place, amigo," Matt said, watching Clint dismount. "I have been treated well."

"How would you like to see some new country?" Clint asked the big Kanaka. "However, we may not receive much of a welcome."

Matt tilted his massive head. "As long as it is no closer to the stocks, or to the *alcalde*'s *juzgado*, I would like new country."

"And you can set yourself right with the *cholos* if things work out."

Hawk followed their conversation with interest but said nothing. Clint turned to him. "And you, mi amigo, do you have any love lost for the Yokuts?"

Hawk did not answer. His look said enough.

"Then ride with us," Clint said. "We don't know the country, though the track shouldn't be difficult to follow. They've stolen over a hundred horses, including some of the finest breeding stock in Alta California."

Truhud, the *paxa*, who had been standing in the shadows nearby, strode forward, speaking the guttural Chumash language in harsh tones to Hawk, who returned harsh words in kind. Then Hawk stomped away, and the *paxa* gave Clint a victorious look with his arms folded.

His eyes cold and hard, Clint glared at him, but the man did not flinch. Chahett stepped from a group of girls and smiled at Clint. The *paxa* strode toward her in anger.

"Hey!" Clint shouted, and Truhud turned and glowered. Clint had his knife in hand, running a thumb across its sharp edge, offering its warning as he glared at the shaman. "If you hurt her in any way, Truhud, you'll answer to the blade." Clint's voice was steady and cold, and it was obvious that the shaman understood.

Hawk rode up, leading another saddled horse for Matt and two spares. He motioned to Matt to mount up. Two of the animals carried water gourds and had *jerga* bedrolls tied to their carved saddles.

The *paxa* shot a last condemning look at Hawk, then spun on his heel and marched away.

Matt labored up into the saddle, and the stout pony expelled a breath. "I hate horses," Matt mumbled as he settled into the carved saddle.

"But not as much as you hate walking," Clint said with a smile, then glanced back and waved at Chahett. He spun the horse and headed out.

Once they were far from camp, Hawk rode up beside him. "These Yokuts— how were they dressed and in what manner was their hair?"

Clint explained in detail as much as he could remember.

"Ton Tache," Hawk said, confirming Clint's belief that the Chumash would be of great help. "I know a faster way. If they're pushing a big band of horses, they'll move to the Always Star, then toward the sun birthplace through the valley the Spanish call Cuyama. It is the easiest way to drive so many, and there is good water most of the way."

Clint figured the Always Star must be the North Star, the only one that remained fixed in the Northern Hemisphere, and the sun birthplace must be the east where the sun came up. He questioned not picking up the obvious trail of the horses, but he had sought this man's help, and he would take it. Hawk reined to the north, and Clint followed, Matt bouncing along behind, his lumbering bulk making the mustang he rode look like a tiny Welsh pony.

It's a good thing we have extra mounts, Clint thought, eyeing the rugged country ahead. Then he turned his attention to the trail, and Hawk dropped back beside him.

"When we reach the land of the Yokuts," Hawk cautioned, "the land of the elk, we must be on our guard. They will take you and the Kanaka for Mexicans, and they would love to have my skin. There was a time when I helped the mission padres round up Yokuts and bring them to the coast."

"Are there many of them?"

"As the stars in the sky," Hawk said.

"How long before we reach this land of the elk?"

"Before the sun takes its dip into the sea, but then it is still a great distance to the Tache village."

Clint rubbed the stock of the revolving breech rifle in his scabbard and made sure the pistol was secure in its saddle holster. As usual, he was riding into trouble.

A great country, this Alta California, he thought. *Never boring, at least.*

Twenty-two

Estoban's heart ached as he kicked his way through the charred remains of the hacienda.

"There is no sense trying to save that," Estoban instructed Juana, who was sorting through scorched china dishes. He attempted a smile but feared his sincerity was lacking. "We will find more dishes that your mother likes better."

"This china was my favorite," Juana said. But the tears she felt did not come. She, like the rest of the family, had no tears left. Without comment, she began to throw the china into a wheelbarrow.

Tía Angelina also helped with the cleanup, but Juana's mother, Doña Isabel, stayed in the caleche, her hands clasped across her breast, rocking back and forth.

It could have been worse, Estoban realized, had the *matanza* not been windowless to keep the flies and rodents at bay. He had climbed to the roof and found burned-out torches where the Indians had tried to set fire to the *brea* he had hauled from the seep near the ocean to seal the flat-planked roof. Luckily, the heavy tar had not ignited.

Yes, it could have been much worse.

He gazed over the ruins and resisted the impulse to throw up his hands and walk away.

"*La paciencia todo lo alcanza*," María, his faithful old house servant, said quietly to him as if she read his mind. His mouth curved in an attempt at a smile. Yes, patience does attain everything. It was patience, he knew, that had bred the finest palomino Andalusians in all the Americas. And it would be patience that rebuilt the hacienda and barn.

Estoban moved from room to room, working alongside his people. Even old Dora, who had been married to Luis for more years than Estoban could remember, worked and hid her grief, except for an occasional tear.

And Muñoz—Muñoz, who had had the foresight to herd the women and children into the *matanza* in the first place. He must remember to give Muñoz his pick of the remuda, if he got them back, and a fine silver-conchoed saddle and bridle.

These were only possessions, he reminded himself, looking at the charred ruins of a lifetime of work. He walked out front to the caleche to comfort his wife. *She is not so strong as Juana and Angelina*, he thought, hearing her sobs.

If only he and the vaqueros had been here when the Yokuts attacked.

At the head of the column of vaqueros, Inocente and Ramón drew rein and let the heaving horses catch their breath. Ahead, the wide valley they crossed narrowed to a cleft between great slabs of sandstone. The mountains beyond were mottled green and tan, sandpaper oaks and slabs of sandstone. It was a place known to them as Las Piedras Estrachas, the narrow rocks.

"It is a bad spot," Inocente said, pushing his hat back off his head. "A very bad spot."

"They know we follow," Ramón said. "But we have no choice. It would take hours to go around."

"Perhaps only half of us should go, until we know they do not lie in wait?"

"I will go alone, amigo," Ramón snapped.

"No, Ramón, we will all go." Inocente motioned to the men, and they spurred their horses forward.

They slowed as they left the cover of the oaks and the sandstone cliffs loomed above them, but Ramón clattered on ahead. Inocente and the others studied the narrow climbing trail for a second, then charged ahead.

Cha sat high on a cliff overlooking the narrow trail below and shook his head in satisfaction. He had sent the bulk of his men ahead to catch up with the twenty braves who had driven the horses out. He and nine others with firesticks waited, and it looked as if their patience would be rewarded.

One vaquero rode fifty yards ahead of the others. Cha

signed to his men not to fire and warn those still out of range, then was relieved when the vaquero waited for the others to catch up.

The men moved slowly into range. Training his sights on a fat vaquero, he squeezed the trigger. The musket bucked, and the man below flew out of the saddle. Almost as one, the other Yokuts fired, and the ravine was a jumble of screaming horses and men.

Vaqueros leapt from their saddles and clambered into the cover of rocks and buckbrush. Three were down by the time the first of the return fire came. Cha signed again, his men reloaded, and the next volley slammed into the horses.

The stallions snorted, whinnied, screamed, and ran riderless back down the trail. Two vaqueros broke from the cover of their hiding places and raced after them. A shot took one in the back, and his arms flew out as he slammed into the dust.

"It is good," Cha said, pouring powder and ramming a ball into place. "A good place for a trap." He rubbed the stock of the old musket. Yes, it was different this time.

Again the Yokuts fired and reloaded, but this time Cha brought his hand across his chest, making the sign for leaving, and they slipped away over the rocks to the mustangs. Silent as shadows fleeing a rising sun, they were gone.

Two vaqueros lay in the dust, the trail soaking up their blood. Another had crawled for a few yards into the rocks before the musket ball stilled him. One horse lay dead in the trail, its feet out stiff with the shock of violent death.

Ramón carefully scanned the rocks above, looking for a target. Nothing. They had ridden right into the trap. He had not been thinking straight. His blood ran too hot. Deciding his revenge would cost the lives of his amigos if he did not collect himself and hunt these Yokuts as he would the puma or grizzly, he settled back into the rocks to wait. He would be more careful next time.

He leaned against a rock, out of sight of the cliff, and collected his thoughts. It would take them hours to regather their horses, if they could find them at all, and the Yokuts raiders would be hours ahead before the Californios could follow.

But even if he had to go on alone, he would. A bead of sweat formed on his forehead and rolled down his cheek. He brushed a fly away. No more shots came. Raising his head, he scanned the rocks. *Stick your head up, Yokuts bastard. Give me a target.* Nothing.

Inocente looked over and regarded his friend, who rose above the rock, offering himself as a target to the Indians, studying the escarpment. "Careful, Ramón," he cautioned. "These Yokuts devils have learned to shoot. We are foolish to even try to follow." They were outnumbered, almost equally gunned, and already going into the country of the Yokuts, following the cat into his lair.

Clint, Hawk, and Matt paused, listening to another shot that echoed to them from a mile or more ahead.

"I know where they are," Hawk said. "The trail narrows into a deep climbing canyon at Las Piedras Estrachas. It is a good place to keep the wolf at bay while the herd moves forward."

"Should we ride to help?" Clint asked.

"Then we too would join those under the guns of the Yokuts. I know a way around. It is hard riding, but we could get in front of them. Then we would be the ones holding the high ground."

"Then let's ride," Clint said.

He heard Matt grumble, "Maybe the stocks weren't so bad," but the Kanaka followed his lament with a guffaw, and as always, a smile covered his face.

They moved off the trail and crashed into the buckbrush. It pulled and grasped at them, scratched and punished, but they pushed through.

The cover opened, and they found a narrow streambed and began to climb into the high mountains. After a mile of hard going, they stopped and changed horses. Clint looked at Matt's exhausted horse and decided to let the Kanaka ride the big roan while he took the smaller Indian mustang. They might have days of this ahead of them, and it would not do to lose a horse to a lame leg.

They reached the head of the creek, where it flattened out to its source in a high plateau, and the riding became easy through massive live oaks and digger pines. Then, after crossing through a low patch of waxy-leaved red-barked manzanita, they started back down. The game trail was narrow and steep down a sandstone face, and the horses slipped and slid, but Hawk charged on.

They had been ten hours in the saddle. It was late in the day by the time they moved through a heavy glade of buckeye trees. As serious as his mission was, Clint could not help but admire the long groupings of white blossoms hanging in profusion among the velvet leaves of the deep green trees.

The glade opened onto a mile-wide sand-bottomed valley between steep rock outcroppings. A large muddy stream meandered through it. No one spoke as the sun beat down. Saddle leather creaked, the horses blew and snorted, and a man slapped at a fly.

Again they changed horses, and when they had resaddled and allowed the horses to drink in the slow-moving stream, Hawk urged his horse into a canter. A roadrunner broke from the brush in front of them, a freshly caught lizard kicking in its long beak. It paced them for a few yards before it veered away. After a mile in the valley floor, the horses well lathered from laboring through the deep sand, Hawk found the tracks of the horse herd and turned back south. He worked his way up into a group of towering rocks, ramparts that overlooked a trail where over a hundred horses had passed—the way the rest of the Yokuts raiders would follow, Hawk assured them.

"Are you sure they have not passed already?" Clint asked.

"I am sure those who waited in ambush have not. See how the grass has sprung back up from the tracks of the animals? These came this way this morning."

They tied the horses deep in an offshoot arroyo where they would not be easily found, then made their way up into the rocks.

"Have you used a pistol?" Clint called to Matt.

"Never one with more than one shot."

"Just keep cocking and pulling the trigger." Clint gave it to him, along with its powder horn, caps, and balls.

Matt wandered down closer to the trail since he did not have the range of the long gun. Finding a place large enough to hide his big frame, he hunkered down into the shade of a rock ledge.

Hawk carried bow, fox-skin quiver of arrows, lance, and ax. He moved off silently.

Now we wait, Clint thought, and made himself as comfortable as he could.

* * *

Ramón and Inocente were angry at themselves. They had
ridden right into the Yokuts trap. Always before, Yokuts
parties had hit and run, but their muskets had changed all that.
Now three good men lay in the dust, and two more carried
lead balls, one in his leg and the other in a shoulder. Five of
twenty were out of the fight. And how many more if they could
not run down their stock? Odds were, most of the horses were
halfway back to Rancho del Robles Viejos, or what was left of
it.

"Should we try to work our way up into the rocks?" Ramón
asked, thinking aloud.

"I think we should wait until dark. We are at serious
disadvantage with them holding the high ground."

"But you will ride on with me?" Ramón asked.

"I told you I would, amigo. Unlike your friend, the Anglo,
I will never turn from a fight. I ride for you, and for Don
Estoban and Juana."

Rather than argue Clint's mettle, Ramón remained silent.
The more men he had with him, the more Yokuts blood he
could shed. He settled down against a rock with his back to the
Yokuts' position and rolled a smoke. Far across the shallow
canyon from where they waited, Ramón spotted three of their
horses grazing among a stand of digger pine saplings. He
carefully plotted the fastest route to them.

Shadows became one, and only the mountaintops remained bathed in setting sunlight when they heard one of the
other vaqueros call, "They have moved out."

"Follow me," Ramón said, taking off at a run for the place
the horses had stood.

Inocente ran along behind for half a mile until they
reached the saplings; then they slowed to a chest-heaving walk
and puffed along until they spotted the horses. Ramón's and
Inocente's well-trained animals were among the five they
found. They quickly mounted and headed back.

By the time they returned to the spot where they had
been pinned down, two of the other vaqueros waited with
their horses, but the rest had not been found. They left three
of the animals behind, instructing the two vaqueros to stay
behind and get the two wounded men to Don Nicholas Den,
who, with three years of medical school, doubled as the town
doctor.

With Inocente following, Ramón urged his horse up into the narrow trail leading into the rocks where the Yokuts braves had waited to rain down their deadly fire.

Worried that they might be lured into another trap, he carefully picked his trail for the first few hundred yards. But there was no sign of the heathen, just the clear trail of eight or ten horses over the earlier muddled trail of one hundred.

It was dark enough that the canyon was beginning to lose detail. Clint heard the muffled clattering of unshod horses' hooves before he saw the rapidly approaching Yokuts band. He counted. Three against ten. He hoped Matt could shoot straight, for they must make every shot count.

As soon as the band was within range, not more than a hundred and fifty paces away within the narrow confines of the steep ravine, Clint sighted on the leader and fired. The crack of the rifle echoed up the canyon, and the rider's horse went down.

He used the ring to advance the cylinder but did not fire. The leading Yokuts brave on the ground quickly swung up behind another, and they galloped forward. As Clint had hoped, they figured he was armed with a musket and would have to reload. They advanced another fifty paces, slipping and sliding down the narrow cleft, and hunkered low in the saddle. Matt rose up from behind a rock and began firing the pistol. The revolving breech spit fire in deadly rhythm, and Indians began to fall.

Hawk rose from behind a clump of buckbrush on the far side of the ravine and loosed an arrow. He dropped down, then stood and fired another almost as fast as Matt's revolver.

Another Indian fell.

The Yokuts riders searched for a target for their muskets, believing there must be a dozen vaqueros in wait, but they saw only Matt.

At thirty paces, they fired at the huge target of a man. With surprising agility, Matt scrambled up the rockface and dived to the cover of a clump of buckbrush.

Clint's second shot knocked a brave from the saddle, but the Indian riding behind spotted him and raised his big .50 caliber, its cavernous muzzle only twenty paces away. Then came the flash and billowing smoke of its blast.

Clint thought his head must surely be blown away. He

flung himself against the rock, banging his head as rock chips stung his face.

He tumbled from his perch and would have fallen thirty feet directly into the path of the oncoming riders, but he caught the ledge. Dragging himself back up, he recovered his Colt. He wiped blood from his cheek where the rock chips had splattered him, then worked the ring of the Colt again.

Across the ravine, Hawk's third arrow thunked into a Yokuts brave's painted belly. The Indian doubled, clutching the arrow with both hands, and dove from the saddle.

Still, five came on. Clint fired again. A paint horse went down as the rider took a slug in the chest and rolled off its back, jerking rein. The horse was quickly up and running. Blowing pink frothy lung blood, the Indian crawled a few feet, then stilled.

The Indians passed thirty feet beneath Clint's perch, so close he could hear their breathing, but he could not see them for the overhang. He ran to the far side of the rampart rock, sighted on the back of a thickset Yokuts brave who crouched almost neck-to-neck with the buckskin he rode, and squeezed off another shot before they were out of range.

The Colt bucked in Clint's hands, and he thought he had missed, but the Indian slowly slid from the carved saddle as the three remaining braves pounded on by. The warrior clung to the horse's reins with a death grip, then fell and was dragged for a few feet by the bucking horse until the reins were jerked free and the buckskin abandoned him, following the three Indians still mounted.

By the time Clint had worked the ring again, they had disappeared into the willows lining the streambed. The last of the gunshots echoed up and down the canyon. The silent stench of gunsmoke rose from the body-strewn cleft.

Clint, Matt, and Hawk had been as effective as a small army. Clint whooped and held the Colt high in victory, then moved back around the rocks until he could see the backtrail.

His joyous mood darkened when he viewed the scene below. Hawk strode up the bottom of the ravine, going from man to man, recovering his arrows, collecting a pair of muskets for himself, and finishing the wounded Yokuts with his blade.

Matt sat on a rock overlooking the grisly scene. For the first time since Clint had met him, he was not smiling. Clint climbed down the steep rockface and joined him. Hawk walked toward them, pausing once to run his knife into the sand.

"Six here," the tall Indian said.

"And one more out in the flat," said Clint.

"Seven. It is good. I will get the horses."

"No damage to either of you?" Clint asked.

Matt showed Clint the holes in his shirt just under his arm from a .50 caliber lead ball coming and going, and a missing boot heel. "They shot my boot."

Clint laughed.

The Kanaka eyed the rotating breech of his Colt. "If I had more holes in this thing for slugs, I would have got more Yokuts."

"Reload. They may be back. I have three shots left, my friend. You should not be so eager . . . but then again, you did well."

"I thought they would turn and run. But they came on. They are very brave men."

"Humph," Hawk grunted. "These are dead men. They can be brave again in the next life. It is better to be alive like the fox than brave and dead. I get the horses."

He jogged away with an arrow notched on his bow even though he carried two Yokuts muskets.

Twenty-three

Ramón and Inocente drew rein, listening to the rever-berating echo of several faraway shots.

"*Por Dios!*" Ramón said. "The *soldados* must have been waiting at the bottom of the ravine."

"It sounds as if the Yokuts devils have run into trouble," Inocente said. "Let's ride. Maybe we can trap them between us and whoever they fight with."

At a dead run, they headed down the canyon. It was a mile before they reined up their panting horses to study the three men who stood beside their mounts in the trail below—and the Yokuts bodies scattered along the ravine bottom. The vaqueros pushed their horses slowly forward, eyeing each twisted body they passed. Then they drew rein and dis-mounted.

"Clint!" Ramón stared in disbelief. "Did the rest ride on in pursuit of the Yokuts?"

"The rest? No, there are only the three of us. Where are the rest of your people?"

"The Yokuts ambushed us and scattered our stock. We lost five men. Two killed, three wounded."

They were silent for a moment.

"This is a lie!" Inocente's voice rang out. He glared at Clint, then at the Kanaka and the Chumash. He dismounted and waved his arm at the devastation. "There were many men who did this."

Clint stepped within striking distance of the equally tall vaquero. The heat of battle still coursed through his veins. "You know, you pile of donkey dung, I've had about all of you

166

I can stand. I'll be happy to stomp you into a greasespot right here if you can't keep your mouth shut."

Inocente stood speechless. He had figured this man for a coward. Anger flooded him, and he moved forward to answer the challenge.

But Ramón did not give him a chance. He stepped between the two. "We need every man, Inocente, and I would hate to see you skewered on the end of that ugly knife my Anglo friend carries before you have a chance to get your *patrón*'s stock back. Save your crowing for when we get back to the pueblo. Not now. Now we have more important business." His voice lowered. "My father and the others are not yet cold, and the Padilla stock will be dripping grease into Yokuts cooking fires in the Ton Tache if we do not hurry."

Inocente cut his hard gaze from man to man, then turned and shoved his foot into his *tapadero* and mounted. "There will be another time."

"That is my sincere hope," Clint snapped. With his hackles still up, Clint stormed to his horse. Inocente stared after him.

Mounting with a swing into the saddle, Clint reined around to face the whiplash-thin vaquero. They sat silent for a moment.

"There's only a hundred or so more Yokuts raiders," Matt said, breaking the tension. "Then we can go home."

"You're right, Matt," Clint said, nudging his horse down the trail, "but next time they will be ready. It won't be so easy."

Blood-red shafts of light escaped from dark clouds on the western horizon and painted the sand of the wide valley spread out before them, but they turned their backs to the setting sun and rode east. They rode hard until it was as dark and ominous as a snakehole, then fell exhausted in a cold camp by the river. A lonely wolf on a far ridge welcomed them with a lament while they unsaddled and hobbled their horses. Matt and Inocente took the first two watches since they had slept the night before.

Cha's jaw was set, his shoulders tense. Behind him, seven braves lay in the dirt—seven who would have to find their own way to the spirit world. And one of those with him would soon be unable to stay in the saddle.

Worse, they had lost many muskets.

The country was becoming drier as they moved farther and farther away from the influence of the sea. Soon the tree cover would be gone, and they would begin the descent into the Ton Tache. Before the light completely faded, Cha sought some rosemary along the riverbed, found it, and paused to pack the ragged hole in the thigh of his brave. Even then, he could not get the bleeding to stop.

Cha remounted and whipped his horse. He would catch up with the herd and the rest of his men during the next sun, then find a place.

A place of his choice.

A place to end this.

But first they must rest. As the last of the sunlight vanished and the sister stars lit the night, he led his men away from the streambed and a quarter mile up into the nearby wooded hills. They camped beneath windblown piñon pines. Cha stood the first watch while his men foraged for packrat nests and robbed them of the fat pinenuts of the piñon. Their hunger satisfied, the men fell into a well-deserved sleep.

Cha sat on a granite outcropping and scanned the dark valley below to the accompaniment of a chorus of coyotes and the sudden screech of the cat-who-had-lost-his-tail. A bobcat had been successful in his hunt, Cha decided, hearing the cry of a rabbit in the jaws of death.

Cha pondered. It would not do to lead these white men back to the village. He must resolve this problem long before then. But against the man with the firestick that sounded like the woodpecker he would need more men. Tomorrow he should catch up with the rest of his warriors and the herd.

He shuddered at the thought of the huge man who had stood near the edge of the trail, a man the size of the great bear who had fired as fast as the crow cawed. This was a new problem, a firestick that did not need to be fed. But no matter how big nor how many times the man could shoot, he could not defeat a hundred men with firesticks and a thousand arrows. That is what Cha must bring against them.

As the moon clawed to the top of the sky, Cha awoke one of the men to take the watch, then fell asleep to the groans of his wounded comrade who tossed feverishly and still wept blood from his wound.

When he awoke, the eastern sky was the color of the wild rose, and the man was quiet. The blood that soaked the earth

beneath his leg was the color of old iron. They found a slight
depression in the ground and hurriedly loosened the soil and
scooped it out until it was deep enough to accommodate the
warrior. Facing south, he was placed in a semisitting position
in the grave. They placed his weapons with him, his charm bag
on his chest, and covered him with little ceremony.

They rode on.

Clint, Matt, Ramón, and Inocente rode abreast in the
wide sandy valley flanked by rocky mountains spotted with
gray-green digger pines. They did not talk, just concentrated
on what lay behind each bush ahead as the horse's hooves beat
a steady dirge. The mottled hills of oaks, piñon pines, and
sandstone lay behind them. Now they rode between the
barren hills of the western border of the Ton Tache.

Hawk ranged far and wide, always studying the horizon,
unwilling to be caught bunched with the others. They trailed
two extra mounts and chewed jerky as they urged the horses
across the sand, passing an occasional clump of buckbrush or
willows near the river. They watched continually for ambush
but knew that if it came, it came. There was little they could
do, for they followed, and a follower could easily be circled
back upon or simply ambushed.

But no one suggested they turn back, for all knew that
Ramón would go on, even alone. And Inocente too seemed
driven. Even when Matt occasionally broke the silence with a
comment, Inocente remained silent, as did Ramón, who
seemed intent on only one thing—blood.

The river disappeared into the sand, reappeared a few
times, then, soon after they watered the horses and filled their
goatguts for what Ramón said would be the last time in at least
a day's ride, disappeared for good. But the horse tracks
continued. The valley widened and became a grass-covered
plain several miles across. They reined up and rested their
exhausted horses.

"At least the chance of ambush is less," Clint said,
surveying the barren landscape.

"It would seem so," Ramón quietly agreed, "but do not
underestimate these Yokuts men."

Clint shaded his eyes with a flat hand and studied the
country ahead. "There is little place to hide."

"For you, for me, but not for the Yokuts. This country is

much like the floor of the Ton Tache, except there it is occasionally swampy or marshy since it is a basin for the water from the high mountains beyond. This is country the Yokuts is used to, country like that in which he hunts every day. Do not relax your guard."

Sometime later, they reined up, again rested the stock and wet the animals' muzzles with kerchiefs. Clint changed to the roan, Matt to the palomino, and they moved on.

As the sun rose higher in the sky, it grew perceptibly warmer than the coast had been, and the heat of the country was confirmed by withered brush and dry grass. The hills flanking the wide valley stood brown and treeless, and even the salt grass lined only the ravines where the last water had flowed during the spring rains.

They slowed to a walk, mopped the sweat from their brows, and talked little.

The riverbed was now only a flood plain with deep-cut sides of sand and sandstone, and no brush spotted the wide flat valley floor. A single dying cottonwood, which had thriven in a better time, stood forlornly in the distance near the deep cut of the gravel-lined wash where a few of its primary roots had been exposed. Still the tracks of the horses and Indians stretched endlessly onward.

As they neared the twisting barren branches, Inocente suddenly jerked his horse to a standstill, and the others drew rein and followed his gaze. Only a quarter mile away, partially hidden in a deep cut where the low ravine-seamed hills swelled from the dry valley floor, twenty Indians sat their horses.

Clint and the others spun their animals, but before they could give them the spurs, a half mile behind them twenty more rode out of a ravine and spread out across the valley on both sides of the deep wash.

The roan pranced nervously, reflecting his rider's feeling, then they whirled back to the east and saw another twenty gallop out from behind a deep cut to take up a position in front of them.

"Only a hundred or so to kill," Matt whispered, palming the Colt.

Clint slipped the long gun from its scabbard. "You said you wanted to kill a thousand, Ramón. Looks like there's a hell of a start for you right—"

Before he could finish, the earth at their feet exploded upward in a cloud of dust. Indians who had buried themselves in the sand rose out of the dirt like clay men, ten or more, with axes and lances.

Clint and Matt fired at the same instant, and two went down. Ramón drove his horse into one and knocked him aside while another swung his ax at Matt. The big Kanaka caught the Indian's wrist and snapped it with an audible crack. The man fell and rolled away in pain.

Matt fired again, and another brave went down. Clint worked the ring and rotated his breech from the saddle of the rearing roan whose hooves kept two more Yokuts warriors and their lances at bay. Clint fired again and blew one Yokuts into the dust while another retreated from the fearsome weapon.

Hawk's ax flashed, and his mustang charged in and out of the fray. As he fought with one, another leaped on the back of his mount and both men tumbled off into the dirt. Hawk bled from a deep gash in his shoulder but beat the warrior to his knees, smashing the man's skull with the ax.

The Indians gave ground before the onslaught, and Hawk swung back into his saddle. Gravel flying behind, bent low, they spurred for the nearby riverbed. Without hesitation, the animals leapt down the six-foot cut to the sand bottom. The men gathered in a tight bunch in the riverbed, then saw the twenty Yokuts riders from the north, five of whom carried muskets, reach the dry stream on the far side.

Clint and Matt jerked rein on one side of their animals, forcing them to the ground, then dropped beside them, pinning their heads down and using the horses as cover in the flat gravel wash. They aimed carefully, picking their targets. Musketballs kicked sand in their faces and whined around them as the first of the group from the north pummeled into the riverbed not forty paces away. The Colt bucked, spitting flame, and a brave was blown from the saddle. Another grasped his side, wavering and reining his mustang out of the fray. Clint worked the ring. Another Yokuts fell to Matt's handgun.

Hawk knelt beside Clint, bow in hand. He loosed two for every shot of Clint's with deadly accuracy.

Cha signaled his band up and out of the ravine. The cattle riders' attention was fixed on those attacking from the west and north. They could be on them before the cattle riders knew they came, but the chattering fire of the men panicked his braves, and they reined away.

"Fools!" Cha shouted. "Dungeaters!" But they reined their horses around in confusion and rode for the cover of the bank.

Five of the Yokuts who had buried themselves charged into the riverbed. Ramón and Inocente, with no time to reload, remained astride their mounts and uncoiled their reatas. Their rawhide loops snaked out and caught two of the Yokuts men.

The vaqueros spurred away, then circled the three that followed, catching them in the web of reatas and using the screaming Yokuts they dragged for dead weight. Arrows cut the air around them, and Inocente laughed viciously as one of the Indians' arrows skewered another. Against the animals' instincts, the horses were driven into the braves, who fell beneath them. The vaqueros dismounted and with their knives finished the two they dragged, then recovered their reatas and rode back to where Clint and Matt knelt firing at the retreating Yokuts braves.

The twenty from the west reached the wash, less than a hundred yards away, and leapt their mounts into the gravel bed. Ramón and Inocente reloaded. Matt fired his last shot, then reloaded madly. The twenty Yokuts warriors approaching from the west converged with a dozen survivors from the northern group, pounding toward the five Californios. Clint and Matt took careful aim. One rider fell, then another. A horse somersaulted into the gravel, his rider slamming into the dry bed not to rise.

With none of his own arrows left, Hawk scrambled to gather those of the enemy protruding from the sand. As fast as he could notch and fire, he returned them to their owners.

Just as Ramón and Inocente finished reloading, Clint carefully sighted and blew one of the leaders of the western group out of the saddle. His horse stumbled and rolled, and Indians, horses, and gravel exploded in a roiling tangle. Those still mounted split to ride on each side.

Matt sidestepped an ax hurled by a screaming warrior but in doing so stepped into the path of another. The second man's ax glanced off Matt's thick neck. Sahma, trying to drive his braves forward into the killing fire, decided he must take on the giant of a man himself. He gave heels to his mount and bent low in the saddle.

Unfazed by the blow, the huge man spun to face him. Lance in hand, Sahma charged, But the huge man sidestepped the lance and wrapped his mighty arms around the animal's neck as it crashed into him. Sahma managed a glancing blow to the man's head with his stone lance, but still he clung to the mustang's neck, and the animal went down.

Blood poured over the big man's face from his split scalp, and the taste of victory flooded Sahma's soul. Then one of the man's massive hands clamped on his neck, and he felt the other hand slip his own stone knife from his waistband. The shaft of his lance broken by the fall, Sahma grappled for the stone knife, but the huge man seemed to envelop him. He saw the massive fist coming but could not block the blow.

He was unconscious when his own knife split his breastbone.

Clint spun and felled another brave with his Colt.

Inocente fought a warrior chest-to-chest, each man's knifehand locked in the other's grip.

Clint sighted on the Indian's back, but feared he might hit Inocente with the shot and instead palmed his knife. The gleaming blade flashed across the ten paces and buried itself to the hilt in the small of the Indian's back.

The man sagged in Inocente's grip. Inocente reached down and plucked the knife out of the warrior's back, wiping it on his *calzonevas*. He hurried to Clint's side, flipped it, caught it by the blade, and offered it back to Clint.

"*Gracias*," he managed, then recovered his musket and began to reload.

The remaining braves regrouped a hundred yards beyond in the riverbed. Cha madly tried to get his men to ride into the fight, but with the constant roar of weapons they had bolted, and only his most trusted two remained at his side. They rode within range, leapt from their horses, and dropped to the ground, sighting carefully. The muskets barked, and their shots were returned in kind.

A musketball from Cha's musket creased Clint's shoulder. Another careened off the saddle of the roan he crouched behind and smashed into his cheekbone, bloodying it and knocking him backward, a hammerblow but not a penetrating one. He backhanded the blood away and fought on.

Cha ordered his remaining men to their horses.

"They hesitate," said Ramón, stumbling up beside Matt and Clint.

"Then let's encourage them to keep going," Clint said, and dropped to the ground. From the prone position, he quickly fired the last two shots from his rifle. One Indian flew from the saddle, and another horse went down, its rider scrambling to double with another.

With whoops that echoed down the riverbed, the Yokuts decided they had had enough. They spun their horses and galloped away.

The stench of black powder lingered over the dry wash, and it was quiet but for the moaning of two wounded Indians.

Matt limped to Clint and Hawk, lying behind the roan. "Clint, I could use a hand," he said.

Clint saw that an arrowhead protruded from the fleshy part of the Kanaka's bicep. He rose and looked to Ramón to help but saw him tending a musketball wound in Inocente's thigh.

Hawk walked along the wash, plucking grass to pack his own shoulder wound.

"Sit, amigo," Clint said to Matt. He grabbed his goatgut from the saddle of the roan, which had struggled to its feet.

Two arrows protruded from the horse's side, two more from his broad chest. The roan sank to its knees, then rolled to its side, driving the arrows even deeper. Clint cursed the loss of the animal as he saw blood bubbling from his muzzle.

He took Matt the water, then walked to the side of the roan that had carried him so well. He stroked the red's neck, clamped his jaw tightly, and fired, making sure the animal was out of its misery.

Moving back, Clint knelt beside the Kanaka. Matt grimaced as Clint snapped the head off the arrow protruding from the back of his arm. He handed the big man his knife with its leather-covered hilt.

"Bite on this, amigo."

Matt clamped down on the leather, and Clint jerked the shaft back through the wound. Matt slowly rolled to his back, the knife falling to his chest, the whites of his eyes showing like mother of pearl.

Clint grabbed the goatgut and poured a little water on him. Matt sputtered and sat back up.

"Sorry, amigo," said Clint, "but no time for rest now."

Matt looked sheepish but gathered his strength and lumbered to his feet. "Hate blood almost as much as I hate horses," the Kanaka mumbled.

Clint reached over and pulled Ramón's silk bandanna from his head. He wiped the blood away from Matt's face and his own cheek, then used the scarf to bind Matt's arm.

Matt's tired but warm smile returned. "Our blood mixes. We are brothers now."

"Suits me," Clint said. "Hope we stay that way for a long time." But he wondered how long it might be. His own furrowed shoulder pained him. More a burn than a cut, it slowly wept blood. Shielding his eyes with a blood-covered hand, he studied the horizon.

Wounds or no wounds, they would press on. They still did not have the horses.

Twenty-four

Even Estoban's wife, Doña Isabel, did not know where he hid the family gold. He had waited until tonight to check on it since he did not want to be caught by the Yokuts raiders should they return, and he did not want to be found out by any of the family or servants.

The last guitar had quieted and the last campfire burned to coals. It was time.

Muñoz had performed a far greater service than he had known when he had locked the women and children in the *matanza* and kept the savages at bay. Only trusted Alfonso had known the location of the gold, and only through necessity, should anything happen to Estoban before he had a chance to pass on the secret. Now he would have to choose another confidant.

He had great hope for Inocente. The young vaquero had matured in the last few years, and Estoban held a secret hope that he would become a part of the family should Juana ever mature enough to judge the true value of a man. Inocente had his faults. He was not particularly handsome, and he was impetuous, as hot-loined young men can be. But he was all man and all vaquero, and he watched after the Padilla interests like a man possessed. These were qualities that Estoban valued highly, and though Inocente was a mestizo, they were qualities he would like to see mixed with pure Castilian Padilla blood.

In the darkness, Estoban smoked a cigar and walked from campsite to campsite to check on his people. Many families from other ranchos had come to help, and all seemed to be asleep. Only Muñoz, the boy who was rapidly becoming a man in Estoban's eyes, was awake, and he proudly stood guard.

Estoban stepped into the *matanza* with a bucket, removed the plank covering of the three-foot-wide, two-foot-deep adobe bloodsump below the meathook where the fresh carcasses were hung, and began digging out the dried blood and offal, placing it carefully in the bucket. Each time he filled the bucket, he carried the mess to the pigpen and dumped the bucket in their feed troughs.

It was a dirty, stinking endeavor, but he was already filthy from the salvage work. He was opposed to feeding offal to his sows, but he was more opposed to wasting anything.

It took eight trips before he reached the bottom of the well. Again he walked outside and carefully checked around. The camps were quiet. After removing the planks that lined the bottom, he dug away a foot of blood-soaked earth until he heard the clunk of the iron box.

He grunted and heaved it out, pulled it open, and removed one of the leather pouches to check its glittering contents. He smiled in satisfaction. He replaced the box, then the earth and the boards. It would take a man with a hearty constitution to dig through this mess in hope of finding a man's treasure. He chuckled to himself as he worked and thought of what kind of loco man would hide something valuable under this filth and stench. Other men would choose a place under their beds or in their clean water wells. No, this place was a stroke of genius.

Stepping outside, Estoban pulled the door shut. A nightbird called, and far away a coyote yipped. "It is not so bad," Estoban said quietly in response to the coyote's lament. He leaned against the *matanza* and lit a cigarillo.

The hacienda would be rebuilt, the *establo* would be rebuilt. Only his loyal and trusted vaqueros could not be replaced. He mourned them, for they were men of his time, men he had looked up to as a boy. And of course he mourned the loss of the blood stock. The proudest Andalusian palominos in Alta California. With years of clever trading, his father before him had assembled the best, and Estoban had spent his life continuing and improving the line.

Please, Lord, Estoban prayed silently, *let Inocente return unharmed and with the brood stock. Return our sixty years of*

*patient work—my father's work, my work, and your work,
Lord.*

Clint sat on a small rise, looking out over their backtrail.
They had backtracked to the last of the Cuyama River water-
holes before they rested. They agreed that the Yokuts would
think they had returned to Santa Barbara, that they needed to
rest and assess their damages before pressing on to recover the
stolen horses.

Satisfied that they were not being pursued, Clint rode
down to the side of the pool to join the men. Inocente's leg was
stiff, but the ball had passed through cleanly, and Matt's arm
had only limited use, but it was his left and he shot right-
handed. Matt's scalp had been laid open with a three-inch
gash, and his neck was bruised and swollen, but he seemed
hardly to notice. Hawk was unscathed, with the exception of a
scrape across his face from a Yokuts ax and a knife wound in his
arm that seemed to bother him little. Clint had a burn on his
shoulder from a musketball, but it had done little more than
weep blood. His cheek was slashed and bruised, and he had a
healthy knot on the back of his head from banging against the
rock wall.

"What do you think, Ramón?"

Clint walked over and sat on a rock near Ramón, his head
propped up on his saddle. Ramón glanced up with a question-
ing look. "That wound of Inocente's is the worst," Clint
cautioned. "Maybe he should return to Santa Barbara."

"That is up to Inocente. I go on with the darkness."

"Tonight?"

"As soon as it is dark."

"Then I go on too."

"*Bueno,*" Ramón said. He rolled a cigarette and offered it
to Clint, who declined, then handed it to Hawk, who accepted
with a nod. Ramón rolled another.

"And you, Hawk?" Ramón asked.

"I will ride with you and Clint. I have not yet had my fill
of killing Yokuts."

As they talked, Clint walked to where Inocente lay, his
hat over his eyes. "The leg getting stiff?"

The vaquero slipped his hat to the side and squinted up at
Clint but did not answer.

"Your leg is bad," Clint continued. "I've seen wounds like that go green and more than one die from the like."

"You came to cheer me up, Anglo?"

"No, I came to suggest that you return to Santa Barbara where Don Nicholas can treat that properly."

"While you go on?"

"While the rest of us go on. Since Matt's hurt fairly bad also, he can ride along with you if you wish."

"Since when did you become the *capitán* of this expedition?"

"I only—"

"You are rude and insulting, as usual. You take care of yourself, gringo, until I have the opportunity to deal with you."

"By God, man." Clint stormed away. "If pompous were an acorn, you'd be an oak."

He sat down near Hawk and Ramón, who looked up at his Anglo amigo and smiled. "He will learn one day that a sharp tongue cuts your own throat."

Hawk glanced over at the wounded vaquero. "He is half Chumash, from the tribe in the high mountains where the condor lives. He wishes to be Castilian, like his keepers."

Clint just shook his head.

"Whatever he is, too bad he wouldn't go," Matt said with a grin. "That would leave more Yokuts for the rest of us."

Even Hawk smiled at that.

Cha rode to a hill where he could see his backtrail for a great distance, then watched carefully as the fading light lit the sky with the last colors of day. Below him, the herd worked its way among the tules to the shores of the lake the Spanish called Buena Vista. It had been a hard ride from the Cuyama Valley, and a sad one. Yes, he had a hundred horses, but he had traded one man for each five. And in the camp below, another half dozen nursed wounds that might take them to the spirit land.

It had been a costly trip.

He only hoped the price had been paid in full.

The vaqueros with firesticks that spoke like the woodpecker had ridden back toward the sea. Maybe they had had enough.

Maybe, but still he would keep a careful watch.

* * *

As shadows deepened and the first bright star glimmered in the east, Clint and the men rode east with the last remnants of a burned orange sky at their back. The moon was waxing, so each night had been brighter. That and the fact that the country had little cover made traveling relatively easy.

Clint grudgingly admired Inocente. The man managed to mount with his stiff leg, and all through the long night of steady riding, never complained. Maybe he had been wrong about Inocente Ruiz. He was a tough, hard man who gave no quarter, a man who would stand and face his enemy. He had proven himself competent and a good man to have at your side. Sometimes it was better to be teamed with a skilled enemy than a clumsy friend.

Beside him, Hawk rode silently. He knew the first good water adequate for the number of horses the Yokuts were driving was the lake called Buena Vista. And he was proved right.

The steady nine hours of riding paid off. As night began to creep into morning, they sat overlooking the fires of the Yokuts camp on the lakeside flat a mile below.

Clint admired the big lake beyond, rimmed with tules, willows, and cottonwoods. The first hint of light shimmered crimson on its dark surface, and he marveled at the valley that stretched out before him with its silhouetted guardian mountains beyond. The valley looked to be a two-day ride across, and to the north it went on and on.

Mist drifted from the valley floor and over the surface of the lake, obliterating some of the view. Clint rode up beside Ramón. "There are the horses—and the Yokuts. How do we separate the two?"

"They are confident we have given up the chase," Ramón said, "or that we'd not attack so many, or they would have no fires. It is good."

Hawk agreed. He studied the scene, then pointed to the far end of the five-mile-long lake. "They will stay close to the water until they pass that place where the hills meet the shore. Then they will swing to the north where the valley opens up."

Ramón studied the lay of the trail. "That narrow spot is our best chance, maybe our only chance. They will ride behind the herd, and the herd is our best weapon against their numbers."

"A stampede?" Clint asked.

A wry smile curved the corner of Ramón's mouth. "Rather than the Yokuts eating our horses, we will see if our horses can eat the Yokuts." He uncoiled his leg from the pommel and found the stirrup in its leather *tapadero*. "Are you ready to ride, amigos?"

Each man settled into his saddle, resigned to the coming confrontation, and no words were necessary. As they rode away, Clint appraised his battered but far from beaten comrades. Inocente seemed clumsy in the saddle, which was far from normal; Matt, favoring his arm, was even clumsier than usual. Hawk rode with determination but obvious weariness, while Clint's head pounded with each hoofbeat. With his swollen and bloodied face, he looked more seriously injured than he was.

But Ramón gave no quarter. He seemed dead set on making this personal war end here. Quirting his horse, he leapt washes and crashed through sagebrush. Driving animals and men, he cut no slack for the harsh country. It took an hour of hard riding through the hills before they sat astride lathered horses on a ridge looking down at the spot where the hills dropped in sharply to a narrow flat at lakeside.

They worked their way down a narrow game trail, watered the horses, then backtracked to a ravine and took positions ten feet apart in the gravel bottom. Unseen by the approaching Yokuts, they blocked the sixty-foot narrows the herd must pass through.

Each man checked his weapons and his tack, smoked, or sat quietly beside his horse. The sun hung in the midmorning sky before they heard the neighing and hoofbeats of the approaching herd. Still they waited while the sun baked them and flies pestered men and animals.

"Ready." Ramón looked up and down the line as the men mounted. He shoved his flat-crowned hat off his head to his back, then gave the spurs to his mount and was up and over the edge.

The herd was only fifty feet from the ravine when the charging riders, waving jackets and shouting, stopped them in their tracks. A paint mustang leading the herd reared and turned, panicking the others who piled up against the spooked leaders. Clint and Matt fired their revolving breech weapons, and the two reverberating shots in the narrows were enough.

A hundred animals turned on the Indians and stampeded into them.

Half of Cha's band fled into the lake, plunging through tules as horses sank to their knees in the deep mud, lunging and falling. The other half headed for the steep hillside. Fighting to scale the shale slope, an Indian pony reared and dumped its rider to the ground. Screaming, he tried to fend off the surging wall of animals, but sharp slashing hooves hacked him senseless.

Matt and Clint kept up a steady barrage of rifle and pistol fire, scattering the Indians, driving the horses. The leader and five other Yokuts spun, gave heel to their horses, and rode to stay in front of the herd.

As they pushed the herd and drew even with the Yokuts who had split from the main group, Clint and Matt fired two shots each, and two more Yokuts rolled from their horses to enter the spirit world.

It was all Cha and his half-dozen riders could do to stay ahead of the stampede, but they managed until the narrows widened and they were able to gallop away to the side and let the animals pass. Cha and two other braves who also carried muskets dropped to the ground on a knoll to wait. As the horses surged past, the Indians took aim at the cattle riders who pushed them and fired.

Spotting the threat, Ramón, Clint, and Hawk dropped low and to the sides of their horses away from the waiting Yokuts. Matt, with his huge bulk, was unable to do much to lessen himself as a target. Inocente could do little more than crouch—bending low with the stiff leg was nearly impossible.

Matt, hindered by his wounded arm and wanting to save the remaining shots in his pistol, still managed to lift his musket and fire, but his shot only kicked sand in front of the waiting Yokuts. A musketball furrowed Matt's broad back, careening off his shoulder blade, almost knocking the big man out of the saddle, but he held fast, recovered, and galloped on in pursuit of the herd.

Inocente fired his long gun one-handed, and a Yokuts musketeer who was fighting madly to reload flew backward, his weapon slung upward. A tall Indian sighted carefully and squeezed the trigger. The weapon bucked in his hands, spit flame, and Inocente flew from the saddle. Unseen by the others, Inocente hit the ground rolling. The ball had smashed through his shoulder.

The herd, and his amigos, pounded on.

By God, we've made it past the first test—we have the horses, Clint thought, slowing to a steady lope. *Now can we keep them?*

He looked over his shoulder and saw Matt, his back bloodied, but all his concentration on the moving herd in front of him. Hawk and Ramón rode side by side, low in the saddle, the wind blowing the Chumash's hair and the vaquero's braided queue straight out behind them.

And Inocente? Where the hell was Inocente?

Clint reined his horse around in a slow circle to search for his sometime enemy, sometime comrade, and saw him two hundred yards behind. He was struggling unsteadily to his feet.

Two Yokuts stood on a knoll only sixty paces away, but apparently they had not seen the fallen vaquero behind them. Their attention remained focused on the disappearing herd.

Maybe I can get to the son of a bitch first, Clint thought. Putting his spurs to the big palomino, he brought his *romal* across the animal's powerful rump. He was within a hundred yards when one of the Yokuts turned to see what it was that brought the loco rider back into harm's way and spotted the dazed vaquero.

Both warriors ran for their mounts. They swung into their wooden saddles and spurred toward the wavering bleeding vaquero who stood facing them in defiance, knife in hand.

Clint snapped off a shot at the Yokuts braves, but the hammer clunked with a thud on an empty cylinder. In one fluid motion, he sheathed the Colt, came up with his reata, and shook out a loop.

One-handed, the brave leveled his musket at Clint, and the big-bored weapon bucked and spit fire. Clint jerked back in the saddle, the ball careening off his leather belt. He reeled with the blow of the lead ball with the sickening dread that he had been gut-shot. Feeling no pain, he fought for and found a stirrup he had lost and glanced down to see a crease in his belt—no blood—and again had his loop circling.

At fifty feet the other Indian leveled his musket on Inocente. Clint cursed silently at the distance, still too far for his reata. But the Indian hesitated, waiting for his horse to bring him closer. Clint's loop whistled out, opened wide in front of the two galloping Indian ponies, and caught both animals' front legs. Clint dallied and veered away.

Both animals went down, their legs jerked from under them. The Indian's musket fired into the air. The Yokuts braves plowed facefirst into the dirt not ten feet in front of Inocente who stumbled forward and drove his blade into the back of one of them.

Clint spun his horse and headed for the vaquero. Inocente staggered away from the dead brave, but the other regained his feet, raised his ax, and charged with a scream. Clint veered the big palomino, and the horse crashed into the thick-chested Indian, sending him sprawling into the dust. The exhausted palomino collapsed to his knees, and Clint flew over his head. He hit rolling and rose to face the Yokuts brave.

Sidestepping a whistling blow from the brave's ax, then another, he backed away, desperately trying to stay out of reach. Again the brave swung the heavy sharpened stone, enough to crush Clint's skull with even a halfhearted blow. Reeling away, Clint's heel caught in a clump of sage, and he slammed to his back.

With an ear-splitting scream, the brave victoriously raised the ax. Before it could fall, an arrow thudded into the man's chest, driving him back. The ax tumbled from his hand as he grasped the fletched shaft with both hands and sank to his knees. A trickle of blood flowed from the corner of his mouth as he fell face forward, driving the obsidian head of the arrow out through his back.

Clint struggled to his feet, his heart beating like a pounding drum, and turned to see Hawk casually sitting his horse, bow in hand, notching another arrow.

Clint and Inocente ran for the palomino. With a sweep of his knife, Inocente cut the loop of the reata, still binding the Yokuts' horse. As Clint reined the horse around, Inocente reached up with his good arm and hooked Clint's elbow into his. Clint spurred the powerful *caballo* away from the pile of Indians and ponies, swinging Inocente onto the back of his mount.

"I will coil your reata, Anglo!" Inocente's voice rang with what Clint read as sharp criticism as the line dragged behind the horse. "Had I not cut it, you would have lost it."

Hawk reined up beside them. They slowed to a trot. Clint

took the coiled reata from Inocente and tied it to his saddle. He felt like giving the man riding behind him the elbow and leaving him in the dust for the Yokuts. But he did not; instead, he quietly steamed in his own juice.

They rounded a sage-covered hill, and Clint saw Ramón leading Inocente's runaway mount. The nervous stallion pranced and sidestepped as Clint drew rein, and Inocente slid from the animal's back.

Ramón tore Inocente's bloodied shirt away, studied the wound through the vaquero's shoulder, then temporarily packed and bandaged it as best he could with pieces of the cloth. Inocente clamped his eyes shut and winced but said nothing.

He tried to mount but could not. Exasperated, he cursed under his breath. Ramón stepped forward and pushed Inocente up into the saddle on his next try.

"*Gracias*, amigo," Inocente said. He turned to Clint, and Clint realized that what he had read as criticism in Inocente's tone was really the cold efficiency of the man. Without emotion in his voice, Inocente continued. "I will reweave your reata for you when we return to Santa Barbara, as soon as I regain the use of this arm. It was a fine reata, and you are as fine an *hombre del lazo* as I have ever seen. *Gracias*, mi amigo."

"*De nada*," Clint said, surprised at the man's compliment. Clint grinned widely and shook his head as Inocente reined his horse around.

He trotted away, and Ramón reined up beside Clint.

"*Hombre del lazo*, eh? The *lazodor*. El Lazo, the Anglo. *Chihuahua!* No one in Santa Barbara will believe it." His laugh rang across the valley as he nudged his horse ahead and began to hum a lively Mexican song.

When Ramón had finished his tune, Clint broke into an even more lively sea chantey. An hour later, they caught up with the herd, Hawk, and Matt. Matt was kneeling on his tree-trunk legs beside a patch of rosemary, and Hawk was treating the wound in the big man's back.

Clint dismounted and walked to Inocente. "Let me help you down so Hawk can care for that shoulder."

"Do stallions need help running?" the vaquero grumbled. "Do eagles need help flying?"

He tried to swing a leg over the saddle, but his dark eyes

rolled up in his head and he passed out, pitching forward. Clint caught him as he fell. By the time he came to, Hawk had his wound bandaged and bound as best he could, a travois constructed, and Inocente lashed securely to it.

"It is the way we haul meat back to camp," Hawk said, a smile flickering at the corners of his mouth.

Inocente looked up at him and growled. "I can ride," he complained loudly as they began to drag him behind the herd.

"As stallions run and eagles fly?" Clint said to the vaquero, a hint of amusement in his voice. "Even they have to rest sometimes."

"Maybe your Chumash half can ride, vaquero," Hawk added smugly, "but your Spanish half is beat to hell. You have lost a great deal of blood. With rest, your strength will return. I would suggest you allow at least the Spanish half the comfort of the travois."

"Comfort, hell." Inocente cursed him quietly, then winced as the travois hit a bump.

Twenty-five

It took two long, hard days to reach Rancho del Robles Viejos. After a day and a half in the travois, Inocente decided he would prefer dying in the saddle. He was sure the jarring drag would kill him if his wounds did not.

Clint, pushing the herd, had time to assess and admire Estoban's beautiful palomino brood stock. But as fine as the others were, none were finer than Diablo del Sol, the golden horse that had carried him through so much. He regretted the loss of the red roan, but returning the palomino to Don Estoban would now be like losing a part of himself.

As the herd neared the burned-out hacienda, those who worked cleaning and salvaging stopped to watch. Estoban picked his way out of the blackened beams of the *establo*, and Juana followed close behind.

By the time the stock was driven into the pasture and the men had dismounted, old Estoban's eyes were filled with tears. With a cry of delight, Juana ran forward and threw her arms around her mare.

Hawk walked over to a group of Chumash employed on the rancho and renewed old friendships.

Estoban threw his arms around Inocente. "*Madre de Dios, mi hijo,* you have saved a lifetime of hard work. Anything you want is yours—anything."

Inocente looked over at Juana, who had Florita haltered and was leading her from the herd to join the men. To his surprise, she returned his look with equal warmth.

Estoban stood beside his *segundo* and rested his hand on Inocente's shoulder affectionately.

"Easy, *jefe,* my shoulder." Inocente took his eyes off

187

Juana, then pushed his hat off his head. "You are grateful to the wrong man, *patrón*. Ramón, and the Anglo, El Lazo—"

"El Lazo?" Estoban interrupted.

"Lazo, the Anglo, as fine a hand with a reata as any I have seen. And the Chumash, and the Kanaka—all were more responsible for the return of your beautiful Andalusians than I."

Don Estoban Padilla removed his hat and looked gratefully at Inocente, Hawk, Ramón, Matt, and Clint. "I thank you all."

"What Inocente said about the rest of us is not true." Clint stepped forward. "Not true at all. Each of us played a part, none greater than Inocente."

"It is good," Estoban said, returning his hat to his head. "But there is serious news for us all." He turned, his eyes on the only Anglo among them. "News has come that Mexico and the *Estados Unidos* are at war. They are fighting in Texas, and soon we suspect there will be fighting here."

The news chilled Clint like a dip in ice water. His country was at war with Mexico and consequently Alta California. He looked from face to face, but saw only smiles.

Estoban stepped forward and laid a hand on Clint's shoulder. "As far as we are concerned, you are one of us, El Lazo. A vaquero first—whatever else you wish to be is unimportant."

Juana dropped the halter lead and walked over to Inocente. She kissed him lightly on the cheek. "You brought back not only my Florita but something even more valuable."

"What is that?" he asked, his face suddenly flushed.

"Humility, mi Inocente. It is a most admirable trait in a powerful, handsome man. An occasional smile is also admirable."

Inocente reddened even more and as usual had no answer for the beautiful girl, but he managed to curl his lips up slightly.

"Now each of you must select a horse from my finest," Estoban said. "Who will pick first?"

The four men turned to Clint. He accepted the honor without hesitation, for he knew exactly what he wanted and cherished the opportunity. He walked back to Diablo and grabbed up his reins. "If it suits you, Don Estoban, I'll stay with this old fella. We're kinda' gettin' partial to each other."

"A good choice, amigo," Estoban said. Clint wanted to shout hooray on receiving the don's gift. Instead, he stroked the horse's withers.

They spent the night camped at the rancho, and in the morning, Estoban added five thousand *reales*, the equivalent of five hundred American dollars, to each man's poke—in the form of golden Spanish doubloons.

Hawk, now a rich man with a beautiful stallion and a poke full of gold, prepared to ride back to his village. Clint walked with him when he went to saddle his stallion.

"It's not my way to stick my nose in others' business," Clint said, watching his Chumash friend bridle the dappled gray he had selected.

"If something burdens you, lay it aside." Hawk reached for the carved saddle and set to the task.

"You can't go backward, Hawk. The way your people used to live was fine, but if I've learned one thing, it's that things change."

Hawk mounted and bent to stroke the stallion's neck. He paused and looked into Clint's eyes. "But not always for the better."

"That's true, but nothing ever stands still, and nothing ever goes backward. There's a war between Mexico and the United States, and if the United States wins, California will be a territory . . . and things will change even faster. The courts of the United States will not accept some of your old ways, and much trouble will come to the Chumash."

Hawk extended his hand to Clint, and they shook. "I will think on it, my friend."

"Think hard on it. You can lead your people out of the darkness."

"And into what? More darkness? Disease? We are of the past."

"But you don't have to be. Look forward."

With a rueful smile, Hawk brought his fist across his chest, and Clint returned the sign of friendship. Hawk galloped away. Clint hoped the next time he saw him, the tribe would be embracing the best of the new world even as they clung to the best of the old.

After Hawk left, Clint, Ramón, Inocente, and Don Estoban rode out to Santa Barbara, following the caleche with the

Padilla women, who would stay at the Camacho hacienda until Estoban was able to rebuild their own. They would arrive in time for the last two days of the celebration of the feast of Corpus Christi. Though they had lost a great deal, there was still much to be thankful for.

While Ramón went to pay his respects to his father's grave next to the mission, Clint found Padre Javier, who was busily overseeing the preparation of a massive meal for the poor.

"This is a good time for you to be here, my son," Padre Javier said, smiling, "for the *Charleston* has come and gone."

"I saw there was no ship in the harbor. Do they know of the war?"

"No mention was made of it. The *Charleston* should be visiting other ports and should not return to Santa Barbara again for months. You should be safe here for a while."

Clint felt the heat at the back of his neck. Hearing of what Sharpentier would do to him was getting old. But he clamped his jaw and made no comment. The padre was only trying to help. He changed the subject.

"Don Estoban seemed to be strangely unconcerned about the war . . . a surprise to me."

"For years," the priest said, "Mexico City has been far from Alta California, not only in distance, but in many other ways. Even though they deny it, they have stepped away from Mother Church and have let the missions go to ruin. It is too soon to tell, but this may prove to be a blessing to us all. God works in mysterious ways."

Clint let that soak in a moment, then changed the subject. "I'm sorry, Father, but I lost the horse Don Nicholas loaned me. He fell to the arrows of the Yokuts horse thieves."

"Too bad, but better him than you or the others." The padre shook his head. "The meal is almost prepared. Then I must go to the fandango, as should you. We will stop by Don Nicholas Den's on the way and you can explain the matter to him."

"And return the guns," Clint said without enthusiasm. He had grown very attached to the Colts.

Ramón joined them, and the three walked through the decorated streets of the pueblo to the don's hacienda. Don Nicholas greeted them warmly, led them to a sideboard, and poured each of them a generous dollop of Irish whiskey. "To the victors."

They raised their glasses. Then Clint gave him the sorry news. "I lost the red roan, Don Nicholas. He took several Yokuts arrows meant for me. If you will tell me what he was worth . . ."

"He died a noble death, saving a brave son of Ireland. Consider him my gift to the cause."

"Thank you." Relieved that the don seemed proud of the horse's part in the Yokuts' punishment, Clint leaned against the back of a tall straight leather-backed chair. "I did manage to return with your fine weapons. I'll tell you—and I shouldn't, for I'd like to buy them —they are without peer." With Sharpentier still a threat, he would need more than the knife he carried.

"Buy them?"

"If you would consider parting with them."

"Leave them here until the celebrations are over, and I will think on it." He laughed. "Come to think of it, I would hate to have a Celt march through the world unarmed." Then his expression changed, and he rested against the edge of a dark mahogany desk. "I understand the death of my old friend Alfonso Diego was well avenged."

"Not to my liking," Ramón said, "but it will do until I have another opportunity."

They talked awhile longer, then Don Nicholas rose and walked them to the door. Clint, the padre, and Ramón left for the fandango, which was being held in the square in front of the presidio.

Ahead of them they could see the crowd gathering. More than two hundred, dressed in embroidered velvet, chiffon, satin, and silk, filled the road and the grassy area of the square, drinking, laughing, and dancing to the lively rhythm of violins, guitars, triangles, and flutes. Many vaqueros sat astride their horses, commenting on the beautiful women and wishing they too had one on their arm. Several vaqueros waved to Ramón, and men Clint had never met called out to him, "El Lazo." He waved and laughed, enjoying the camaraderie.

Then, only a block from the square, he glanced up. From between two adobe buildings a group of men moved in front of him, blocking his way. Clint sucked in a breath. A scowling Captain Quade Sharpentier, in full-dress uniform, backed by ten sailors armed with muskets and cutlasses, stared back at him.

Clint stopped in his tracks.

"There are eight more behind us," Ramón said quietly.

With a glance back, Clint recognized the smirking face, the massive shoulders, the rotting teeth, and the bald head of Skinner, his old first mate. Skinner hawked and spat into the street, then cocked his head to the side and stuck out his tongue grotesquely as he held one arm up high, miming the hangman's noose.

"You have no authority here." Padre Javier stepped in front of Clint to face the captain. "Your warrant is no longer valid. Mexico and the United States are at war."

"I come with the greatest authority"—Sharpentier smiled sardonically—"musket and cutlass. If you doubt that authority, I may just run up the Stars and Stripes over that pile of mud you call a public building."

He stepped forward and glowered at the priest. "Get the hell out of the way."

"I've no dog in this fight," Ramón mumbled. Spinning on his heel, he gave them his back and strode across the road. Clint's shoulders sagged as he watched his trusted friend slip away.

Ramón was the last man, he thought, to run from a fight. Clint looked desperately for a way out but saw none. Resting his hand on the hilt of his knife, he cursed himself for leaving the Colt behind with Don Nicholas. *I'll not ride acorn's horse without a fight,* he swore.

The sailors behind closed to within paces, as did those in front. Turk stepped in to face Sharpentier.

"Wait, Captain. Wait just a moment."

"Stand aside."

"Not till ye hear me out."

"Speak quickly. We've a neck to stretch, and since we are technically at war with these greasers, I see no reason not to use that big oak in the square and add to the decorations of this falderal party. Maybe they'll give us a reason to take this town as well."

Clint shifted slowly, easing his back to the adobe wall. Then he unsheathed his knife—and a dozen sailors leveled their muskets at him.

"Ryan," Sharpentier snarled, "I'd as soon hang you with the added weight of a few musketballs. My line is stout enough."

"But he was below, Cap'n," Turk protested.

"What the hell are you talkin' about, man?"

"Ryan. When we grounded the *Savannah*, Ryan was below. He was never called to watch."

The men behind the captain stirred, muttering quietly among themselves. Wishon stepped out of the crowd. "And he be no shirker, Captain. I can speak to that."

As they argued back and forth, Clint noticed more and more mounted vaqueros passing in the road, and Ramón, Don Estoban, and Inocente were among them, their looks deadly serious.

Sharpentier clutched Wishon's collar in his fist. "Stand aside, you Ethiopian sogger, unless you want to join him."

"Let's hang the bastard!" Skinner shouted, and the men charged forward.

A sharp blow knocked Padre Javier aside and musket butts, fists, and feet drove Clint to the ground. Through a haze of pain he heard a few scattered musket shots. Then his attackers began to career away. Clint's vision cleared, and he realized he was no longer being held.

Screaming obscenities, sailors were being dragged in every direction, the road a jumble of horses, lines, and men.

Matt, his huge arms circling his foe, was locked chest-to-chest with Skinner while the first mate rained great thumping blows on Matt's head. Blood flowed from Matt's nose and ears, and through the bandages from the wound in his back, but still he squeezed. Skinner's eyes bulged. He flailed his arms, gasped and groaned, then uttered a gurgling choke, and his eyes swelled even more. They rolled up in their sockets, his huge head fell to his shoulder, and his arms went limp. Matt dropped him to the sidewalk, but Matt was not smiling.

Straining, the veins popping out on his face and neck, Matt hefted Skinner chest-high by his throat and crotch, and flung the first mate against the adobe wall. The wall crashed away, and the first mate tumbled through in a cloud of dust.

Matt wiped at his bloody face and grinned at Clint. "Should make walls from good teak, like in Sandwich Islands."

The *alcalde* rode up, leading a detachment of *cholo soldados* carrying lances and muskets. He shouted at the vaqueros, who reined their horses and dragged their charges back to where Clint struggled to his feet.

Ramón, with Quade Sharpentier at the end of his reata,

pulled to a stop in front of the *alcalde* and Clint. He doffed his hat. "I have roped the goat, Lazo. Do you wish to have him now?"

"I have no need of the bastard," Clint said, brushing himself off.

Sharpentier lurched to his feet, shed the loop, and staggered over to Don Francisco Acaya. The captain's fancy uniform was covered with dust and dung from the streets and his beard was dirt-brown, but he managed to speak. "I have a warrant," he sputtered.

Wishon and Turk, who had managed to flee inside the hacienda to avoid the loops, stepped out of the hole where Skinner had disappeared. "We're with ye, Clint," Turk said. "I know ye're innocent."

Matt stepped forward and addressed the *alcalde*. "You should have a warrant for Captain Sharpentier, sir. I saw him knock your guard out and break into your armory."

"That's a bloody lie!" Sharpentier shouted.

Matt took a step toward Sharpentier, and the captain's eyes widened.

Don Francisco, his opulently uniformed chest puffing out, turned to his captain of the guard. "Take the Anglo *capitán* to the *juzgado*. We will straighten this out after the fandango." He turned back to Clint and Matt. "You two will report to me when the fandango is over. We have unfinished business: the matter of my stock and this Kanaka's escape. If it were not for your service in punishing the Yokuts—"

Dragging a dirt-spitting *marinero*, Don Estoban reined up and dismounted nearby. "I can vouch for those men, *Alcalde*."

Don Francisco pondered for a moment. "Then I will leave this matter to you. I am satisfied with their service to the pueblo and hereby grant them a pardon—this time. I will not miss the bullfight."

The *cholos* marched Sharpentier away at lancepoint, and Skinner stumbled to the opening in the wall, a broken man. Grinning, Matt took a step toward him, but the first mate held up his hands. "All I want is to get back to me ship. With Sharpentier in jail, she is my responsibility now."

The *alcalde* glared at the first mate. "Then take her away from the shores of California. Until this war is settled, I do not want to see her in the harbor."

"We'll sail with the tide," Skinner said, pleased by the turn of events.

Clint moved between Matt and Skinner, nose-to-nose with the big first mate. "Take your mates with you." Skinner backed away and began to gather his men. Several carried those who could not walk, and they limped away to the safety of the ship.

Clint clasped Matt on the shoulder. "Come on, brother. Ramón and I will buy you a mug of *aguardiente*."

Matt backhanded the blood from his nose.

"But only one," Clint amended.

Inocente dismounted, favoring his shoulder, and limped along with them. "I will buy the second," he said.

Coiling his reata, Ramón trotted his horse up beside them. "Lazo! Inocente and I were going to capture the *oso grande* next weekend. Since he is unable to hunt for a while, you will ride against the grizzly in his stead."

Clint glanced at Inocente.

"It is true, amigo," Inocente said. "You may borrow my reata as I have not yet mended yours."

"We need a grizzly," Ramón said. "The one captured for the bull-and-bear fight has escaped. It has been rescheduled for next week."

"*Gracias,*" Clint said with a smile. "I need a little excitement."

Epilogue

A little more than three months after the Corpus Christi festivities ended, Sharpentier was serving a six-month sentence in the pueblo *juzgado*. Clint and Matt lounged in the square in front of the presidio watching the afternoon *paseo* of señoritas and their *dueñas*.

They noticed a ship entering the harbor, a ship Clint had never seen before. He and Matt wandered down to the waterfront and watched while she dropped anchor. A Mexican stood awaiting the longboat, a spyglass in hand. Clint borrowed it.

"By the saints!" he said. "She's a U.S. frigate."

The longboat breached the surf, and ten musket-toting marines in full battle attire and fieldpacks unloaded and fell into snappy formation behind a man resplendent in a commodore's brass-buttoned uniform. Six navy bluejackets remained with the longboat. The marines started forward in precise unison, then the commodore paused when he noticed the sandy-haired blue-eyed vaquero.

"You there!" He motioned Clint over. "I'm Commodore Robert Field Stockton of the United States Navy, and I'm here to take possession of the entire Santa Barbara Presidial District. Where will I find the *alcalde* of Santa Barbara?"

Deciding to play it safe, Clint, gave him directions in heavily Irish-accented English.

"Thank you," the commodore said. "And your name?"

Clint hesitated a moment. "El Lazo of Santa Barbara, but

196

by birth and blood, Kilkenny County, Ireland, and I'm at your service, Commodore."

The commodore nodded another thank-you, and he and his contingent of marines quick-stepped away. The men glanced from side to side as they moved up Calle Principal. When they reached the square unopposed, they dropped the serpent-and-nopal banner of Mexico and ran up the Stars and Stripes.

El Lazo watched with mixed emotions. He was a wanted man by the government of the Unites States. He would have to be gone from Santa Barbara before Captain Quade Sharpentier was released from the *juzgado*, but even so, he felt his chest swell with pride at the sight of the red, white, and blue banner.

And he knew if there was to be a fight, no matter how he was torn by allegiance to new friends, he would have to stand on the side of Old Glory.

Times were changing in Alta California. And times were changing for John Clinton Ryan, a good man with line or *lazo*.

Historical Notes
and
Acknowledgments

The first Europeans found the California shore and its offshore islands well populated with natives. Several thousand Chumash, called Canalinos by the Spanish, occupied the Santa Barbara Channel area, including the offshore islands. As many as twenty-five thousand Yokuts occupied California's great central valley. Though in some ways not so advanced as the Plains Indians, these tribes had an intricate society with well-established religious and social mores.

The Chumash and Yokuts used *pestibaba*, a strong native tobacco, and *toloche* (jimson weed), a highly toxic plant, for their religious ceremonies. (For those adventurous and foolhardy few who might be tempted, the use of jimson weed will blind you, if you are lucky enough to survive its consumption.) The native medicine men were skilled and were not condemned for burying their mistakes. They could blame it on Sup, their god. If their subject died, he had obviously displeased Sup.

The early Chumash believed that the killing of their firstborn strengthened the subsequent offspring, and among other practices abhorrent to Anglos, believed in the free exchange of women, including sisters, among the adult men. The author has taken some liberty (literary license if you will) in suggesting that a group of Chumash might have returned to those beliefs as late as 1846.

The Chumash native weapons were well developed,

though their bows were small and their arrows short. The Yokuts used both short and long bows and *atlatls*, throwing sticks. Both tribes used axes and lances. They could not kill the formidable grizzly, but the weapons were sufficient to take any other game native to California and took their share of men.

Most game was caught by snare or trap, and the fishtrap in the marshy valley was common. Poisons were also used to stun fish and bring them to the surface for easy gathering.

Native basketwork, particularly that of the Yokuts, was as intricate as that of the Plains tribes and often far superior.

The great interior valley of California, now known as the San Joaquin and Sacramento valleys, was primarily populated by Yokuts. The word *Yokuts* is not plural, but like Crow or Apache, is the tribal name. The Yokuts society was much like that of the Chumash, with the notable exception that only the chief could have multiple wives.

The tribes of central California seldom fought. The Yokuts were divided into several tribes of up to four villages each. Tribal boundaries were well defined by watersheds or waterways, and disputes were settled by tribal elders.

Trading was a way of life for the California Indians, and they ranged far and wide, trading extensively with the distant Mojave and Paiute Indians of the deserts. Abalone-shell ornaments found their way into the pueblos of faraway New Mexico and Colorado.

There is disagreement among archaeologists regarding the whaling done by the Chumash. Some claim the whalebones found in middens came only from beached whales, though there is good documentation regarding their wonderfully constructed *tomolos*, thirty-foot canoes of split, lapped, and tar-caulked planks. Unfortunately, none survive to grace museum halls, where we might gaze in wonder at the workmanship of these patient early craftsmen.

The introduction of the horse changed the California natives much as it changed the Plains tribes. In addition to transportation, California natives, whose primary protein staple had been the acorn, developed a dependence on the horse as a food source. From 1830 to 1850, raids on the horse herds of the missions and ranchos of the coast by the Miwok and Yokuts from the interior were commonplace. Horses were stolen and driven to the interior not as riding stock but as meat for the butcher's knife.

The Mexicans considered constructing forts in the passes to keep the Indians at bay—particularly at Pacheco Pass—but California was segmented in its politics and never loyal to the governors appointed by Mexico City. Therefore, few public projects were completed.

Point Conception, near Santa Barbara, and its neighbor to the north, Point Arguello, have claimed many ships over California's history. Point Arguello is known as a ship graveyard.

Calle Principal, in Santa Barbara, is now known as State Street.

The *alcalde* of Santa Barbara in 1846 was actually Nicholas (who later changed the spelling to Nicolas) Den, an Irishman who took Mexican citizenship, married a señorita, and acquired by grant one of California's oldest, most beautiful, and most prestigious ranchos—Rancho Dos Pueblos, just north of Santa Barbara. Due to the economic reversals of his family, Den had been forced out of an Irish medical school in his last year, but the knowledge he gained there brought him the title *doctor*, though he discouraged its use. Rancho Dos Pueblos was one of the first places named in California, having been mentioned in Cabrillo's log on October 16, 1542, when his unwieldy caravels, the *San Salvadore* and the *La Victoria*, both flying the flag of Spain, anchored offshore and spotted two almost identical Indian villages on either side of a creek. Later in the twentieth century, Dos Pueblos, demonstrating the area's ideal climate, gained fame as an orchid farm.

Mexican independence in 1820 and the emancipation of the Indians in 1835 resulted in the downfall of the mission system. Mexico felt the Franciscans were loyal to Mother Spain and coveted the land and great herds of the missions. The conversion of California neophytes peaked shortly after the turn of the nineteenth century, and most of the coastal Indians were converted to Christianity. The interior, always ignored by the Spanish and the Mexicans, held what was left of the California natives, and they, like the coastal natives, would be tamed by the white man's diseases far more than by his weapons.

Nicholas Den and his partner, Daniel Hill, an American who also sought Mexican citizenship so he could partake of the land-grant system, were instrumental in protecting Mission Santa Barbara from the nepotistic greed of Governor Pío Pico.

They conspired with the priest to lease the mission, thereby saving it from the governor's gavel. Pico sold Mission San Juan Capistrano and its thousands of acres to his brother-in-law for seven hundred and fifty dollars. Pico, with his bags of gold, fled to Mexico during the Americanization of California.

Today, Mission Santa Barbara ranks as the most visited of western historical shrines. The altar candles of Mission Santa Barbara have been burning continuously since Padre Lasuen first lit them in 1786.

In 1848 California boasted a population of some 14,000 Mexicans and an estimated 30,000 Indians. But the cry of gold was heard around the world. By 1852, 350,000 Americans, Chinese, Peruvians, Australians, and many others had flooded her shores, and until Lincoln restored the ownership of the missions to the Franciscans in 1865, the mission system was virtually destroyed. The women of the tribes of California were assimilated into the white race, leaving the pure Indian strain almost unheard-of in the Golden State.

Today, the former glory of the missions is only a memory, but thanks to the intelligence, education, and tenacity of the learned padres, a memory that has been well recorded.

Until the gold rush, the interior of California was virtually unexplored. A few Spanish and Mexican expeditions made their way around the interior valleys, mostly to punish Indian raiders. But Mexico considered the territory of California as the land extending from the coast to the Rocky Mountains, even though the coastal areas of California and the Rio Grande watershed—Taos, Sante Fe, and Tucson—were the only areas settled. Sante Fe, like California, did not depend upon Mexico or faraway Mexico City. Sante Fe (the oldest European city north of Mexico on the North American continent other than St. Augustine in Florida) traded with Missouri and Arkansas via the Sante Fe Trail, and California traded with the ships of many nations plying the Pacific.

Americans considered a United States stretching from ocean to ocean to be their "manifest destiny." When Texas became a republic, she too looked at New Mexico and California with covetous eyes, seeking those areas mostly as a method of convincing the States that Texas must be annexed. The Texas president Lamar went so far as to launch an expedition to take Sante Fe but failed.

His navy was armed with the Colt revolving breech rifle

and his Rangers with Colt revolvers, the forerunners of modern arms. Fifteen Texas Rangers actually fended off eighty musket- and breechloader-armed Commanches, killing or maiming forty of them and proving for all time the value of the revolver.

If it cannot be said that the vaquero of California had no peer as a horseman, at least not without starting a range war between California and the other western states, it can certainly be said that he was equal to any in the world. The horse was his life. He treated his horse with respect and ruled him with utter authority, and sometimes disdain, for horses were numerous. At one time, over five thousand head were driven off the cliffs of the Irvine Ranch simply because they were competing with the cattle for forage. A halter-broken horse would bring five dollars in California when a wild one would bring fifty in Fort Smith, Arkansas.

In addition to many other sources, the author is particularly indebted to the following writings:

Arnold "Chief" Rojas, 1897–1988, whose many books on the California vaquero are not only informative but a joy to read. As a working vaquero, Rojas spun a tale as if you sat across a campfire from him.

Frank F. Latta, 1892–1983, the ultimate chronicler of California Indians. Latta, a born ethonographer, personally interviewed hundreds of surviving Indians from 1923 until his death. His knowledge and writing regarding the daily life of the Yokuts were invaluable.

Other works of particular interest:

The Californians, the magazine of the California Historical Society.

The exploration reports of Fages and Crespi.

The exploration reports of Anza and Font.

From Cowhides to Golden Fleece, by Underhill.

A Scotch Paisano, by Dakin.

The Land of Poco Tiempo, by Lummis.

If you enjoyed Larry Jay Martin's
EL LAZO, you will be thrilled
by his next novel for Bantam:

AGAINST THE 7TH FLAG

Here is an exciting preview of this new Western
novel, to be published in May 1991. It will
be available wherever Bantam Books are sold.

Turn the page for a preview of
AGAINST THE 7TH FLAG, by Larry Jay Martin.

With a whisper of death, the lead ball buffeted the air. John Clinton Ryan jerked back on the rein.

He could not tell where the shot came from but it splattered sandstone in the trail's narrow cleft a few paces in front of the palomino, and made the stallion snort and back-step. Deciding the shot had come from the front, he dropped low in the saddle, wheeled, and spurred the big horse.

Then he heard the echoing shout, "*Alto!*" and looked back over his shoulder. Three riders. He had no reason to run from Californios, so he jerked rein. His palomino sidestepped, jittery with the sound of clattering hooves as the three vaqueros swept down from the escarpment above. Clint spun the stallion to face them.

Bursting out of the buckbrush, the first of the riders pulled rein so hard his roan stallion set his hindquarters and slid to a stop in the trail in front of Clint's horse. The vaquero glared, hard-eyed, at the gringo—then at Clint's revolver, cocked and leveled on the man's ample belly. The Mexican's own single-shot cap and ball remained stuffed into his belt. The other two riders reined up behind the first, muskets lying across their saddles. Diablo, Clint's palomino, tossed his head impatiently, wanting to keep up the trail-eating lope they had been moving at since they had left Santa Barbara at daybreak, four hours ago.

"You are on the rancho of Alonso Mendoza," the first rider snapped. Then his narrow gaze swept up and down Clint, noting the Spanish boots, *calzonevas, chorro, jerga* shirt, and flat-crowned hat. His eyes never left Clint as he hawked and spat in the trail, raising a tiny puff of dust. "You are dressed like a *paisano* . . . but you look like a gringo." The two with the muskets began to inch their muzzles up.

Clint shifted the barrel of his Colt revolver to center on the belly of the second man, the tallest of the three. A scar marked the man's face from forehead to cheek. The eyebrow had healed slightly out of line and the eye carried a white slash across the pupil. His lips curled upward, showing teeth, but his musket muzzle slowly lowered.

Clint spoke accentless Spanish. "You *hombres* shouldn't be shooting at peaceful travelers. This Colt has what they call a revolving breech. "He spoke softly. "Eight shots." He let that soak in, then added, "Enough to feed you two rounds each, with still enough left to drop a rabbit for dinner." The third man lowered his worn musket also and smiled, but hollowly, without confidence.

Clint nodded, let down the hammer on the Colt, but kept it palmed. The fat vaquero in the lead noticeably exhaled, then his look hardened. "Had we been shooting at you, gringo, you would be lying in the trail now."

"A back-shooter might accomplish that . . . but not a man who faced me." Clint let his hard stare dissolve into an indulgent smile. "I was unaware I was on a rancho," he lied, "or I would have called at the hacienda. Am I not on Camino Real, a road open to all travelers?"

"You are," the last of the three said, urging his dappled gray forward beside the fat vaquero's roan. He pushed his flat-crowned hat back off his head and studied Clint, looking down a long regal nose. "You have not answered *mi amigo*'s question. You are a *gringo Americano*?" he asked, fingering the musket.

"Is it the custom in Alta California to rudely question a traveler? Not that it's your business, *hombre*," Clint said, "but I'm an Irishman, by birth and El Lazo of Santa Barbara by choice." He failed to mention the fact he carried papers identifying him as an American seaman, had been raised in Mystic, Connecticut, and had come to California as a member of the crew of an American merchantman.

The three men remained a half-dozen paces away. Then the long-nosed man with the scar looked him up and down. "You are called 'the lasso.' An honorable name, but one I doubt would be given to an Anglo." He laughed and the others joined him. Finally, the fat one collected himself.

"Tell me, light-haired, blue-eyed Irish vaquero, how did you get the name, El Lazo?"

"It was given to me by a vaquero who does not talk so much as you three, who taught me the use of the reata, and who would never be so rude as to laugh at a traveler."

The laughter died down.

Clint raised the Colt enough to convey a threat. "Now stand aside, and let a peaceful rider pass on the King's Highway."

Two of the vaqueros backed their stallions, but the long-nosed man gave no ground. He studied the unusual weapon.

"Are you sure you're not one of the *gringo marineros* who has lowered the Mexican banner and raised the invader's flag at Monterey and Santa Barbara?"

"And," Clint added, "at Sonoma and Sutter's Fort, I have heard. At the moment, I answer to no flag, nor any man's. Now move aside." Clint motioned with the Colt. The man's gaze dropped to the revolver. With the skill befitting a Californio vaquero, he jerked his horse around. The gray had to rear in the narrow trail and dance on his hind legs to make the turn, but the rider stuck in the saddle as if born there. The three of them spurred their horses, kicking up shale and gravel, and reined away up the hillside threading between the heavy buckbrush and sandpaper oaks back to the escarpment where Clint had first spotted them.

He holstered his Colt revolver and hoisted his revolving–breech Colt rifle an inch in its scabbard—just enough to make sure it rode free and easy.

It was a narrow escape.

In the last few months, California had become a boiling cauldron of distrust and suspicion. Not only was the explorer Fremont raising the flag of the United States over every Mexican governmental building in Northern California, but as usual, the Californios were fighting amongst themselves.

Clint Ryan was a man without a country. Not that the U.S., his adopted home, did not want him—they wanted him so dearly they had a warrant out for his arrest.

He waited until the vaqueros topped the ridge, then touched the palomino's sides with his long-roweled spurs. The big animal leapt into a gallop beneath the canopy of gray-green scrub oak and dark green buckeye. Summer was on the land, and the grass on the hillsides lay in golden contrast to spotted clumps of musty digger pine, Clint felt better when he cleared the narrow cleft and could see open trail ahead.

A reata snapped taut across the trail in front of his galloping stallion. He jerked rein but was on the trip-line before the big horse could react. The animal's legs caught the line and Clint sailed over his head. He hit rolling, losing the reins as Diablo pulled away.

He rose, spitting dust. Trying to clear the dirt from his eyes with one hand, he clawed for his Colt with the other. He had it halfway drawn when a second reata closed around his arms and jerked him off his feet.

The Colt spun away.

He recovered his stance and fought against the pull of the noose, only to have a musket butt slam into the side of his head.

Clint went down in a heap.

Lieutenant Edward "Ned" Beale leaned on a hitching rail in front of the presidio of Monterey, the military headquarters of the pueblo, and watched explorer Captain John Charles Fremont's party approach. Fremont's scout, Le Gros Fallon, stood next to Beale with a Hawken rifle resting in the crook of his arm.

Beale glanced up at the huge, hulking mountain man. "I presume that's Fremont in the lead. Who are the men flanking him?"

Behind the explorer, five chisel-featured, buckskin-clad Indians, armed with Hawkens, saddle pistols, knives, and tomahawks surveyed the pueblo. Among them rode another man, a thick-shouldered red-headed Anglo in merchant's dress, with his Black slave a half-length behind.

"Delawares. The cap'n keeps 'em as sorta personal guards. The one on the paint horse following Fremont is their leader, Chief James Sagundai." Fallon leaned on the rail, propping his rifle next to him. "The city suit is Archibald Gillespie. He come all the way to Oregon to fetch Fremont back."

Behind the lead guard, one hundred and fifty riders and fifty spare mounts followed two by two.

"That little fella's Kit Carson." Fallon pointed to the first pair of riders following the Delawares and Gillespie. "And Alex Godey rides a'side 'im. That big ol' boy behind 'em is Stutterin' Zeke Merritt. He's the one what stole about two hundred head of Castro's horses and shamed his fancy dan Lieutenant Arce."

"So this is the California Battalion," Ned said. "They're a rough-looking bunch."

"Man don't need no fancy-dan doodads to fight, Lieutenant Beale," Fallon snapped.

"No offense, Mr. Fallon. They look like hard men who can accomplish a difficult task. If it comes to that, General Castro and his mounted lancers will be a formidable foe."

"We'll take 'em as they come," Fallon said. "These men all crossed the high lonely, some with young'uns and stock to look after. We practiced up by kicking the hell out of those murderous Maidus on the way here. These men'll meet any test."

The big scout straightened up from the rail. "And each of 'em signed a pledge to protect the settlers hereabout. Cap'n promised twenty-five dollar a month, and beef and flour to the boys' families while we're ahunting Castro and the greasers." Fallon eyed the last of the column that passed. "I got to join up and show the cap'n the campsite I picked."

"I'll be happy to buy you a mug first . . . or later," Ned said.

"No time, but I'll not forget the offer." Fallon extended a callused hand the size and texture of a bear paw.

"It'll still be good the next time we meet." Ned shook the man's hand, and watched him mount his big buckskin. The sixteen-hand horse looked small under the massive Irish scout. Fallon reined away and loped up beside the tall, ramrod-straight captain of the California Guard—the Bears, or *Osos*, they called themselves.

Ned considered taking a mug, even if alone, then looked beyond the little pueblo on out at the harbor. Commodore Sloat's flagship, the *Savannah*, lay at anchor. The *Cyane* and *Levant*, sloops-of-war, and Commodore Robert Field Stockton's *Congress*, a frigate and the finest ship in the fleet, also tugged at anchor rodes. A formidable fighting force in any man's navy. It was a good thing, for John Bull, as the British were known, was baring his teeth. The British flagship *Collingwood* had been spotted at sea and had boldly made several California ports over the last two months.

The mug would have to wait. Ned had to get back to the *Congress*. He didn't want to miss the upcoming meeting with John Charles Fremont, Commodore John Sloat—the commander of all the Pacific forces—and his own immediate superior, Commodore Robert Field Stockton.

As master of the ship, a position responsible for all shipping and stowing of stores as well as inspecting all ship's equipment and keeping the log, Beale had been well qualified for the position of Stockton's personal secretary, and had proved more than equal to the task. Stockton had recently promoted him to acting lieutenant. Ned was sure he would be ordered to attend the meeting.

Ned had an acute interest in the possible conflict between John Bull and the U.S.A. over California and Oregon. His first important assignment as a midshipman had been an exciting one. On his first voyage aboard the *Congress*, Stockton had hoved to alongside a Danish ship, the *Mariah*. When he discovered that she was on her way to Liverpool, he assigned Beale, a fledgling officer, the job of donning civilian clothes and going to England to spy to find out what the British planned for California. Ned spent almost a year of his life ashore, in merchantman garb, listening to rumor and fact, and trying to determine the difference. On his return, he reported to President Polk himself, and to Secretary of the Navy George Bancroft. He reported that Britain was preparing her fleet for war—a report that had already been confirmed by the American Consul to Britain.

After catching up with the four-hundred-eighty-man *Congress* at Callao, Peru, Ned was now back at the duty he was trained for, duty that might very well include battling the British—a fearful proposition—the French, or the Russians over the territory the Mexicans called Alta California.

Rumor had it that General Castro wanted to separate northern Alta California from southern, where Governor Pío Pico kept his residence. It was said that Castro would appeal to either John Bull or the French to help him keep his newly independent territory free—and under his dictatorial power.

Rumor also had it that the Mexican government had pulled out of Mazatlán, taking the archives with them, an act which foretold an American-Mexican war. But so far, no word of war had reached the Pacific fleet. It was an exciting time. As Ned made his way back to the beach and the waiting shore boat, he hoped Commander Sloat was up to the challenge. Secretly he questioned the old man's capabilities. He wished Stockton were in command. But it was a wish he wisely kept to himself.

When he reached the beach, Ned turned back to survey the scene. He could see Fremont and the Bears less than a mile away approaching the cypress-covered knoll Fallon had picked for their camp. It was a high spot, one with a commanding view of its surroundings, but one that suffered from a continual wind, Ned decided after studying the flagged cypress with all their foliage on the lee side.

The adobe walls and tile-and-thatch roofs of the Monterey pueblo stretched up the hill away from the water. Horses, goats, donkeys, and pigs roamed the streets, as well as a few *carretas* pulled by oxen and loaded with goods. None of the sandal-clad Mexicans going about their business seemed threatening. The customs house, the biggest building in the pueblo other than the mission, rose from the beach beside the harbor. The new twenty-nine-star flag of the United States—a flag that did not yet represent the new state of Texas—waved over it.

Monterey had long been the first port of call for any vessel wishing to trade in Alta California. Trade goods were taxed and a license issued at the customs house under the control of the *commandante* of Northern California, General José Castro—a situation that angered his southern rival, Governor Pío Pico. Beale knew that Pico had ordered the customs house moved to San Pedro, where he could control California's primary source of revenues, but Castro and his men had taken to the hills when the powerful flotilla anchored. Sloat, with Stockton's encouragement, raised the American flag over Monterey—in the guise of protecting American settlers. If Stockton had anything to say about it, the business of Mexicans in California was at a standstill for all time. But Stockton was not the commander of the Pacific Fleet, Sloat was. And Sloat was hesitant to act decisively until he heard from Washington.

Ned whistled to his two oarsmen, who sat nearby on empty barrels chatting with two lace-clad señoritas and their fat *dueña*, or chaperone. The two oarsmen reluctantly tipped their ribbon-trimmed hats to the ladies, then hurried over to take up their oars.

Clint Ryan came to slowly.

His head pounded and he could not quite get his surroundings in focus. He closed his eyes tightly and worked his jaw, sore as a boil from the blow. He tried to reach up and touch it, then realized his hands were bound tightly. He opened his eyes and waited until the multiple images in front of him came together.

He was tied to the thick, rough trunk of a live oak. His hands were bound behind him, and a reata encircled him and the tree several times, making it difficult to breathe. Five men sat around a fire nearby, the three he had met in the trail and two others who he presumed had tripped his horse.

Clint glanced over at a picket line, where the vaqueros' horses were tethered to a taut reata stretched between two oaks, and was relieved to see Diablo standing among them. The big horse stood on all four feet, not favoring a leg. Apparently he was all right.

Scar-face glanced over and noticed that Clint's eyes were open. He rose from his spot by the fire, brushed off his *calzonevas* as he approached, pushed his hat back off his head, and stood in front of Clint.

"Did you have a pleasant rest, gringo? El Lazo, the vaquero, fell off his *caballo*." He guffawed.

"Why the hell am I tied up?"

"It is my privilege to ask the questions, not yours."

"And who the hell are you?"

"I am called Cicatriz . . ." He smiled. "But my friends call me Cica."

And well named, Clint thought eyeing the ugly scar on the man's face. *Cicatriz*, the scar.

"Am I your friend, Cica?" Clint asked. "This is no way to treat a friend."

"You can be my friend, Anglo, for a few hours. Then I must hang you, or shoot you if you prefer."

Clint studied the man, who grinned like a dog eyeing a bone. The men behind him began to laugh quietly.

"Is it against the law to travel the King's Highway?"

"It is against the law to be an *Americano* in Alta California. Besides, I like your horse and fine guns."

"Ah, so the patriot is nothing but a horse thief after all." Clint ran his tongue over his teeth, still gritty from his tumble off Diablo. He spat onto the ground near Cica's feet.

"You are arrogant, Anglo. We will soon see if you are as good a dancer as you are a talker. How well do you do the hangman's fandango?" His men laughed. "If you dance well, I may take you down from the limb and hang you only a little at a time. But already I tire of your talk." Cica turned to his men. "Get him on a *caballo*."

Two of the vaqueros jumped up, hurried to Clint, and untied the reata that bound him to the oak. Another ran to the picket line and untied a rank brindle-colored mustang.

Clint's mind raced. He was about to be hanged by Mexicans who had no idea they were carrying out the sentence of the Americans.

"You do the gringo's work," Clint said, and spat again on the ground.

Cica spun from deciding which limb to throw his reata over and studied Clint. "What do you mean, I do the gringo's work?"

"I am a wanted man in the United States. I, of all people, have no wish for the United States to rule Alta California."

"And why would the gringos want to stretch the neck of such a fine vaquero as 'El Lazo?'" Cica asked sarcastically. His men aligned the brindle-colored horse under the straightest, strongest-looking limb, and two of them hoisted Clint up. The animal sidestepped nervously. Clint bunched his legs under him and kicked away from the saddle. He and both men crashed to the ground.

With his hands tied behind him, Clint was unable to gain his feet as quickly as the Mexicans, who kicked him repeatedly in the ribs. He tried to roll away from the blows, turning and jerking to protect his head, but the boots found their marks. His head swam, and blood flowed freely from his nose and lips. His ribs and stomach throbbed with pain as the Mexicans jerked him to his feet again.

This time, four of them lifted him into the saddle beneath the dangling reata. Two men stood on each side of him, holding his legs in place. Cica adjusted the loop over Clint's head and pulled it tight around his throat. For the first time, his stomach flooded with dread.

"Are you sure you do not work for the gringo?" Clint desperately goaded.

"I work for no man," Cica snarled.

"I thought you worked for Don Alonso Mendoza," Clint said, his wind constricted by the tight noose.

"My friend only told you that you were on the rancho of Alonso Mendoza," Cica corrected. "He did not say we worked for him."

"Get him here before you hang me. He will straighten this out," Clint said.

Cica laughed. "If Don Alonso was here, he would hang me, not you."

"A common thief," Clint managed to choke out.

The men stepped away from the sides of the horse, and Cica raised a revolver—a pistol Clint recognized as his own Colt.

"I am a very uncommon thief, thank you. You will not need your horse or guns where you are going, gringo." Cica grinned widely. The Colt spat flame, and the mustang plunged out from under him.

Clint tried to yell "Bastard!" but the word would not come as the noose jerked hard against his throat.